Every Game You Play

Every Game You Play

Ted Darling crime series

Two missing women. One will die.

L M Krier

Cover design DMR Creative
Cover photo Neil Smith

EVERY GAME YOU PLAY

ISBN 978-2-901-77300-9

Contents

About the Author

L M Krier is the pen name of former journalist (court reporter) and freelance copywriter, Lesley Tither, who also writes travel memoirs under the name Tottie Limejuice. Lesley also worked as a case tracker for the Crown Prosecution Service.

The Ted Darling series of crime novels comprises: *The First Time Ever, Baby's Got Blue Eyes, Two Little Boys, When I'm Old and Grey, Shut Up and Drive, Only the Lonely, Wild Thing, Walk on By, Preacher Man, Cry for the Bad Man.*

All books in the series are available in Kindle and paperback format and are also available to read free with Kindle Unlimited.

Contact Details

If you would like to get in touch, please do so at:

tottielimejuice@gmail.com

facebook.com/LMKrier

facebook.com/groups/1450797141836111/

twitter.com/tottielimejuice

http://tottielimejuice.com/

For a light-hearted look at Ted and the other characters, please consider joining the We Love Ted Darling group on Facebook.

Discover the DI Ted Darling series

If you've enjoyed meeting Ted Darling, you may like to discover the other books in the series:

The First Time Ever
Baby's Got Blue Eyes
Two Little Boys
When I'm Old and Grey
Shut Up and Drive
Only the Lonely
Wild Thing
Walk on By
Preacher Man
Cry for the Bad Man

Acknowledgements

I would just like to thank the people who have helped me bring Ted Darling to life.

Beta readers: Jill Pennington, Kate Pill, Karen Corcoran, Jill Evans, Alison Sabedoria, Emma Heath, and The Dalek, for editing assistance.

Police consultants – The Three Karens

Special mention for Hilary for all her kindness and patience in updating me on Stockport and suggesting locations for cover photo-shoots.

Thanks also to Kate Bendelow, author of The Real CSI: A Forensic Handbook for Crime Writers for her permission to adapt one of her anecdotes to create the 'randy Rottweiler' scene.

And a very special thanks for all Ted's loyal friends in the We Love Ted Darling Facebook group (especially Larry). Always so supportive and full of great ideas to be incorporated into the next Ted book.

To Mr Wolf

Thanks to whom I now have to avoid the sun
which gives me more time to spend indoors with Ted

Author's Note

Thank you for reading the Ted Darling crime series. The latest volume, Every Game You Play, continues with cases begun in Preacher Man and Cry for the Bad Man, so is best read as a follow-on to those. The books are set in Stockport and characters do use local dialect and sayings. For example, 'I'll do it if I get chance', without an article or determiner, is common parlance. Ted and Trev also have an in joke between them - 'billirant' - which is a deliberate typo. If you have any queries about words or phrases used, do please feel free to get in touch, using the contact details in the book. I always try to reply promptly to any emails or Facebook messages. Thank you.

Chapter One

'Please don't be afraid.'

The man's voice was soft. Sibilant. It somehow scared her more than harsh abuse and threats would have done.

The hand reaching out to her was like a paw, trying to stroke her hair. She flinched away, trying to press herself as far up against the wall as she could. The old-fashioned radiator dug painfully into her back as she tried.

'I wouldn't hurt you for the world. You're so beautiful.'

His words made her cringe. Especially as it was not a word many people used about her. Not that she was ugly. She just never bothered with trying to beautify herself. Her hair had greyed prematurely and was now flecked with silver highlights. Unfashionably short and wiry. Hairdressers always despaired of trying to do anything to combat its rebellious nature. When she could be bothered to go to one.

'I'm so pleased you came to find me. I knew you would, one day. Ever since the first time I saw you outside the supermarket that time.'

'But I didn't. Like I explained, I'm doing market research. I came to ask if you'd do a survey on a chocolate cereal bar.'

Now his tone was chiding, his look one of patient indulgence.

'But we both know that isn't true, don't we? Don't be embarrassed. I know you felt the same when our eyes met. I should have come to find you. But I've always been rather shy. My mum always told me I'd never get a girl. "Too shy by half, Gordon. You wouldn't say boo to a goose," she used to say.

What would she say if she could see me now? Here, with you. Like it was always meant to be.'

His hand moved towards her face now, trembling slightly, as he tried to touch her skin. She attempted to pull away, trying to shuffle as she sat. But he had secured one of her wrists to the radiator with a pair of tights before binding them both together. Not tight enough to hurt her, but enough to restrain her, uncomfortably.

'Please don't touch me,' she begged, trying to keep any note of disgust or panic out of her voice. All she could think was that at least his hands were clean. Scrubbed pink, the nails immaculate, smelling strongly of soap. His clothes, too. With every movement he made, she picked up wafts of a flowery detergent. She could even identify it. It was one she'd done market research on previously.

'Would you say the fragrance reminds you more of spring flowers or a summer breeze?'

That was one of the questions she'd had to ask. Standing in the foyer of a shopping centre, accosting anyone coming out with their laden trolley. She'd thought it a pretty daft question. They often were, but it was a job.

He pulled his hand back. As if he had touched her and the contact had burnt.

'I'm sorry. You're quite right. We should take it slowly. Savour every moment. There's no hurry. After all, we have the rest of our lives together.'

She shuddered at his words. This was her worst nightmare come true. They'd covered it in training. Always let someone know where you were going to be working. Check in frequently. Keep your phone switched on so you could easily be tracked.

When she'd got on the bus that morning and realised she'd left her phone at home, she'd so nearly got off to go back for it. But she had a quota of calls to make and she was behind already. A pounding migraine the day before had meant she'd had to cry off before she intended to. She'd been pleased to find just the right profile to answer her questions. He'd seemed pleasant. Harmless enough. She'd happily gone through to the small kitchen of the flat when he'd courteously stood aside to let her go first.

Everything had happened so quickly she still wasn't quite sure how. But here she was, sitting on the scrupulously clean floor, immobilised and terrified. All she could do was try to reason with him.

'I think you've perhaps mistaken me for someone else. I'm afraid I don't remember having met you before, or even seen you. It's quite all right, though. If you'd just be kind and untie me, I'll be on my way and I promise not to say a word to anyone about this little misunderstanding. You can keep the chocolate bar, too, and I hope you'll enjoy it.'

He was smiling at her now. Hanging on to every word she said. He spoke as if explaining something obvious to someone not all that bright.

'I don't mind that you made the first move. It just makes me love you even more. Because you came to me. I'm going to take such good care of you. I promise you that. I will love you so gently and so intensely. Because you're mine now and I'm never going to let you out of my sight again.'

Detective Chief Inspector Ted Darling's heart was pounding in his chest. His breath came in a series of ragged gasps and grunts. He knew he was a lot fitter than many officers of his rank, even though he was forced into spending far too many hours desk-bound these days. He counter-balanced it by spending as much time as he could practising his martial arts or going hill walking.

But his current activity was testing his fitness to the limit. He'd been summoned to play squash with his Chief Constable. Or as Ted always thought of the experience, an exercise in ritual humiliation.

The Chief, Jon Woodrow, was a proper copper. He might spend a lot of his time lately as a public figurehead, more politician than policeman. But behind the image was a man who still bore the scars of service in the front line of policing. Dealing with bottle-wielding drunks on a Saturday night and coming out the other side, bloodied but on top.

The Chief had played squash to a high level; national championship standard. He used it as a means to assess officers under his command. He had a lot of time for Ted. Although he'd never been beaten by him, at least Ted gave it his best shot and always went down fighting.

As ever, he was gracious in victory, shaking Ted's hand, congratulating him on a good effort then insisting that the winner should buy the drinks which would follow their showers. It would be fruit smoothies, not alcohol. Ted didn't drink, the Chief wouldn't at his sports club.

Following the custom of their infrequent matches, Ted made a token offer of paying for the drinks and the mascarpone-topped carrot cake they both opted for. The Chief was insistent.

'Thanks, boss,' Ted told him as they went to find a table, waiting for their order to appear.

'Ted, behave yourself, for goodness sake. We're neither of us on duty and you know my name. I've never understood why someone with your reputation for being a bolshie little sod is such a stickler for all this rank and form stuff. All that sir and ma'am went out with the Ark in most forces, including ours.'

Ted never looked his age. Just into his forties, he could easily pass for ten years less. The grin he gave at his Chief's words made him look younger still.

'You'd be surprised how much meaning you can put into a simple word like sir when you need to.' He left just enough of a pause before he added, 'Sir.'

'Cheeky sod,' the Chief laughed good-naturedly.

Ted had had endless heated debates with his father on the same subject. Joe Darling had been a miner, a Trade Unionist, a thorn in the side of management. He'd hated to hear his son on the phone to senior officers calling them sir and ma'am. He said it was demeaning, made Ted no more than a hired hand.

Ted's train of thought was broken by a man coming over with a tray holding their refreshments.

'Afternoon, Chief, Mr Darling,' he greeted them, putting glasses and plates in front of them.

'Thanks, Larry. Put that on my tab, will you, and if Mr Darling tries to pay, just ignore him.'

It was always the same ritual, and Larry was a party to it. Ted tried to pay every time and had never yet succeeded.

Once they'd been left alone and had started on the refreshments, the Chief became serious.

'I wanted a chance to talk to you, Ted, away from work. I know you'll have been sweating with the prospect of this inquiry hanging over you. I'm as keen as you are to get it done and dusted then you can get back to doing what you do best. I know you didn't want to take time off, but I hope you made good use of the week's break to try to relax a bit.'

For the first time in his career, Ted had had a recent case he couldn't bring to a conclusion. He'd had no shortage of suspects. Simply not a shred of evidence against any of them, and tight alibis for all of them.

He hadn't wanted to take time off but the ACC (Crime) had insisted, and had made it clear he was to have no contact at all with his team whilst on leave. Ted had managed a long weekend in Wales with the unwanted time on his hands, visiting his mother with his partner, Trevor. But Trev had to work all week which had left Ted on his own for too much of the time. Going over and over the case notes obsessively to see if there was anything he could possibly have missed.

'I've had a quick look at the files and I'm blowed if I can see anything you could or should have done differently,' the

Chief told him. 'So I'm fairly confident the inquiry will just be a rubber-stamping job. But it needs to be seen to be done and to be impartial. Then we can all move on. Which is why I have a suggestion which I wanted to run past you.'

Ted took another bite of his cake. He suspected he needed the sugar hit for whatever the Chief was about to propose. He was, as ever, dying to get back to his team and get on with his job. But even if he wasn't suspended or under any suspicion of wrongdoing, there would inevitably be a cloud hanging over him until it was all sorted by an independent inquiry.

When under stress, Ted would normally have booked a hard training session with his Special Skills instructor. But Mr Green was now retired. Gone back to live with the family he hadn't seen in years, goodness knows where. Ted had instead filled his time with punishing training hikes, running up and down Jacob's Ladder a few times with a heavy rucksack on his back.

His boss and friend, Jim Baker, was recovering from a heart attack and meant to take gentle exercise, so Ted had taken him out and about so they could at least talk shop while they were both on enforced leave. But being coppers was what they both liked best and Ted, for one, was prepared to do anything it would take to get back to it as soon as possible.

'You know Gerry Fletcher, of course,' the Chief continued. 'You've probably heard that he's left GMP and gone up to Preston. He's got a wider remit too. Not just Complaints and Discipline, but inquiries into other forces.

'Now I know you've met him socially through Jim. But I don't think you've ever served together, have you?'

Ted shook his head, already guessing where the Chief was going and thinking of all the ramifications. If Fletcher was no longer in the Greater Manchester Police Force but serving with neighbouring Lancashire, he could be seen as impartial.

'Gerry has the advantage of being readily available. He's got a few bent coppers who need his attention but he's enough of a sadist to enjoy making them wait and sweat it out. He's got the designated team, the experience, and even if he's met you socially, I think we both know his impartiality is beyond question. This would mean we could get this whole business out of the way quickly and get you back to work properly. But as you know him, I thought I'd run the idea past you, as a courtesy.

'I don't think you have anything to worry about. But you know as well as I do that Gerry takes no prisoners. If you've made a balls-up anywhere, no matter how small, he'll find it and he'll hang you out to dry. So what do you say?'

'Fine by me. I just want to get it finished so we can get on with things. The team and I have unfinished business on this case.'

The Chief shook his head emphatically.

'Not you,' he said firmly. 'Even if and when you're cleared, you'd do well to stay away from personal involvement in this case. It's too much of a hot potato. Unless things change dramatically and you suddenly find evidence you've not had to date, of course.'

Ted opened his mouth to object, read the Chief's expression and wisely closed it again.

'What you put your team onto is up to you. But I need you personally to back off. What did you make of the letter that lad left before he died? Is that the truth, do you think?'

'I'm not convinced. It would be the perfect revenge, to leave something like that, trying to implicate others. He probably wouldn't have realised we couldn't act on it either way, without corroborating evidence.'

The Chief nodded this time.

'I agree. Load of old bollocks, if you ask me. Right, I'll give Gerry the green light. Let's get this show on the road and put the past behind us. And I mean it, Ted. You back well off, whatever happens. We can always reconsider, if circumstances change.'

'I don't even know your name,' he told her. 'I think I fell in love with you from the moment I first saw you, but I don't know what to call you. You know I'm Gordon. I told you that. Mum used to call me Gordy. But what do I call you?'

Her mind was racing, trying to think of the best thing to do. She was going to get out of there. Soon. Of course she was. It was just a matter of time. So was it a good idea to give him her name before she escaped? Might he come after her and find her again?

He saw her hesitation and smiled at her.

'I'll know if you don't tell me the truth. I feel I know a lot about you already. But I don't like people playing games with me. We need to be perfectly honest with one another. Especially as we're going to spend the rest of our lives together.'

She tried to suppress the shudder his words provoked and not to let her voice betray the fear she felt. She made eye contact with him as she replied. She'd read or heard somewhere that it was always best to try to remain calm and rational when being held captive. To try to engage on some level with the captor.

'Tara. It's Tara.'

'Tara. That's a really beautiful name. It suits you.'

Again he reached out a hand. She steeled herself not to recoil as his fingers made soft contact with the side of her cheek. The fear she was suppressing was giving her an urgent problem, though.

'I really need to go to the bathroom. Please. I won't do anything, I promise. I just need to go.'

'Of course! I'm so sorry. How rude of me. I should have showed you where everything is. I'll just release you from here. But please promise me you won't do anything silly. I really mean you no harm. I would never, ever hurt you, believe me. But even if you start to scream, the old lady in the next flat is stone deaf. And the family the other side don't speak any

English. I think some of them might be illegals. They hardly ever come out.'

As he spoke, he reached for a kitchen knife and gently cut her free. Then he helped her to her feet and guided her to the bathroom. She waited for him to leave her alone to use the toilet but he stood in the doorway, watching her expectantly. She noticed he still had the knife in his hand, held down beside his thigh. His adoring gaze at her frightened her more than anything. Before she could stop herself, she was trembling all over and had lost bladder control.

'Oh Tara, darling, please don't be frightened of me. I would honestly never hurt you. Ever. I'll let you into a little secret. You will be my first. My first love and my only love. There, there, please don't cry, my darling. I'm going to run you a nice warm bath and help you to clean yourself up. I still have some of my mum's things you can wear while I wash your clothes for you. Then I'll go out and buy you something new.'

His touch was gentle as he folded her shaking body into his arms and pulled her against him. It was a tender embrace but she could feel the thrust of his erection against her as he soothed her, stroking her hair and murmuring in her ear.

'We have all the time in the world, my darling. You're here now and I'm going to make you mine and keep you safe. Forever.'

Chapter Two

'Which side of the bed do you prefer to sleep on, darling?'

Gordon had led her into a small bedroom with what looked like a three-quarter sized double bed. First he'd washed her, thoroughly and intimately, in a warm bath filled with a rose-scented foam. Despite the warmth, she'd sat shivering, trying to keep her arms wrapped round her and her legs squeezed tightly together.

The ordeal seemed to last an eternity. Slowly, gently, he'd lifted each foot out of the water and held it up, kissing and licking each toe in turn. Then he'd run the soapy flannel languidly the full length of her inner leg, stopping just before he reached her most private parts, before repeating the same on the other side.

He was making low moaning noises in his throat as he stroked her. She tried to keep her eyes from the prominent bulge in his trousers. She welcomed the tears that filled them, blurring her vision. She tried to take her mind to a safe place, to detach herself from her surroundings and what was happening to her. She thought of Micki, her little cat, and hoped she would be all right until she could get home to her. She always left her plenty of dried food and fresh water and there was a cat flap but she knew the cat would be missing the company.

'I'll be home soon,' she kept silently telling herself. 'If I just let him do whatever it is he wants, perhaps I can convince him that I need to go home to get my things so I can move in with him. Please god let it be quick and let me get out of here alive.'

She tried to look at him dispassionately, gauging how much of an ordeal it would be to sleep with him, even if she didn't want to, to have a chance of getting out of there. She put him at around her age, mid forties. Medium sized, reasonably well built. Above all, he was clean. Obsessively so. Everything about him was scrubbed and spotless. His teeth – all his own by the look of it – gleamed and gave off a strong minty fragrance.

'What features do you look for when buying toothpaste?'

'How important is it to you to feel confident in prevention of bad breath?'

The survey questions sprang unbidden to her mind. At least they helped to take her mind off what was happening to her. And at last he had finished washing and rinsing her. He helped her up, carefully, considerately. Guided her over the rim of the bath, then folded her into a large, fluffy bath sheet which gave off the same flowery fragrance as his clothes, carefully patting her dry all over.

Keeping hold of her with one hand, he reached into a cupboard in the corner of the bathroom and pulled something out of it.

'You'll have to have one of my mum's nighties, just for tonight, until I can go out and buy you something much prettier. It will be too big but it's only for one night.'

He slipped it deftly over her head and let its folds envelop her, falling almost to the floor and ballooning around her. Then he reached under it to remove the towel, hanging it over a rack. He handled the manoeuvre so deftly she wondered how many times he'd done it for his mother.

He eyed her appraisingly and smiled.

'You look wonderful. Shall I dry your hair for you? It seems to dry quite quickly with that short style. I would prefer you to let it grow. I would love to feel your hair against my skin as we lie in bed together.

'Now, I'm sorry about this part but it's just a precaution, until I know I can trust you. Until I know you're not just playing a game. Pretending to feel for me as I do for you then trying to run away as soon as I fall asleep.'

As he spoke, he was quickly tying her wrists back together with a fresh pair of tights. His mother's, she presumed. When he'd finished, he led her into the bedroom, indicated the bed and asked her preference for sides.

The panic started again. He was going to rape her, she felt sure, and she didn't know if she could stand it.

'But I don't want to sleep with you!' she blurted, aware of the rising note of hysteria in her voice and desperately trying to control it in case it excited him.

'Of course not, my angel. I understand that and we're not going to do anything until you're ready to give yourself to me fully.'

It's not that,' she gabbled desperately. 'I don't go with men. I'm a lesbian.'

Now his expression was sad, his tone reproachful.

'Please don't lie to me, my darling Tara. It's so hurtful. I know you're as excited as I am and perhaps that's what frightens you. But I promise you, you are in full control of what happens. I don't want to rush you. I want it to be beautiful for both of us. All the more so as it will be my first time.

'Come on, just lie down here, like this, and I'll spoon around you, so I can hold and protect you all night long.'

He half-lifted her onto the bed and pulled the covers over her. She could feel his strength and realised his build was deceptive. He would be difficult for her to struggle against. He laid her on her side and fastened the tights to the wrought iron bed-head.

Then he walked round to the other side of the bed. She heard the sound of him undressing before he slid in between the sheets as she lay with her back to him. Feeling vulnerable. Unable to see what he was doing. He slipped one arm under her neck, laid the other softly over her shoulders so she was held in his embrace.

She felt his body move closer until they were in full contact. Felt again the press of his erection against the back of her buttocks. His breath on the back of her neck as he began to move rhythmically against her. The sudden dampness from his rapid climax.

His voice was thick with emotional tears as he whispered, 'Oh my darling, I can't wait for the moment when you give yourself to me fully and freely. But I'm a patient man. I'm prepared to wait as long as it takes. We have all the time in the world.'

Ted was surprised to see Maurice Brown's car swing into the parking space next to his as he returned to work on Monday morning. DC Brown was not known for his punctuality and Ted was in well ahead of his start time, itching to get back to work.

'Morning Maurice, couldn't you sleep?'

'All right, Ted?' Maurice greeted him cheerily as he got out of his car, informal as ever outside the station. 'I knew you'd be in early today so I thought I'd come in to make sure you were all right. I bet you've been fretting about being away, especially with the inquiry hanging over us. You know me and the team are behind you all the way, right?'

His customary kindness made Ted feel bad about his jibe, especially as Maurice followed his remark by reaching out to give Ted a companionable pat on the back. It was a warm and affectionate gesture, typical of Maurice. Ted had to steel himself not to recoil. He was never good at the touchy-feelies but he wouldn't have hurt Maurice's feelings for the world. Maurice might have been a Grade A skiver but he was also the kindest, most compassionate man Ted had ever met.

They fell into companionable step side by side to cross the car park. Ted appreciated the solidarity but he was quick to correct Maurice.

'Hanging over me, Maurice. No one else. If anyone goes down for this, it will be me.'

'Won't come to that,' Maurice told him cheerfully.

They'd reached the door to the station so Maurice switched into work mode, standing aside to usher Ted through first with an ironic, 'After you, boss.'

It was good to be back. Even when Ted was confronted with the pile of accumulated paperwork from a week away from his desk. His DI, Jo Rodriguez, would have done his best to keep on top of anything urgent, but most CID officers these days found themselves drowning under the tide of forms and reports. Resignations were already happening because of it.

With a sigh, Ted decided that looking at it all wasn't likely to achieve anything so he put the kettle on and made a start on sorting it.

He didn't seem to have achieved much before there was the welcome distraction of a knock on his door and Jo strode in.

'Am I glad to see you back in charge of the European paper mountain, boss. Any ambitions I had to go for DCI melted away in the face of that lot,' he nodded at the piles on the desk. 'I tried to keep on top of it and develop some sort of system but towards the end of the week it defeated me, I'm afraid, and it probably shows.'

He cast a critical eye over Ted as he continued, 'Have you lost weight? I hope you've been relaxing, rather than fretting?'

Jo was observant. Ted had dropped a few pounds with all the physical exertion he'd put himself through. He must have mowed the lawn at least five times, just to keep himself occupied. When he was under any sort of stress, Ted's answer was always punishing physical activity.

'I tend to run up and down mountains when I'm feeling stressed,' he confided.

'And are you? Stressed, I mean? Is there any news of the inquiry?'

'I played squash with the Chief on Saturday. Or rather, I was once again soundly thrashed by him. He wanted to check I was okay with Superintendent Fletcher leading the inquiry. He's switched forces and is available. I just want to get it over and done with now so I agreed.'

'The Grim Guardsman? I know of him and his reputation, of course. But we shouldn't have anything to worry about, surely? We've all gone over our notes again and again and I can't see what we could have done differently.

'By the way, just a word on the QT. Forewarned, and all that. I got it from a friend. That lad Antoine's father, Louis Martin, is in the Rotary Club. So is our Chief Super. Apparently Louis has been making mutterings about us harassing his son and the other lads. Nothing official yet, as far as I know, but not what we need at the moment. We've not touched the case in your absence, as you instructed, pending the inquiry.'

'If everyone's in, can we start briefing? I just want us all to get back to normal.'

'They're all here. I think Maurice must have slept here, he was in before any of us.'

They often briefed in the main office, unless they had a big case on. Ted was keen to touch base with everyone, to find out what had been going on in his absence.

'Right, team, settle down,' he said to begin with.

There was a ripple of laughter from all present. DC Jezza Vine got up and walked over to Ted, holding out a gift bag.

'We all missed you, boss, so we had a whip-round for this.'

Puzzled, Ted rummaged in the bag and pulled out a mug, printed with his catchphrase. He was touched and smiled round at them.

'You load of soft beggars. But thank you. Right, what have we got on?'

'Probably a nice easy one for the figures, boss,' one of his sergeants, DS Mike Hallam told him. 'A woman got fed up of telling her husband to stop picking his nose at the table and being ignored, so she picked up a cast iron frying pan and whacked him round the head with it. Killed him outright. She's not denying killing him, just claiming she never intended to do more than injure him to make him stop.'

'Well, that's a first. What else?'

His other sergeant, Rob O'Connell, spoke next.

'I've finally been able to see the bent bishop, boss. The one who was accused of indecently assaulting young boys. The nursing home for clergy that he's in seemed to keep fobbing me off, saying he had various infections and wasn't up to being spoken to, but I kept asking.'

Ted was watching Rob as he spoke. He didn't look altogether on form. A bit more designer stubble than he usually favoured. Dark circles round his eyes telling of poor sleep patterns. He'd been the senior officer on the scene when their last case had ended with a young man going under a train. Added to that, Ted knew Rob himself had been subject to abuse whilst he was being fostered as a boy. That would explain his use of the word 'bent' in the context, which he wouldn't normally use in front of the boss. He made himself a note to have a quiet word with him as soon as he could.

'I've got something I want someone to look into,' Ted told them. 'While I was at home, my neighbour called me to go round there. She's an older lady and she's just discovered the internet for banking and credit cards. She told me she was on the phone to her bank who'd called her to alert her to fraudulent activity on her account. She was very pleased with herself because she said she'd rung the bank back so she'd know it wasn't a scam. They were just going through her details with her and needed the security code from the back of the card but she was having difficulty reading it, so could I read it out to the nice young man on the phone for her.

'Said nice young man said he couldn't speak to anyone other than the card-holder. I said he could probably safely speak to me, but when I told him I was Detective Chief Inspector Darling of the GMP he suddenly remembered an urgent appointment scamming someone else. He'd clearly done the old trick of not disconnecting the call when he phoned Mrs Adams so of course she got straight back through to him when she called back.

'So who wants it? It'll need a follow-up visit afterwards just to let her know what we've found out and to advise her again never to believe anything like that without checking it out first. Steve, can you check the details out online and then perhaps Maurice, could you go round and work your charms on Mrs Adams?'

DC 'Virgil' Tibbs spoke next.

'Boss, I know we weren't supposed to be touching the other case until after the inquiry. But I had a drink with Sal in the week and I happened to ask him if his friends in Fraud knew anything about either Louis Martin or his son Antoine.'

DC Sal Ahmed had left the team to go back to his speciality, Fraud. He and Virgil had always been friends and had stayed in close contact.

Seeing the boss's disapproving expression, Virgil hurried on.

'I know, boss, but it was just a question over a drink. I didn't think anything would come of it. But I hit pay-dirt. Sal says it's all a bit under the radar at the moment but they've been keeping a close eye on them both – father and son - and so have Drugs. It seems the father is well known as a supplier of quality recreational drugs, mostly coke.'

'I thought he was supposed to be a pillar of society? Football sponsorship, Rotary Club and all the rest of it?' Ted asked him.

'Apparently that's where he finds some of his biggest clients. He's supplying half of Greater Manchester's elite, it seems. Hospital consultants, bankers, barristers, solicitors. Allegedly even some high-ranking police officers.'

'So what's Fraud's interest in it, if they're drug offences?'

'Here's where it gets interesting, boss. There's been a suggestion which has set Sal and his team sniffing about. It's thought that Louis launders his drugs money very carefully indeed, which makes him even harder to catch. And one theory is that young Antoine's so-called online currency trading may be how he does it.'

'Now that is interesting. I'll give Sal a call myself for more info but keep me in the loop on this one if you hear any more before I do. But officially, we do nothing at all with anything related to that case until after this inquiry is finished. And I hope to hear today or tomorrow when it's going to be starting.'

It was mid-afternoon before he heard from his immediate boss, Superintendent Debra Caldwell. A quick call to tell him that Gerry Fletcher would be arriving to start the inquiry on Thursday, and promising to catch up with Ted soon.

Ted finally found the time to go downstairs for a catch-up with Inspector Kevin Turner.

Kev looked up as Ted entered his office.

'Mind-reader. I was literally just about to pick up the phone to tell you we have a missing person which might possibly be one for a joint operation. She's called Tara MacNamee, mid-forties, works in market research. Lives alone, but it was her supervisor who contacted us. She's not heard from Tara since Friday and she's concerned because she's usually very good at keeping in touch. And she's not sent in her work from the end of last week, which isn't like her at all.

'She's tried phoning her but it just goes to voicemail. We checked and the phone is in her house so my officers gained entry and there's no sign of her anywhere. There was a little cat which looked hungry so my lads fed it and left a note to contact us, in case Tara turns up. The supervisor has no idea exactly where she might have been working and she uses public transport rather than her own car. So it looks like she could have been missing for four days now.'

Chapter Three

'Eat your breakfast, dear. You're not eating enough to keep a sparrow alive. Would you like me to make you something different? It's no trouble.'

He'd made her toast. Wholemeal. With real butter and what looked like home-made strawberry jam. He'd cut the crusts off and served it in obsessively neat quarters. He hadn't given her a knife and when she took a sip of the tea, made just the way she had asked for it, she found it was cool. He must have added cold water to it. So that wasn't a potential weapon either. He was clever.

'Did you sleep well? I went out like a light.'

She hadn't. She'd lain awake most of the night, tense with fear with what he might do to her next. It was hard to get comfortable with her hands tied like they were, even if the knots were not tight and there was some stretch in the tights.

He'd fallen deeply asleep soon after climaxing against her and had barely stirred all night. She'd kept trying to inch away from the hot, intimate contact of his body moulded up against hers. But at her slightest movement, his arms would tighten briefly around her while he muttered something indistinct. She hated that. It was a long time since she'd let anyone share her bed for more than a couple of hours at the most.

She'd been dreading the moment he woke. Wondering if he would make more demands on her when he did, and if he would want to take things further. She was surprised and relieved when he woke and announced he wouldn't come near her until they had both had a shower and brushed their teeth. The night before he'd produced a toothbrush, still in its wrapper, and an unopened tube of toothpaste, from another bathroom cupboard which appeared to be stocked with all sorts of supplies. As she'd brushed her teeth, she'd wondered if she could break the brush quickly against the wash basin and have a sharp enough edge on the plastic handle to fight him off and escape. She'd quickly decided the uncertain outcome didn't warrant the risk.

Once again he'd stood and watched her in open admiration as she used the toilet. Then he'd gently removed the nightdress and stood her under the shower, washing her meticulously. Soaping and rinsing, soaping and rinsing. Over and over in some bizarre ritual.

Next he'd taken out a clean pair of tights and secured her to the towel rail while he took a shower. She'd wanted to look away. Especially as he'd soaped himself until he achieved an erection, all the time looking at her, a smile playing round his lips. But her eyes were locked in repelled fascination. Like a rabbit gazing at the weasel which would soon despatch it.

'Soon, my darling. Very soon.'

Then he turned the shower to cold and blasted away all trace of soap and of his arousal.

The clothes he'd washed for her the previous day were clean, dry, folded and smoothed free of any wrinkles as he'd taken them out of the machine. He helped her to put them on, untying her from the rail while he slipped her arms into the T-shirt and sweatshirt she'd been wearing when she arrived. Much less than twenty-four hours ago, yet it seemed like a lifetime. An eternity.

She'd asked him for her glasses, which he'd put away somewhere. Although she didn't need them for close to, she felt more vulnerable than ever without them. He'd simply smiled and said she looked so much prettier when they weren't masking her face, and he was sure she could soon adjust to going without.

'I'll go shopping today to get you some things. More clothes, for one thing. And food. Just tell me what you like to eat. I enjoy cooking. It would make me very happy to cook for you. Do you need anything in particular? You know, intimate women's things? I don't mind buying anything like that, I won't be embarrassed.'

She almost shuddered. She'd just finished a period. She couldn't stand the thought that she would still be here, with this weird man, for the next one. She would have to use all of her cunning to get herself out of this situation. And soon.

'I'll go to the big supermarket, where we first met. I can get everything I need there, including some clothes for you. I know your size, from washing your things. I'll never forget that moment, when I first saw you. You were interviewing someone and just for a moment, you lifted your head and looked directly at me as I was coming out. I felt the connection then, and I knew you must have felt it too. That's why you came to find me. I should have been brave enough to be the one to find you.'

'Oh no,' she told him hastily. 'It wasn't like that at all.'

Now he'd mentioned where he'd first seen her, she could pinpoint the day. It was only two weeks ago and he'd clearly been obsessing about her ever since. She wanted to put him right, without making him angry. She had a feeling it would not be in her interests to anger him.

'I'm very short-sighted. I need my glasses for distance but not for reading. So when I'm writing down responses, I often take them off. So I honestly wouldn't have been able to see you clearly.'

She saw his face start to cloud so began digging.

'But the attraction must have been so strong that I felt it even without seeing you clearly.'

He beamed his pleasure at that, reaching out a hand to hold hers briefly, then immediately going to the sink to rinse away any toast crumbs. For the brief second his attention was off her, she looked wildly about for anything with which to defend herself while she made a break for freedom.

As if reading her mind, he turned back towards her with surprising speed and smiled at her again.

'All the doors are kept locked and only I know where the keys are. I got into that habit because of my mum. Her mind started to wander a bit and she would often try to get out on her own. I like to keep those I love close to me. For their own protection. There's no way out.'

Tuesday morning briefing and Ted was pleased to have a live, ongoing case to take his mind off the fact that in two days' time, Superintendent Gerry Fletcher would be going over every note, every interview tape of his last case. He would leave no stone unturned and would pounce, like a hungry raptor, on the slightest procedural slip-up.

'Jezza, I want you to liaise with Uniform and go with them to the house. I checked and there's still no news of Tara MacNamee so she is still officially missing. Uniform have checked the house out from the point of view of a Misper but I want trained eyes in there to see if it's a crime scene. Make sure you preserve it if so, check in with Jo and we'll get CSIs in there if you think there's a need. Her mobile phone's in the house so get that to Steve to check out anything and everything on it which might help us. And let's check on her bank and credit cards. Have they been used since she was last seen, and if so, where?'

'Are we certain she's not just taken off for a long week end somewhere and forgotten to tell anyone?' Mike Hallam asked.

Ted shook his head emphatically.

'She left the cat. With apparently not enough food for that long. Jezza, check with the neighbours to see if someone was meant to feed it but forgot. Generally speaking, cat owners think of their pets when they're planning a few days away.'

He was speaking from his own perspective. He and Trev spent a fortune on live-in pet-sitters on the rare occasions they managed to get any time away together.

'I'll talk to the Super in a minute about press releases and getting some posters up. Jo, can you organise a full background check on Tara and any known associates. We know nothing like enough about her at the moment to form a picture, so let's start digging. And Jo, this one's yours to run, while I drown under admin. Just please keep me in the loop at all times. Let's try to get this lady safely back home to her pussy-cat, and soon.'

Once they'd finished, Ted went down to see his Superintendent, the formidable Ice Queen. Despite her reputation, her attitude to him had thawed considerably of late. She was as stiff and formal as he was and they were still a bit wary in each other's company. He'd been surprised not to have been summoned to see her before now but guessed she was probably, like him, wading through paperwork.

'Good morning, Ted,' she began, her tone formal, but at least not calling him by his rank. 'Would you like coffee? I hope your break did you some good. And you're quite happy about it being Superintendent Fletcher leading this inquiry?'

'Anything to get it over and done with as soon as possible.'

He thanked her as she handed him coffee, then laid out for her what he needed for the Missing Persons case. They were interrupted by her desk phone. She replied, listened briefly, then handed it to Ted.

'This sounds as if it might be important.'

'Sorry to bother you, Chief Inspector, but I have someone asking for you by name and being very insistent,' the switchboard operator told him. 'They won't give a name or say what it's about. They just said to tell you Mr Green gave them your name. Will you take the call?'

'I think I better speak to them in the circumstances,' Ted

told her, looking quizzically at his Super for her nod of consent.

A man's voice spoke. One he'd never heard before.

'Is that DCI Ted Darling?'

'It is.'

'And you know who Mr Green is?'

'I do.'

'The name Gayboy means something to you?'

'It does.'

Ted was being wary, his replies guarded. He had no idea who he was talking to or what it was about. He wasn't about to give anything away.

'And so does the codename BRIOCHE?'

'That too.'

'Right. I'm not being melodramatic here but I'm risking a big op, not to mention my life, in talking to you. But it's something I feel strongly about and I can't let it lie. Are you alone?'

'Not currently.'

'In that case I'll call you later.'

'I could call you, if you give me a number.'

'No chance,' and the line went dead.

'That sounded enigmatic,' the Ice Queen commented.

'It was. A mysterious anonymous caller who needs to talk to me. Told me it was Mr Green who put him in touch.'

Her eyebrows went up at that. As a former Firearms officer herself, she'd also had the pleasure of some of Mr Green's specialist training.

'I thought you told me he'd retired?'

'That's what he told me. And you know as well as I do that he wouldn't give out anyone's name unless it was on a strictly need to know basis. The caller will phone again later on. I'll keep you posted.'

'It's really very kind of you to offer to go out shopping for me.

But I don't want to put you to the trouble and expense. Wouldn't it make more sense if you just drove me to my house, if you have a car, so I can get some of my own things to bring back here? And then I could make sure my little cat has enough to eat.'

He frowned at her words.

'You have a cat? Oh dear, that won't do at all. I can't abide cats. I could never have one in the house. Such dirty, disgusting creatures. I would have thought you'd have got rid of it before you came to find me.'

'But I didn't know you'd feel the same way as me,' she said quickly. 'That you'd want me to stay so soon. It's all moving so fast.'

Humour him, she told herself. She'd heard that was the best thing to do with obsessive people. She knew she wasn't physically strong enough to be sure of getting away from him. All she could do was to try to keep a cool head and to outsmart him somehow. It seemed to be working. He beamed with delight at her words.

'Isn't it, my love, and doesn't that make it all the more exciting? I just hope that very soon now you'll be ready to move things to the next level. But I won't press you, I promise.'

'So will you take me to my house to get my things? And sort something for Micki? Please?'

His expression changed again, as swiftly as throwing a light switch. Artful, cunning.

'First you need to show me I can trust you entirely. Too many people have tried to play mind games with me. I soon got wise to all that. When you win my trust you will have it, and my undying devotion, for the rest of your life. I promise you that. But it's just a bit too soon for that. Once you're lying underneath me, with me inside you, and we're gazing into each other's eyes, then I will know. I will know that you are mine for ever.

'For now, I need to know you will sit here and wait quietly for me while I quickly go and buy you all the things you need. So come here, my darling.'

He pulled her towards him, his touch still gentle, then spun her round so her back was to him. Deftly, he retied her wrists behind her, then whipped open a drawer and pulled out a clean tea-towel. He rolled it into a sausage and firmly, but without hurting her, pushed it into her mouth and tied it securely at the back of her head.

She'd started to cry now, shaking her head from side to side, making whimpering noises, trying to implore him not to leave her like that. Ignoring her, he used his foot to sweep her legs out from under her, without ever hurting her, and guided her down to the floor where he proceeded to tie her hands to the radiator. Then he covered her head and face with soft kisses while he whispered to her.

'I am so, so sorry, my angel. I will be as quick as I possibly can. You just need to find a way to make me trust you completely then I won't have to do this any more. As soon as you learn you can trust me and give yourself to me, our life together is going to be so wonderful.'

'Are you alone this time?'

'I am.'

'I'll be brief. I'm putting myself in danger even speaking to you. I need to see you face to face, as soon as possible. The witness Mr Green delivered. Her life's in danger. I'm in London but I don't want to meet here and I don't want to come there. Could we meet in Birmingham? A café near New Street station? I'll give you the address.'

Whoever it was on the phone, they were speaking of a young woman, a witness to paedophile activity. Mr Green had sprung her from custody to order and delivered her to a shadowy group who called themselves BRIOCHE.

'I need to be here on Thursday and probably for a few days

from then.'

'It won't wait that long. This is urgent.' His tone sounded impatient now. 'Look, Mr Green led me to believe you were a man of action and that's what I need. I need to talk to you tomorrow. I'm not saying anything more on the phone so can you get yourself there tomorrow or not?'

'Give me a time, preferably early on, and I'll be there. How will I know you?'

'You won't but I'll know you. I'm looking at a photo of you online now. Be there. I'm not pissing about when I tell you lives depend on it.'

Chapter Four

'Birmingham?' Trev's tone sounded as if Ted had announced he was setting off to find the source of the Nile. 'That's way off your patch. What are you up to?'

'Nothing,' Ted said evasively. 'It's to do with a witness on a case. I might need to make some arrangements for her, that's all.'

Trev's blue eyes were studying Ted's face while Ted tried to hold his gaze and not look shifty. Trev could always read him like a book.

'If it's just a case of sorting out witness protection, why are you going to Birmingham, of all places, yourself and not sending one of the team? Ted, you keep promising to be more open, to stop bottling things up. You're still not telling me everything. I'm at least trying to be tidier in the kitchen, like you asked me to. '

Trev did most of the cooking, ironing and cleaning because his hours were more regular than Ted's. The house was always spotless but Trev was pathologically untidy. It was always Ted who picked up the piles of discarded clothing, moved dishes from wherever they were dumped to put them in the dishwasher.

Stuck in the house on enforced leave, when he wasn't out running with his backpack, Ted had resolved finally to tackle his partner about his untidiness. When Trev got home from work, shedding his motorbike leathers in the hall and leaving them in a heap as usual, Ted was there to greet him and lead him by the hand up the stairs.

'I realised something today. Even after all this time together, there's still a thing or two I can teach you in the bedroom.'

'You have my undivided attention,' Trev said delightedly. 'Teach away.'

Trev headed for the bed, anticipation on his face, but Ted steered him skilfully past it and into a corner of the room by the window.

'You see this strange creation here in this corner? This is called a laundry basket. And these things here on the floor? Those are your kecks. Miraculously, every day, they somehow manage to levitate themselves into that basket then later, as if by magic, down to the washing machine.'

Trev was laughing out loud now. He knew it was true. He always blamed it on growing up with servants. And Ted had compounded his bad habits by appearing happy to keep picking up after him.

'It would be marvellous if you could somehow learn the magic spell to at least put them in the basket rather than hang them on the floor.'

'I promise to try harder, Mr Policeman,' he said solemnly, then gave Ted his most provocative grin. 'So if we were to make use of being up here in the bedroom now, you'd want me to stop and put each item of clothing in that magic basket first, before doing anything else, would you?'

Ted was already peeling off his own T-shirt, tossing it carelessly to the floor behind him.

'You could probably leave it for a bit.'

'But why Birmingham?' Trev persisted, cutting through Ted's memories. 'Why do you have to go there instead of dealing with whatever it is from here?'

'Because I need to liaise with someone from London so we both thought it would be easier to meet in the middle.'

'Is this your friend Harry again? From the Met? Things

don't always turn out well when you have anything to do with him.'

'No, not Harry this time, someone I've not met before. I'll get a train first thing tomorrow and hopefully be back in the office by early afternoon. I need to be back because the inquiry starts on Thursday and I want to make sure everything is as it should be.'

Trev reached out to hold his hand across the dining table.

'You're all right with this, aren't you? You would tell me if it was getting to you? You know what you get like if you start brooding and not unloading. Look, I'll show commitment. I'll clear the table and put things in the dishwasher, if you promise to talk to me about how it's all going.'

'Side the table,' Ted corrected him automatically.

They often made a joke about the gulf between their backgrounds – Ted, a miner's lad from the Lancashire coalfields who grew up in Stockport, Trev the son of a high-ranking diplomat, educated in expensive international schools.

'And I promise to tell you as much as I can. But you know it can't be everything, not even to you. You know how the saying goes. If I tell you everything, then I'd have to kill you. And you know I could never do that.'

Ted found the café easily enough, a short walk from Birmingham's New Street Station. It was pouring down so he was forced to go inside. He would have preferred to be out in the open, where he could see everything going on around him.

He had no idea who he was coming to meet so had no way of knowing if they were already inside waiting to check him out before identifying themselves. He glanced round the room while he waited to be served, always alert to potential danger. No one was noticeably paying him any particular attention.

The place was not all that busy. Probably the early breakfast rush of commuters had gone on their way, fortified and ready for work. It was clean, though slightly on the twee side of trendy for Ted's taste. He decided he was hungry enough for a stack of American pancakes with his cappuccino and carried both carefully over to a table he'd picked out earlier as the best vantage point. His specialist firearms training meant he was always happiest when he could position himself so no one could approach him from behind.

Now all he could do was sit and wait for whoever he was meant to be meeting. He made a start on his breakfast, enjoying the sweet stickiness of the maple syrup.

Eventually, well past the agreed meeting time, a man entered the café, shaking rainwater from his uncovered head of dreadlocks, pulled into a man bun. He didn't have a coat on, just a shapeless mohair sweater in bright colours over jeans that were not of the cleanest.

Once served, he carried his tray and walked through the room, looking for a seat. He stopped next to Ted's table and asked, 'That chair taken, mate?'

Ted recognised the voice. It was the man he had come to meet. 'Help yourself.'

The man sat down on Ted's left, taking a drink of his espresso and a bite from his bacon toastie before he said anything else. There was no one sitting immediately next to them and background music would help muffle conversations.

'Before we start, can you take your mobile out, switch it off and leave it on the table where I can see it. Both of them, if you're carrying a work one and your own.'

The man spoke with his sandwich in front of his mouth. It muffled his voice and Ted's immediate thought was this was someone wanting to avoid any chance of lip readers. A copper. He'd have put money on it. He'd guessed as much, from the mention of an op, although the man might have been military or even Security Service.

Ted did as he'd been asked. He only had the one phone on him but he turned it off and left it on the table in plain sight. Then he waited for the other man to continue.

The man took another bite of his toastie and a noisy swallow of the coffee before he said anything else. He kept the sandwich in hands which were none too clean, with dirty nails and nicotine staining down the fingers.

'My name's Ian. I'm a copper. With the Met. Undercover. Deep undercover. I'll give you my gaffer's details before you go so you can check me out if you need to. I've infiltrated this BRIOCHE shower of revolutionaries. They're sort of a twenty-first century Angry Brigade. Been with them two years, going on three, and they're still none the wiser, dozy pillocks.

'I've seen your friend Harry and I've met your Mr Green. He knew I was a copper. I've no idea how. I don't think Harry knows.'

'Mr Green has a way of knowing things. It's usually better not to wonder about the how.'

Ian smiled at that.

'He delivered the witness to us for safe keeping. He found a moment to have a quiet word with me. Singled me out straight away. Told me about you and said if I ever needed someone I could trust one hundred percent, to get in touch with you.

'The group are only interested in the woman as a means to an end. Her testimony really could bring the government down. I've talked to her and it's shit-hot. She's a walking time bomb. I've been getting close to her – very close, if you know what I mean – because I'm worried about her safety. I can't see her being allowed to testify and people in power must know the group has her. If they don't yet, they soon will.'

Ted did know what he meant. He knew all about the so-called 'spy cops' and their methods. Some would form relationships, even have children with members of the groups they infiltrated, who knew nothing of who they really were. It was controversial but sometimes effective.

Ian had another swig of his coffee, bit another chunk of toastie, and carried on speaking.

'The problem now is that I don't think I'm the only infiltrator in the group. Another bloke joined us recently. He checks out. Everything about him checks out. He walks the walk and talks the talk. His cover is just a bit too perfect, though. He sets my alarm bells going. I noticed Mr Green giving him the once-over and it was soon after that he found time to have a quiet word with me and to mention your name.

'My best guess is the new bloke's a Spook. Some sort of government agent sniffing around our witness and seeing how easy it would be to take her out. That's why I've been sticking as close to her as possible. And before you ask, I've made sure she's safe this morning while I meet you. But I need to get her out of there and into a much safer place as soon as possible. For that I probably need your Mr Green again and I don't know how to contact him. Plus it wouldn't be safe for me to do so. I'm too deep into this op to risk blowing my cover now.'

Ted ran his spoon round the inside of his cup, scooping up every trace of the foam from his cappuccino, while he thought of how to respond.

'First off, Mr Green has retired. I may be able to get hold of him but there's no guarantee he would help you. He did the original job at a low rate as it was his swansong. Who would pay this time, if he even agreed to do it?'

'Can't you appeal to his better nature?'

'He doesn't have one. He's a mercenary. He does what he does for the money. If you can't pay him, you won't get him. Next, why are you bothered? If your remit is to infiltrate the group, presumably they're being considered as a terrorist threat, so why does the witness matter to you? And thirdly, why don't you simply make contact with your own control, explain the situation and let them sort it out? That way she's made safe and your involvement isn't revealed.'

'Seriously, Ted? I think you know the answer to that as well as I do. I'm in there to do a specific job. My bosses would probably consider the witness as justifiable collateral damage.

They want the terrorists, not the paedos. Me, I'm different. Can't stand bloody paedos. I've seen first-hand the damage they do and I'd like to see them all castrated with a rusty knife then banged up for life.

'With this witness, we're probably the closest anyone has ever been to bringing them down from the very highest level. But the BRIOCHE lot aren't the people to do it. They're mostly a bunch of armchair idealists. Some poor little rich kids, a few head-cases. None of them up to handling this sort of stuff, if I'm right about the other infiltrator. There's always a chance I'm not, of course, but I'm sure your Mr Green had his suspicions, the same as I have. So can you help or not?'

Ted's mind was working overtime. This wasn't his case; not on his patch. Other than acting as a go-between for Harry, the ex-Met officer, and Mr Green, he'd had little involvement in the bigger picture. But he had been instrumental in bringing one senior police officer to justice on charges related to a paedophile ring, and he knew there was unfinished business to attend to.

It couldn't have come at a worse time, with the inquiry due to start tomorrow. But nor could he simply ignore what he was being told. He knew Harry was constantly in hiding because of the implications of the case. That made it clear that there would be heads rolling at the top of the establishment.

'If it helps you to decide,' Ian pressed on, seeing Ted hesitate, 'one of the reasons I suggested meeting here in Birmingham was that some of what the witness has said relates to offences in the West Midlands and I know you've already taken down some police top brass from up here. So can you help me or not? Without compromising me or my case?'

'I will do. Contact me when you can but don't put yourself at risk. Leave it with me. I'll do whatever I can, but it may take me a few days.'

'Hello, my angel, I'm sorry I've been so long. There was a

clothing sale on so I couldn't resist getting you some lovely things. I hope you've been all right.'

She'd been far from all right. She'd been determined not to cry because she knew how uncomfortable it would be with the gag in her mouth. But she hadn't been able to stop herself. She'd felt so helpless. Unable to detach her hands nor to pull free from the radiator which held her prisoner. She'd given in and let the tears fall, which had left her dry-mouthed, desperately sniffing as her nose ran all over the tea-towel.

He couldn't have been gone all that long but it had felt like an eternity. She'd been unable to find a comfortable position to sit in and had developed cramp in her leg, so painful it made her cry more. Apart from her fears for herself, she couldn't stop thinking about Micki, her cat, and hoping she was all right.

Never in her wildest imaginings had she thought she would have been thankful for the man's return. But she was. The sight of him coming into the kitchen made fresh tears start to her eyes when she thought she had already cried herself dry.

He saw her tears, dropped the shopping bags where he stood and rushed to her side, crouching down to remove the gag from her mouth. His arms enfolded her, one hand stroking her neck, rubbing her back, rocking her gently.

'Oh my poor, poor darling. Did you miss me so much? I'm so sorry. There, there. I'm back now. Gordy's home, my love. Let me untie you, then I'll make you a nice cup of tea and show you all the pretty things I bought for you. I can't wait to see you in them.

'But first I'm going to run you a lovely warm bath with some new scented oil I bought for you. Then we're going to go and lie down together on the bed. We won't make love fully just yet, not if you don't feel ready to, sweetheart. But before we do, for the first time, I want us to get to know every inch of each other's bodies. So there's no clumsy fumbling, like over-eager teenagers, the first time we do. Every single inch, my darling.'

Chapter Five

Ted was in even earlier than usual on Thursday morning, the day the inquiry was to begin. He'd slept badly, on edge about it. He'd tried not to fidget but even Trev, who could usually sleep through an earthquake, had stirred sleepily and asked if he was all right.

In the end Ted slid out of bed, pulled on sweats and went downstairs. Adam, the youngest of the cats, immediately woke, yawned, stretched and padded after him. He was besotted with Ted.

'Go back to bed, young man, it's too early for you to be up and about,' Ted whispered sternly, but Adam just opened a pink mouth in a silent meow and started trying to climb up the leg of Ted's pants.

Ted put the kettle on, made green tea, took a turn round the damp, moonlit garden, cradling Adam in his arms. He finally decided there was no point in trying to get any sleep so he shut Adam firmly back in with the others, showered and dressed, and left for work.

He liked the nick when it was this quiet. It meant he could catch up with things without being disturbed. With never-ending staffing level reductions, there was only a token presence overnight.

He wanted to try to make contact with Mr Green. He didn't have a direct number for him but he always had a paging service he could use. More in hope than anticipation he left a brief message asking Green to call him in connection with the witness, without giving any details.

He was also keen to speak to Harry, the ex-Met officer, the person behind finding the woman. If she was compromised and in danger, there was a good chance he was, too. None of the mobile numbers Ted had for him seemed to be working so he turned to the last email address he had and sent a cryptic message, asking him to get in touch.

He was just about to make a start on the piles of paper still taking up too much room on his desk when his office door burst open unceremoniously and Superintendent Gerry Fletcher strode in.

Ted shot to his feet in a reflex action. Not only was he unfashionably formal – obsequious, his father always flung at him as an accusation, together with 'establishment lackey', in some of their more heated exchanges – but the ex-Guardsman towered over him enough when Ted was on his feet. If he stayed sitting down, he always felt like a hobbit in the presence of a troll.

'Morning, Ted, just to let you know, as a courtesy, that me and my team are here and just about to get stuck in. I understand you've made the conference room available for us?'

'Yes, sir. I think everything you need is there. If not, just ask and I can sort it for you.'

'We'll try and get our work done properly and as soon as we can, but you know we need to be thorough, and to be seen to do an impartial job. There's a strong chance I might need to speak to you or some of your officers at some point, but I think today is likely to be about noses to the grind over the files and reports.'

Knowing that the inquiry was now under way somehow made Ted feel even more twitchy. He was determined not to show it, nor to let the team know he was worried. Ted made a point of always standing between his team and any flak, which was why he was widely respected. Not all bosses were like that. Some would happily throw team members to the wolves to save their own skin.

Instead of saying his usual catchphrase to start morning briefing, Ted simply took his new mug with him and held it up towards the team. There were smiles and a couple of chuckles. They were clearly as tense as he was but appreciated his effort at humour to start the day.

'Where are we up to with Tara MacNamee? Tell me what we now know about her and does it lead us anywhere?'

'Mid-forties, single, no regular significant other,' Jo began. 'Bit of a loner. She came to our attention once a couple of years back. She was spoken to at a party where there was a bit of cannabis being circulated, but nothing to warrant any further action. Personal use, and all that. Other than that, nothing on our records.

'As well as the market research, she does some evening shifts at a gastropub near town. She's not turned up there for any of the work she was booked for and there's been no word from her, which is apparently most unusual. She's one of their most reliable staff members.

'She has a car. A bit of an old banger, by the look of it. It's parked near her house. It doesn't seemed to have moved since she was last seen. Not shown up so far on any cameras we've tried yet, not since there was last any contact with her. She used public transport a lot.'

'Any response so far from the press releases and posters?' Ted asked.

'We're sifting through it now. Some of what we've got is hopeful. As you can see from the white board, we've got a possible sighting on Friday, the day we think she went missing. From talking to her supervisor, with the market research stuff she'd sometimes be based in a shop foyer, that sort of thing. Other times she might go door to door asking questions, sometimes with samples for people to taste or try. For that, she'd usually go into people's houses. Which is why she was supposed to have had her mobile with her and switched on at all times so she could be traced if anything happened.

'It looks like she quite simply forgot to take it with her when she went out. The supervisor said she'd not been well the day before so perhaps she was still not feeling a hundred per cent. Steve's gone all over the phone and there's nothing to suggest she'd gone away, or gone off to meet anyone. So it looks like she went out to work and disappeared after her first call or two.'

Ted was looking at the board as he asked, 'So the only sighting is in Brinnington? If we're looking for anyone with form out there, I don't suppose we'll be short of suspects.'

It was an area with a higher than average crime rate and high long-term unemployment, running at about twenty per cent. Two of its streets had featured amongst the three worst roads in which to live in Stockport, based on a recent police poll.

'Is there any way we might be able to narrow down a bit more where she could have gone from the place where she was last seen?'

Mike Hallam replied, 'There's a slight chance, boss, but it may mean us flooding the area with more officers going door to door, if we can find enough bodies. The supervisor explained how the system works. The researchers have to talk to people from different socio-economic backgrounds. You know the sort of thing, someone retired, someone with independent means, another on benefits, a low income household, and so on.

'This Tara is apparently a good worker. Experienced, reliable. Always puts her work through at the end of each day. And she only started work on this particular survey last Wednesday. So the supervisor has her findings from Wednesday and Thursday and has worked out what profiles she still needed to cover.'

'Now you're going to tell me she was interviewing unemployed, low-income households, which is going to be quite a large percentage, aren't you?'

'The sun always shines on the righteous, boss,' Mike told him. 'She still needed someone employed but in a medium income bracket. So that does narrow it down a bit. Not minimum wage, for sure, and probably not zero hours contract work. We're trying to collate info centrally from here if we can to save time and narrow it down. It will still mean a lot of legwork though.'

'Of course she may have disappeared before she got to find that particular person. I'll talk to the Super about more media coverage. If we can release where she was last seen, that might help. What news from the house? Crime scene or not?' Ted looked at Jezza as he spoke.

'Not, boss, I'd stake money on it. I've been over it in minute detail and there's nothing to suggest she didn't just go out to work as usual and leave her phone behind by accident. The neighbours say she seldom went away. She had a friend in Wales she sometimes went on camping trips with. She would never normally leave the cat for several days without arranging something. The woman next door used to put food out for it and keep an eye on it when Tara told her she was going away.'

'We need to up the ante on this one, everyone. It's nearly a week. You all know the statistics as well as I do and it's not looking promising for Tara at this point. Previous offenders in the area with any form for anything relevant? Assaults? Kidnaps? Anything? Who's on that?'

'Me, boss,' Maurice told him. 'And at the moment it would be quicker to tell you who's not got form up that way.'

'Right, Jo, every available body on this one, please, until we find Tara. Liaise with Kevin Turner and let's throw all the resources we have at it. I need to make myself available here for much of the day for Superintendent Fletcher. So I can mind the shop while the rest of you are out there. Let's get her found, please, and soon.'

'Let's slip you out of these old things, darling, and once I've washed them, I'll put them away. I've bought you some much prettier clothes. Much more feminine. Once I've washed you, you can try them on.'

'Can't I just have a quick shower myself?' she asked him. 'I'm sure they're all lovely, but that way I can get to wear them much sooner.'

She was trying her best to humour him. While he'd been out she'd been turning over and over in her mind the best way to handle him. Could she steel herself to sleep with him, as that was clearly what he wanted? Or would that make him even more obsessive about her?

At least he was clean, she kept telling herself. She'd slept with worse, when she'd had a few. But never anyone who was holding her captive against her will. She'd thought about getting herself drunk and hopefully him too. Then she could just close her eyes, think of England, and as soon as he fell asleep, as he almost certainly would, she might just be able to find a way to escape. Especially if she could convince him not to tie her up while they were having sex as she would need her hands free to make it even better for both of them.

She'd been thwarted when she'd made the suggestion before he went out shopping. He'd looked at her in surprise as he replied, 'Oh no, darling, no alcohol. I want to keep a clear head for our first time together. So I can savour every moment and relive the memory over and over.'

If only she could find her handbag, but she hadn't seen it since she'd first arrived there. He'd taken it away and hidden it the first time he'd tied her up. There was a pepper spray in it. She knew she wasn't supposed to carry one but her work took her into some dodgy situations. One time, alone in a flat with a man, when she'd asked his occupation, he'd told her he was on bail for killing a neighbour. She'd invented a reason he didn't fit the profile and left in a hurry.

Gordon left her hands tied while he ran the bath for her, pouring a generous quantity of foam into the running water. It gave off an overpowering smell of lavender. Positively her least favourite fragrance. It always reminded her of her granny and her maiden aunt, who kept bunches of the plant in their underwear drawers, so they always reeked of the stuff.

Once he was satisfied with the temperature of the water, he turned to her and untied her hands. Then, so slowly it made her skin crawl, he removed her clothes, one item at a time, kissing and licking every part of her body as he uncovered it. She felt her stomach turn over, willing herself not to start retching. She could do this, she told herself sternly. If this was what it would take to get her out of there, then she had to do it. She had to find a way.

Once he'd washed and dried her, he produced the promised clothes. She wasn't sure whether to laugh or cry. There was nothing there she would have chosen for herself. The only thing he'd got right was her size. Everything else, from the ridiculously flimsy and skimpy underwear, to the too-short skirts and flouncy blouses, she wouldn't be seen dead in.

As soon as that thought went through her mind, it chilled her to the bone so she shivered involuntarily. Perhaps that was what this was all about. Perhaps these were the clothes she was going to be found in if he finally raped and strangled her. Or perhaps he would cut her throat as he forced himself on her. Panic started rising in her. Her heart was thudding, her breath shallow.

She shook herself firmly. She had to find a way to get herself out of there. Whatever it took. And that meant keeping a clear head and not giving in to the terror which threatened to swamp her.

He made her try on every single item, then left her dressed in the one he liked best. She was not surprised that it was the one she found the most offensively hideous. Then he tied her up once again to the towel rail while he took another ritualistic shower.

This time he soaped and fondled himself almost to the

point of climax, before blasting himself with cold water, smiling at her the whole time.

'Not yet, my darling. Not yet. I'm saving myself for you.'

Trev was out for the evening when Ted got home. He was with his karate club friends and had said he might go for a drink and a bite to eat with them afterwards. He'd wanted to cancel so he'd be at home, with a meal on the table when Ted got home. But Ted told him he'd no idea what time he'd be back so he should go and enjoy himself.

He'd not long been home and was just fixing himself something to eat from the contents of the fridge when the front doorbell sounded. He wasn't expecting anyone and frankly, he wasn't in the mood for company. He thought he'd better at least see who it was and what they wanted.

As soon as he opened the door, a tall, black-haired teenager flounced past him in a waft of expensive perfume, headed straight for the kitchen and picked up the nearest cat.

'I hate men! They're all bastards,' was her only form of greeting.

With an inner sigh, Ted closed the door and followed Trev's sister, Siobhan, to the kitchen. Teen angst was about the last thing he wanted to cope with but with Trev out for the evening, it would be up to him to smooth ruffled feathers.

'Hello, Siobhan, this is an unexpected surprise. Trev's out for the evening. I could try calling him, if you like?'

She unceremoniously dumped senior cat Queen back on the table she'd picked her up from and let out a melodramatic wail.

'But I need a hug. I need my brother.'

'I can do hugs, if you like,' Ted told her patiently. 'They're not as good as Trev's but I'm all that's on offer at the moment.'

She turned and flung herself at him. He put one cautious arm round her. She may have been his sister-in-law, but he was too much of a copper not to be aware of the potential for misunderstandings with a distraught and impressionable teenager. He asked her what was wrong.

'It's Henry. I was supposed to be meeting him at the stables but I got there early and found him snogging the face off Oliver behind the tack room.'

'Ah,' Ted said. His stock phrase for buying time.

She pulled away from him, her expression furious.

'You don't sound surprised. You knew? Did my brother know as well? You absolute bastards. Why didn't you tell me he was gay? I hate the pair of you as well.'

All Ted's plans for a quiet, relaxed evening to unwind after a stressful day seemed to be flying out of the window. He hated to spoil Trev's fun but he needed reinforcements for this.

'Why don't you let me make you a bit of supper and we can talk about this? I'll text Trev and ask him to come home as soon as he can.'

Chapter Six

'Shewee, you're very welcome to come and visit us any time, you know that,' Ted began. Siobhan had told them she was more than happy to go back to being called by her school nickname, since it was Henry who had objected to it and he was no longer an item.

Ted was busy making tea and toast for everyone. Trev was still in the shower, but at least he was up, much earlier than usual. Ted would normally have insisted that one or the other of them took Siobhan back to school in person. But neither was able to drop everything to do so because of work commitments. Ted had, as usual, been the one to phone the school to assure them that Shewee was safe, just visiting her brother, and to apologise – not for the first time – for any concern she had caused by her unannounced disappearance.

'But you can't keep nicking off school without telling anyone where you're going. One of these days they're going to phone the police and a load of officers are going to be tied up looking for you when they have plenty of other work to be getting on with.'

Shewee leaned over his shoulder to pinch a freshly buttered piece of toast. She spoke round a mouthful of the crust.

'Yeah, yeah, whatevs. Ted, you are so boring sometimes. I can't imagine what my brother sees in you.'

Ted handed her a plate to prevent crumbs and butter hitting the floor as he replied, 'Of course I'm boring. I'm a policeman. I'm paid to be boring. And your brother loves my sparkling wit and endless patience with his sister.'

She laughed out loud at that then tried to look contrite.

'All right, Mr Policeman,' she said, sounding disconcertingly like her brother. 'I promise to try harder. I still think you're a pair of bastards for not telling me about Henry, though.'

'It cuts both ways, Shewee. If you want to be treated like a grown-up you have to accept that sometimes we're going to let you make your own mistakes in life, so you can learn from the experience. We won't do that if we think you're putting yourself in danger, though. So no more disappearing tricks. My team are tied up at the moment with a woman who has genuinely gone missing, long enough to be causing real concern for her safety. If someone did the same as you've just done, at the same time, we'd be stretching resources beyond breaking point and the consequences could be fatal.

'So, it's been nice to see you, but no more unscheduled visits. Trev will take you to the station shortly and see you safely on your way. And don't be too hard on Henry. He may have treated you badly but it's not always easy to come out, even in these supposedly enlightened times.'

He gave her a peck on the cheek and went on his way, his own toast in hand.

'Don't you have to go to work or anything?' she asked him. 'I'll be perfectly all right if you do. As long as you promise not to gag me, of course. I'd need to be able to drink something, at least, while you were out.'

'We have all the time in the world together, my darling,' he told her with a smile. 'I'm signed off on the sick from work. Long-term. I had a few problems when my mum died. I wasn't very well. There was a bit of a fuss. I just have to get my sick-note renewed from time to time. But I can spend almost every waking and sleeping hour with you, while we get to know one another really well.'

She shivered at his words. They were sitting at the table

together, eating breakfast. Her hands were still tied with tights – clean ones every day – and he was keeping anything sharp or hot out of her reach. She was worried by how quickly she was losing her grip on reality. Starting with her perception of time. How long had she been held captive here now? Was it three days or four? Living in a heightened state of fear all the time was playing tricks on her mind. She needed to concentrate. To focus on her main objective – getting out of there alive. She tried another tack.

'Could I have my handbag, please? I haven't seen it since I got here and there are some things in it I would like. I get migraines and I need my tablets for that, just in case.'

His expression changed. He looked suddenly sly. His eyes narrowed. It tilted his usual obsessive appearance to something much more sinister. For the first time she realised he might be totally insane and the thought chilled her to the core.

'I know what you're doing,' he told her. 'If you want your things back, you have to start being nicer to me. Call me something. You never call me anything.'

Stay calm, she told herself. You can do this. Just play along with him. He's not hurt you yet. He would surely have done so by now if that was his intention.

'What would you like me to call you?' she asked him, trying to keep her tone neutral.

'You choose. Something nice. Warm and affectionate. To show how much you care about me.'

'Gordon?'

'That's just my name. Call me something special.'

'Gordy?'

He was frowning his displeasure now. 'That's what my mother called me. I want you to think of a name for me.'

'Dearest?'

His expression started to clear.

'That's better. I quite like that. But something a bit warmer.'

She stifled a hysterical desire to laugh. Her fear was almost intoxicating.

'Bunny?' she tried, in desperation.

He smiled at that.

'I like that. That's lovely. Bunny. Nobody ever called me that before. Now ask me again about your bag, and call me by my new pet name.'

'Please may I have my handbag, Bunny dearest?'

'Of course you can, my angel, because you asked me so nicely.'

Keeping his eyes on her at all times, he went to one of the kitchen cupboards and brought out her battered but much-loved leather shoulder bag. He put it on the table in front of her, smiling at her all the time.

She fell on it, fumbling with the zip, hampered by the fact that her hands were still tied. Wrenched it open. Gazed inside in growing disbelief. Lifted her face to look across the table at him. Saw the smile playing round his lips. If she'd thought herself afraid before, it was as nothing to the fear that seized her at the sight of that smile.

'Bunny is cross with his angel now. I found what you had in your bag. The nasty pepper spray. You were going to spray poor little Bunny in the eyes and he doesn't like that. You pretended to love me but all the time you were planning to hurt me. That's very bad. Wicked. And wicked girls must be punished, until they can be trusted.'

The calm, dispassionate way in which he spoke scared her more than anything he'd done so far. As he took hold of her bound hands and pulled her up from the chair, she opened her mouth to scream. His hand clamped over her face, cutting off not only the sound but most of the vital oxygen she craved. He pushed her, hard, back against the wall, using the weight of his body to immobilise her. The impact forced out what little air remained in her lungs. Stars exploded behind her eyelids for a brief moment before everything went black and she slipped into blissful unconsciousness.

'Trouble, Ted?'

It was Harry's voice, sounding breathless as he often did. Ted knew he was constantly on the move. He'd been hounded and targeted because of his relentless pursuit of paedophiles in high places, which had cost him his job.

Ted hadn't yet made it from the car park to his office. He ducked back into the car, anxious to keep the call as private as possible. He knew Harry would be using a burner phone and would keep it brief so there was less risk of him being traced.

'The witness may be compromised. I got a tip-off which seems legit.'

Harry swore before he went on, 'I thought she was safe. No idea what I can do. I'm having to stay below the radar as much as possible. Can you help? Or our mutual friend?'

'I'm trying to get hold of him to see what he can suggest. It's complicated. There's an undercover op in progress surrounding her current hosts. Our friend spotted their officer. He has a nose for that sort of thing. He told him to contact me in case of trouble.'

He was keeping it cryptic, never knowing who might be intercepting calls.

'Shit! We're so close with this one. I can almost smell success.'

'I'm tied up here. An inquiry into a case. I'll do what I can though. I might be able to sort a safe house and a babysitter. You could perhaps do with a safe house yourself.'

'I'll call you when I can. I'd certainly like not to be looking over my shoulder the whole time. Good luck, Ted.'

He'd no sooner ended the call when Ted's mobile rang again. Another unknown number.

'Why are you pestering me, Gayboy? Have you forgotten I've retired?'

Mr Green. At least he'd called back. Ted hadn't been

convinced that he would do.

'There's a problem. With the witness you delivered.'

'How is that my problem? I did the job I was paid for. A pitiful sum, too.'

'You gave my name to someone. He contacted me. He thinks her safety's compromised. I need help.'

The familiar snort of contempt which was Green's trademark.

'You can't afford me. I know what a DCI earns.'

'The person I spoke to suggested I should appeal to your better nature.'

This time Green laughed. It was not a sound Ted had heard often from him.

'I hope you told him I don't have one.'

'You told me you did the job at a special rate. For your family. For your grandson. The whole operation will be wasted if we can't get her to a place of safety. I can sort a safe house but that's about as much as I can do.'

'So he was what I thought he was? And there's a live op in progress? And the other bloke?'

Ted was used to Green's verbal shorthand. They were on the same wavelength. They didn't need many words to understand one another.

'You were right about that, too. A Spook of some sort, it seems. That's why it's approaching critical point.'

There was a pause, then Green said, 'You do realise this will put you in debt to me for the rest of your miserable existence? That any time I need anything, you're the first person I'll call?'

'If that's what it takes.'

'Sort the safe house. I'll call you in twenty-four hours for the address.'

Green hung up before Ted could say anything further. It might work. If the BRIOCHE group really had been infiltrated by a special agent, Green was the only man Ted would trust to go in and get the witness out with minimum collateral damage. But now he needed to sort out where he could keep her in safety. At least until she could give her evidence on the allegations of historical sexual abuse of under-age children, which looked set to have heads rolling from high up. For that, it was time to go and talk to his boss, the Ice Queen, and ask for her help.

She was an early bird, like him, so he didn't have long to wait before she was in her office. He knocked and put his head round the door to ask when she might have some free time to discuss something with him.

'I have meetings scheduled for most of the day but if you can make it brief, we could talk now, over coffee, if you like?'

As usual, she had set her coffee machine going the minute she walked through the door. She nodded to Ted to sit down, sorted their drinks then took her seat opposite him. He was finding her easier to talk to of late, although their relationship would never be the same as the one he had always enjoyed with Jim Baker. It helped that she knew all about Mr Green, though, and Ted knew she felt the same way as he did about paedophile rings. He outlined everything he knew while she sipped her coffee, listening intently.

'I think we can help and we should help with this. At the very least arrange a safe house and sort out officers to protect this witness. I'm going to pretend I have no idea how she came into Mr Green's clutches in the first place. I think that would be best for everyone, in the circumstances.'

The witness had been sprung from custody not all that far from Stockport, whilst she was being taken from prison for a medical appointment. Allegations had been flying about that she was being held there on a trumped-up assault charge. It had made national headline news when, shortly after her disappearance, the group BRIOCHE issued a statement saying she was with them and making their claims that her testimony could bring down the government.

'I've got the contact details of this Ian's gaffer at the Met, if you want to speak to him out of professional courtesy.'

She surprised him with her answer.

'I think, in the circumstances, it might be better not to say anything. One ongoing inquiry into the affairs of this station might possibly be sufficient for now, don't you think?'

The pain woke her. Dragged her back from the safe, comforting darkness of the deep faint. Her body had been quite happy to stay there after she lost consciousness. It had clearly decided that the world was not a nice place to be in for the moment.

There was a stinging sensation across her buttocks, an angry slapping sound. She realised he was hitting her with something. It felt and sounded like a slipper. She started to struggle, then realised her hands were tied to the bed's headboard, above her head. She was face down and totally naked. She once again had a gag in her mouth. It felt different this time; not as rough as a tea-towel. Possibly a cotton pillow case. She started to struggle, thrashing her untied legs about desperately.

'Keep still! You have to be punished. The more you struggle, the worse it will be.'

She was crying now, great choking sobs around the stifling gag, trying to articulate the word 'Please' over and over. Anything to make him stop. She was so afraid his anger would drive him to something far worse.

It was her tears which finally got through to him. He abruptly stopped hitting her, hurling the slipper across the room where it bounced off the wall. He sat down beside her on the bed, undoing the gag and removing it from her mouth. Then he untied her wrists from the bed-head, though left them bound together as he turned her over, sat her up and put his arms round her.

'There, there, my darling. You were very wicked, but now

I've punished you, I'm sure you won't ever do anything like that to your Bunny again. Will you?'

She was shaking her head violently from side to side, trembling all over. Feeling the power with which he had cut off her airway had been terrifying. She had to find a way to back-pedal, to make him forget what had happened and start to trust her again.

'I'm so sorry, Bunny,' she whimpered. 'I honestly wasn't going to hurt you. I promise you. I just needed to make sure I had my migraine tablets. I'd forgotten the spray was even in my bag. Please believe me, Bunny.'

'Hush, darling, it's all forgotten now. We're going to get back to how we were before this. Come on, I'll take you to the bathroom to wash away those tears and that pain. Then I'm going to let you wash me. So you can show me how really sorry you are for upsetting me, and convince me that you'll never do anything like that again.

Chapter Seven

She was losing weight and it was starting to show. She had the sort of fast metabolism which meant she could eat more or less anything she wanted to without gaining a pound. But the minute she stopped the refuelling, her weight would start to drop. He'd noticed it, too. Expressing concern, which sounded genuine.

'You must try to eat more, my angel. You don't eat enough to keep a little mouse alive.'

It wasn't just being held captive against her will, nor living in fear every moment. She'd always been an active person, preferring to walk than take her car whenever she could. Always out and about doing something. Long hours on her feet in both her jobs. The inactivity and lack of fresh air robbed her of her appetite.

As well as that, his cooking didn't help. He tried his best but all he produced was what she mentally referred to as invalid food. Toast with the crusts cut off at breakfast time. At least she could manage some of that. Soups and broths, from a tin but reasonable quality, for lunch. Mushy, watery mashed potato with a bit of chicken or white fish for supper. One time he served her boiled eggs with dippy soldiers. She'd stared at it in disbelief. What adult ate stuff like that when they weren't ill?

The conversation they were having at the time, coupled with the egg, which she'd always had difficulty eating, all her life, nearly caused her to gag and retch all over the table.

He still hadn't forced her to have sex with him, but she

knew it could only be a matter of time before he did. She'd decided to try a different approach.

'Could we perhaps go away somewhere, Bunny? To a hotel, maybe? For our first proper night together, I mean. I just thought it might be really romantic to do it somewhere new and exciting for us both. Something to make it really special.'

He frowned immediately, shaking his head.

'Oh no, I don't think I'd like that at all. I wouldn't be comfortable anywhere except my own bed. Well, it was mum's bed originally. Towards the end, when she was very poorly, she didn't like me to leave her alone, not even for a moment. I use to lie down on the bed next to her and cuddle her until she went to sleep. That's how she was when she died. Snuggled up in my arms.'

His words made the hated egg lodge at the top of her throat until she felt as if she was choking. She coughed and spluttered, sure it was about to reappear. He hurried to her, gently patting and rubbing her back, fetching her a drink of water, dabbing away the tears which had started to her eyes with a clean towel.

She'd half been thinking about sleeping with him to have done with it. Surely it couldn't be any worse than what she'd gone through already. His story had robbed her of any ability to steel herself to do it. Not in that bed.

She had to get him out of the flat so she could think straight. She desperately needed an escape plan. A proper, realistic one. She told him she thought she might be able to manage some poached salmon with steamed broccoli for supper. When he started to protest that he might not be able to cook that how she liked it, she gave him the details of a ready meal she often bought for herself. He seemed eager to please and promised to go straight out to get it. She asked for strawberry yoghurt for dessert. She specified a particular brand which meant he needed to visit two shops, so it would take him longer than his previous shopping trips.

As usual he tied her to the radiator before he went out. Although he gagged her, he didn't put the tea-towel in her mouth after her coughing fit, just fixed it so it covered it. It was a start.

As soon as she heard the front door close, she started wriggling about to see if there was any way to free her hands. She was soon disappointed and frustrated to find she was as tightly trussed as ever. And no amount of rubbing her face against her shoulder did anything to loosen the gag across her mouth. She swore aloud behind the cloth.

She looked all round her. Although she'd done it many times since she'd arrived there – however many days ago it was, she could no longer remember – there must be something, some glimmer of hope she'd not yet spotted. Even if she could somehow get free from her bonds, she still needed to locate the door keys. And a telephone. She hadn't seen a landline and had never seen him use a mobile phone, nor even carry one with him.

Everywhere was as clean as a hospital operating theatre. He spent most of his time cleaning, wiping down everything with disinfectant, talking to her all the time as he worked. Constantly asking her questions about herself. Telling her about his life, his hopes and dreams. His plans for their future life together.

The kitchen was compact but well appointed. Some of the units and cupboards looked quite new. They were the less fashionable type without plinths. Raised on feet with a small gap under them. They could be a nightmare to clean under, but every day he ran a mop under there. There couldn't have been anything under them, she told herself. But she had nothing else to do and no hope from anywhere else so she might as well give it a try.

Her hands were useless to her, tied as they were. She could only wriggle her fingers underneath one cupboard a couple of inches and there was nothing there. Not even fluff. But her legs were free and thanks to his hideous taste in shoes, she could explore barefoot.

She always favoured trainers or hiking shoes, walking sandals when it was warmer. He'd bought her a repugnant pair of sparkly court shoes with impossibly high heels.

Her hopes had soared when she'd first seen the heels on the shoes. Was he unwittingly handing her a weapon? But as soon as she touched them she realised how flimsy they were. Too much so to risk even attempting to attack him with one. And impossible to conceal in her hand so he'd see her coming a mile off.

At least they were easy to slip out of. But there was nothing. No matter how she stretched and scrabbled about with one foot after another, she could detect nothing at all. Certainly nothing which could help her to escape. And there was no way she could open any of the cupboards with her feet, try as she might. Tears of frustration flooded her eyes.

Even with two shops to visit, it wouldn't be all that long before he was back and she felt she'd achieved nothing. She was no nearer to ending the nightmare and getting away than she'd been before.

Then, just as she was about to give up, she felt something under her toes. Right at the very back in a far corner under a cupboard. Something hard. Metallic. Which made a tantalising chink on the tiles as she tried to hook it out into the open with her toes.

Inch by inch she drew it carefully towards her, craning her neck to see what her treasure was.

It was a nail. A brand new, shiny, smooth, big steel nail. With a wicked point at one end.

It had been so long since she'd believed in any kind of divine being, she didn't know who it was she was silently thanking for her only chance of survival to date. But now she had to be clever. As cunning as he could be. She knew she would only get one chance to use this potential weapon to save herself. She needed to plan and prepare so nothing went wrong.

Carefully, reluctantly, she used one bare foot to push the nail back out of sight until she could use it. Somewhere the intruding mop couldn't snag on it and pull it out into the open. Painstakingly, she managed to wedge it behind where two of the cupboard feet stood next to one another. That way, if she was very lucky, it could stay there, ready for when she'd worked out the next part of her plan.

This time she didn't have to act when he came home, bending to untie her gag and release her from the radiator. As he helped her to her feet, gently kissing her cheek, she gave him the first genuine smile of her captivity.

'I'm so pleased to see you back, Bunny dear. I had terrible cramp in my back, sitting there. I just need to stretch my arms right up above my head. That should ease it.'

Ted bumped into Gerry Fletcher's sergeant as they were both going into the station at the same time. He'd been introduced briefly to him the day before but they hadn't spoken other than in passing. The inquiry team were keeping their distance for now. They would in time probably be speaking to all members of Ted's team and to Ted himself. But not yet. His greeting to Ted was brief and informal.

'All right, Ted?'

Ted nodded back at him, 'All right, Tony,' as they went their separate ways.

Ted had no idea how long Fletcher and his officers would be in the station. Their presence inevitably put everyone on edge. They were there to do a job but they were never the most popular members of any force.

'Are we any further forward with Tara MacNamee?' Ted asked at the start of the morning briefing.

'By working back from the report of where she was last seen in Brinnington, we got lucky and found the person she'd interviewed just before that sighting,' Jo began. 'Unemployed single bloke living alone. He's got form for all sorts of stuff, mostly nicking cars and a bit of housebreaking. There's nothing in his history to suggest violence, especially not towards women. Mike went round after Uniform found him. Mike?'

'He couldn't have been more helpful, boss. He's well used to us knocking on his door but whatever's happened to Tara, he was keen not to be going down for it. Voluntarily invited us to search his place. He even found the wrapper off the chocolate cereal bar he'd tasted for the survey to show us. Gave a good description of Tara and said when she left his flat she was absolutely fine.'

'See that his profile gets through to her supervisor please, Jo. That should help her narrow down even more who Tara might have needed to interview next.'

'Already done, boss. She's still saying someone employed, in a medium wage-earning bracket, so it doesn't narrow it down all that much from where we were already. What about a reconstruction of Tara's last known movements, now we have a definite last sighting? It's been a week. If she's all right, someone should have seen her by now.'

'I'll ask the Super to get onto the Press Office. See if we can get an updated bulletin out on the local news as soon as possible, then look into a reconstruction, if that doesn't bring anything in. Have we traced all her known contacts?'

Jo nodded. 'All bar one traced and spoken to. No one's heard from her for a week now which is unusual. Her cards haven't been used at all anywhere, either. Steve's got her phone and is monitoring traffic to it. Steve?'

'Pretty much what you'd expect, boss,' Steve replied. He was finally much more relaxed and informal, even with Ted. Lodging with retired sergeant Bill Baxter was clearly doing wonders for his confidence. 'Calls from work, getting increasingly concerned about her as it's clearly so out of character. A couple from the friend in Wales asking if she was all right. Nothing at all to suggest she had any plans to go anywhere.'

'And based on her last known location, compared against previous offenders in the area, is anything jumping out? Maurice?'

'We've got a right bunch of charmers scattered about that area, but no one with any known form for kidnap, assault on women, murder or anything that might give us a lead.'

'Anyone got any theories?'

'There's nothing anywhere in what we've found out about her to suggest she's the sort who would go off on a whim without letting anyone know. Especially not work. Both her immediate bosses say she's a thoroughly reliable worker who never lets them down,' Mike replied.

'And then there's the cat, boss,' Jezza put in. 'The neighbour says she would never go off without making sure it was all right. That's completely out of character.'

'Have we spoken to the friend in Wales yet?

'Not yet, boss, that's next on the agenda. She's not answered her mobile when we've tried so she may well be at work and we don't have a work number. We didn't really want to leave a message saying it was the police, in case it panics her into thinking Tara's been found dead,' Jo told him.

'Right, chase her up as soon as possible then, please. If Tara had talked to anyone about any plans she might have, surely it would be her friend. And let's get a look at her computer. If that's still at the house, Steve, can you go round and see what it might be able to tell us? If you can get into it all right. Perhaps she received emails which made her behave out of character. We're presumably keeping the house under observation?'

'Uniform have that covered, boss. They'll let us know as soon as there's any sign either of Tara or of anyone else going to the house.'

'It's looking more and more a possibility that wherever she

went to next and whoever she spoke to, that's where she still is. I just hope she's alive and unharmed. Being held against her will is bad enough but the alternative is worse.'

Ted had warned Trev he had no idea what time he'd get home and that he could well be in work over the weekend, depending on what, if anything, developed with the case. He took a moment to call him late afternoon with an update.

'Did Shewee get back to school safely?'

'Yes, she did. Missed a connection at Bristol Parkway because of a delay, so she got there later than planned but she's there. Have you found your missing woman yet?'

'Not yet ...' Ted broke off as his desk phone started to ring. 'Got to go, see you when I see you.'

'Kev here, Ted. Finally might have a lead for you on the Misper, though it might not be what you were hoping for. An anonymous caller, reckons they saw something suspicious up the top end of Reddish Vale last night. A black 4x4 up near the lakes. It looked as if whoever was with the vehicle may have been dumping something in the water.'

'And they're only just telling us? What's the matter with people? This is up near Brinnington, then, so it could be relevant.'

'It was a bit of a funny call. Bloke refused to give any details. Said he didn't think anything of it at the time but he heard a mention on the lunchtime news that a woman had gone missing up in Brinny, which was when he decided to call us. If you ask me, he might have been up to no good up there himself which is why he didn't want to say anything when he saw the vehicle. Hearing that on the news might just have pricked his conscience.

'I've got officers going there now, and I've asked for Mounted support. They can search a bigger area more quickly than we can on foot.'

'Do we need a dive team, do you think? How reliable is

this info about dumping stuff in the water, would you say?'

'I'm not sure how reliable any of it is, to be honest. But if we don't search and she's in there, we'll get hung out to dry for the delay. Not that it will help her if she's been in the water all night, poor lady.'

'I'll just run it past the Ice Queen and see if she'll green-light it. I think I'll take a run-out up there myself, just to see what's going on.'

Kevin laughed.

'Any excuse to escape the office and the paperwork, eh, Ted? I hope we don't find a body. It would be nice to hold on to a shred of hope that she might still be out there alive somewhere. But after a week, it's looking more and more unlikely with no more sightings and nothing else to go on.

'If only she'd not forgotten to take her phone with her. We'd have pinpointed her long ago if she had it with her.'

Chapter Eight

Ted went to find Jo Rodriguez to tell him he needed to go up to Reddish Vale to direct the search, as he was responsible for the day to day running of the case. Ted asked him if he'd mind if he tagged along. A lot of officers of Ted's rank seldom left the sanctuary of their office. But Ted was a hands-on type. Although he trusted Jo and the team, he still liked to get out into the field from time to time. He was particularly keen to see this latest case brought to an end. He was getting a bad feeling about it. A week was a long time for someone to disappear without contact and with nothing to suggest the absence was pre-planned.

They went in Jo's car and he drove. As usual, the language got a bit colourful whenever traffic was heavy or anyone made a stupid manoeuvre anywhere near him. Most of it was in Spanish, which Jo knew the boss didn't speak. Or at least he thought he didn't until Ted remarked amiably, 'Did I tell you Trev's teaching me Spanish? In case we go there on holiday one of these days.'

Jo let out a shout of laughter.

'Busted, boss,' he said. 'But I bet that's not true.'

It was Ted's turn to grin.

'Just as well I'm not a good Catholic boy like you always claim to be. I'd have to confess that little porky, for sure.'

The police horsebox was already on site when they drove up to the visitor centre to park. The side jockey door was open and the ramp was down, but the back gates were closed and the horses were still on board. Ted and Jo went over to the side door, ID in hand. Ted gave a brief knock on it.

An officer with sergeant's stripes leaned out of the door, clocked their ID and greeted them.

'DCI Darling, DI Rodriguez. Can we talk about where to deploy you?' Ted asked.

'I'm Karen. Climb aboard,' she invited. 'It's easier to brief in here, away from the prying public. You've got four of us. The others are in the back, tacking up. Nice to be out here in the countryside. It certainly makes a change from the streets of Moss Side. You've not got us for all that long though, I should warn you. The horses are getting close to the end of their hours. You can muck about with our shift patterns, but not theirs.'

They followed her into a small living area with seating, complete with cooker, kettle and fridge. They declined her offer of a brew, keen to get the search under way. As they went in, a large bay horse's head appeared round the door from the seating area to the rear of the lorry where the horses were transported, eyeing the newcomers with interest.

Karen had her back to them as she pushed the great head back and shut the door on it.

'You can keep your nose out, Ted, it's got nothing to do with you,' she said emphatically.

She turned back to see Ted and Jo exchanging surprised looks. It was relatively cramped inside so now she could look more closely at the ID hanging round Ted's neck.

'Oops,' she smiled. 'You're a Ted too? That great lump in there is my horse. His stable name is Ted. That's who I was talking to. His real name is Edwin Drood. They all have names from Dickens. Did you know that? And he's a right nosy beggar.'

Ted didn't, but he did know who Edwin Drood was. It was the character he was named after, as his father had enjoyed reading Dickens. Few people knew that and he wasn't about to admit it.

'So what do you need from us, while you've got us?' Karen

continued. 'This is presumably about your missing woman, last sighted in Brinnington?'

Ted nodded and went on, 'We've had a call which may or may not be reliable about someone possibly throwing or dumping something in the water up here last night.'

'Last night? So we're looking for a body, then? I hoped we might be able to help get you a happy ending on this one.'

'We've got a dive team on the way but they're held up on another job. What we need from you is a thorough search of the area around the lakes for any sign of a car having been close to the water. Or anything else which might suggest the tip-off could be reliable.'

'The tip-off mentioned water, rather than the lake specifically? So we need to check the river as well, do we?'

'Good point. Yes, please. Uniform can do the area around here but it might be useful if you can cover further out. We don't have enough info to pinpoint an exact place. It was all very tenuous, but with nothing at all to go on, we clearly have to follow up every possible lead.'

'What if two of us did the lake and river and the other two check out the old railway line area? Hopefully by then your dive team might have appeared. Wouldn't it be great if real life was like fiction on the telly where you'd have dozens of officers at your beck and call in an instant?

'Right, we'd best go and get on and see what we can find for you. The clock's ticking. Once we're done, we'll radio in before we leave. Obviously we'll be in contact sooner if we do happen to find anything of use to you.'

Ted and Jo went to find whoever was in charge of the Uniform presence at the scene. It was another sergeant who was deploying officers to keep interested bystanders away from the water's edge. He nodded a greeting to Ted and Jo.

'D'you want us to start taping an area off yet or just trying to keep people back? Is it a crime scene?'

'Chicken and egg at the moment,' Jo told him cheerfully. 'We won't really know the answer to that unless and until we find a body. Or at least some strong indication that there's one here to be found. Just keep people back as best you can for now. We don't want Joe Public's footprints all over everywhere if it does turn out to be a crime scene.

'Have you got enough bodies to start questioning everyone hanging around, as well as starting the search?'

'I've got dozens of them. All just hanging about with nothing else to do.' The sergeant's reply was heavy with sarcasm. Ted would have pulled him up short but he felt and shared his frustration at the increasing cuts, which were hampering the way they could work.

'Well, you have me and the DI for now, that's two more bodies than you had before,' he told him. It was a mild rebuke, nothing more. 'I'm sure we can talk to a few people while we wait for news from the Mounties or the arrival of the dive team.'

'Thank you, sir.' It was the sergeant's way of an apology. Tempers were constantly getting frayed by the shortage of resources and the inevitable criticism from the public and press for the perceived lack of action and results on cases.

Ted and Jo went to talk to the onlookers. Nobody had been around the previous night so they couldn't find anyone who may have witnessed anything. Inevitably all of them were keen to find out what was going on and to discover whether or not the police were looking for a body. It was no surprise to Ted that before long the familiar figure of the local newspaper reporter threaded her way through the bystanders to come and talk to him.

'Erm, hello, Chief Inspector,' she began, as awkward as she always was. She somehow managed to put some good stories together, despite her apparent timidity. Ted suspected that she played on the image and that people often felt sorry enough for her to say more than they usually would say to the press.

'Hello, Penny, and before you ask, I've no official statement to make at the moment. You can see we have mounted and other uniformed officers searching this area, but that's all I can tell you for the time being. There'll be an official press release as soon as we have something to tell you.'

'I see you have an underwater search unit arriving,' she said, watching the vehicles arrive.

Ted mentally tried out one of Jo's Spanish swear words for size. Typical! The dive team would have to arrive just as he was standing with the press. He really didn't want to have to answer any more of her questions until he knew a bit more about what was going on. Preferably not even then. Penny was certainly nicer than her predecessor, Pocket Billiards, but Ted didn't like talking to the press. He found they invariably misquoted him.

'So you're looking for a body in the lake, presumably, if you've brought divers in,' she went on. 'Is this the missing woman? Last seen in Brinnington? We're quite close to Brinnington up here, of course. You think she'd dead, then? Has there been a development? Or a tip-off?'

'No further comment, Penny. Now, if you'll excuse me, I need to go and talk to the dive team. Any further questions, you know my DI, Jo Rodriguez, over there. I'm sure he'll be happy to help you, if he's able to.'

The dive team comprised yet another grumpy sergeant with tired team members, coming to the end of their scheduled hours. They would do their level best, with the time remaining to them. But Ted understood that, like the Mounted section, the divers' hours were carefully regulated for safety reasons. It was one of the reasons Ted wanted to be there in person rather than leaving Jo to have to deal with smoothing all the ruffled feathers, on top of everything else.

The Mounted officers did their bit but radioed in that there was nothing to report before they loaded the horses up to take them back to their stables for evening feeds.

The underwater team's sergeant kept his officers searching for as long as he reasonably dared then told Ted apologetically that he really would have to call it a day. As usual, Ted took the time to thank everyone personally. All of them were dispirited. Despite hours of searching, they had turned up absolutely nothing which gave them any clue as to Tara MacNamee's whereabouts. The only positive thing to have come out of the exercise was that it looked unlikely that she was at the bottom of the lake.

Ted and Jo were the last to leave the scene and were just getting into Jo's car when Ted's mobile phone rang.

'Irene here, Ted. Duty Inspector. What joys! You probably aren't going to like what I have to tell you, either. We've had another anonymous caller, about your missing lady. I know you've been out all afternoon following up on the other tip-off. This one, which may or may not have been from the same caller, is now saying a dark coloured all-terrain vehicle, an open boot and a splash. But this time at Sykes Reservoir. And I bet you've just stood the dive team down.'

Ted thanked her then, as he rang off, he made Jo chuckle by repeating his Spanish swear words.

'Irene. There's been another call. This time someone claiming to have seen a vehicle disposing of something in Sykes Reservoir. Right on the other side of town. Someone is playing games with us over this.'

Jo had phoned the station earlier and told the team to knock off at the usual time. There was no point in keeping everyone hanging round and not a lot of use in carrying on searching for the missing woman until they'd checked out the tip-off. It wasn't as if they were short of other cases to be getting on with.

'Swift half in The Grapes before we both head home, Ted?' Jo suggested when they got back to the station and went up to clear their desks for the day.

Ted had already phoned Trev earlier to let him know he was likely to be late back. He told him to go ahead and eat, not to wait for him.

'Do you think you and I could play squash together a bit some time?' he'd asked him.

'In all the massive amount of time we get to spend together?' Trev laughed. 'Why squash, in particular, when we barely have time for martial arts together, let alone anything else?'

'Just once I'd like to be able to come close to at least matching the Chief next time he summons me for more ritual humiliation.'

'Well, you know Willow is always saying we can sign ourselves into her club as her guests at any time. So I'm up for it, if you can find the time. Don't be too late home this evening. I've hardly seen you all week and I quite fancy a bit of sport, now you come to mention it.'

Jo got the drinks in, putting Ted's Gunner down in front of him and making a start on his own half of lager.

'Bugger about all that wasted time, eh? Not to mention the budget. Why do people do stuff like that? I've never understood anyone who gets their kicks from seeing the police run round like fools on a wild goose chase.'

'And we've potentially got it all to go through again tomorrow. No way I could get hold of another dive team this evening and no point asking for more Mounted officers if we risked running out of daylight. I'll come in myself tomorrow; I'd like to see this through.'

'Do you think this next one is any more likely to be true than the one today?'

'I honestly don't have a clue on this case. Is Tara being held somewhere by someone who's getting his kicks not just from having power over her but by watching us run round like idiots following false leads? Or is this someone else, not connected with the actual disappearance, who has an axe to grind and likes watching us get it wrong?'

Before they'd left the station, they'd gone over the notes of what the team had been working on while they were both out. It amounted to a big fat zero in terms of tracking down where Tara might be. The team had managed to get hold of the friend in Wales, at last, and she was as mystified as anyone. She spoke regularly on the phone to Tara and reported she'd given no indication of any plans to go anywhere. She'd also confirmed there was no way she would simply take off without making sure her cat was looked after.

Jezza and Rob had been to the pub where Tara worked and talked at length to other staff there. Again, there was no hint of a planned trip away. Nor had anyone noticed any customers paying an unusual amount of attention to Tara while she worked. Neither had she mentioned being pestered by anyone, or having the feeling she was being watched or followed.

From her market research supervisor, they'd obtained details of all the areas she'd been working in for the past month and were busy trying to get hold of CCTV cameras from stores where she'd been based to do shopper surveys.

'It's hours of work but there's just a chance we might spot someone watching her, or interacting with her in some way,' Jo said optimistically. 'And now we've got a few more concrete locations of where she was working, we can get Maurice onto cross-checking them with known offenders in those areas. I think that's about as much as we can do for now.'

Ted and Jo drained their glasses and stood up to leave the pub.

'Dive team first thing tomorrow then,' Ted said as they walked back to the station car park together. 'And let's just hope this isn't another hoax. I'd like to find Tara alive, of course, but at least we'd know where she was if we do find a body. Trouble is, like you said, we're cranking up the budget already with nothing to show for it.

'If she has just gone off somewhere on a whim, she's certainly going to have a lot of explaining to do when she reappears.'

Chapter Nine

Ted's phone pinged with a text message just before he set off to drive home.

'Delivery Sunday midday. Will phone 2hrs before for address.'

Mr Green. Being his usual ultra-cautious self. If he didn't know his final destination himself until shortly before delivering the witness to the safe house, it was less likely that anyone else would know.

Everything was in place to take the witness into temporary protection until a more permanent solution could be found to allow her to testify in safety. Knowing Mr Green, Ted was certain he was not going to be best pleased with the arrangements which were in place to receive her. It was skeleton cover, at best.

The Ice Queen had called Ted earlier in the day. She wasn't in the office but was, as ever, working from home through yet another Saturday. Luckily her teenage sons were used to not seeing much of their mother, even at weekends, and her Traffic Inspector husband arranged his own shifts so he could be with them when she wasn't.

'Firstly, Ted, don't shoot the messenger. I promised you a safe house, which I now have. But the cover is not all I would have wanted it to be. You'll have an AFO on duty round the clock, a team of three working eight hour shifts, one on, two off, as long as is necessary.'

'One?' Ted queried. 'One firearms officer and that's it? You and I both know that's nothing like enough, even if it's twenty-four hour cover.'

'It was a struggle to get that, believe me. It's not our case, so there's no budget allocation for it. The best I can suggest is you put one of our officers there as well. Even if they're not armed, they can at least call help if it's needed. As the witness is female, might I suggest you send DC Vine? I'm assuming Mr Green's will be a flying visit, simply to effect delivery?'

'I imagine so. He's not said. He's being his usual talkative self.'

'And you're planning on being there yourself to oversee the handover?'

Ted hesitated. He was keen to see it through up at the reservoir with the next underwater search the following morning. As if reading his mind, she continued, 'You can safely leave Jo Rodriguez in charge of the search, surely? Your specialist skills would be better used in ensuring this witness's safety until a proper transfer can be arranged. I imagine there must be someone on the Met's team to whom she can be entrusted. With that in mind, I would suggest you draw a side-arm until we're happy she's safely under cover.

'I don't wish to sound pessimistic, but perhaps it would be a good idea if you were to ask DC Vine or whoever you send to record a full testimony from the witness. That way there are statements on record in more than one place, should anything happen to prevent her from testifying elsewhere.'

'Childcare is often an issue for Jezza, because of her brother, but I'll see what can be done.'

'And Ted, one last thing. Don't try and do everything yourself. I'm sure I don't have to remind you that it's one of your mercifully few faults. Delegate. Jo is an excellent DI. Let him show it. Plus you have two DSs. Let DS Hallam, certainly, spread his wings a bit.'

Ted knew she was right but didn't like to be reminded of his reluctance to step back. He let his feelings show with a curt, 'Ma'am.'

The Ice Queen ignored his tone and went on, 'How is DS O'Connell doing? I imagine he's more worried than most about the inquiry?'

Ted had found a quiet moment to talk to Rob. They couldn't discuss the ongoing inquiry but Ted was anxious his DS wasn't piling too much pressure on himself, while it was going on, by taking up the paedophile case on their own patch at the same time. He'd reminded him again that he would always make time to talk to any of his team who needed to air their feelings about anything.

He didn't know how long they would need to babysit the witness. He imagined that Harry would be busy trying to find someone they could trust within the Metropolitan Police on the operation dealing with sexual abuse against children through paedophile rings. Ted knew that this witness had come forward to say that she had tried several times in the past to report what was happening to her and others who were mainly from children's homes. She'd spoken of incidents happening in London as well as other areas of the country she'd been moved to, including the West Midlands.

The names she'd been mentioning had been sufficiently highly placed to put her at risk. She'd first been imprisoned on a dubious police assault charge. Now it seemed that her cover was blown again which suggested a leak somewhere within the police who were handling the case. Ted would know more when he could talk at length to Harry and for that he needed him, too, in a safe place.

Ted made time to speak to Jezza before he finally went home for the day. Trev would be giving up on him at this rate. But knowing Jezza would require time to sort something for her brother, Tommy, he wanted to give her as much notice as possible to make arrangements, if she could. If not, he'd call on Maurice who was always a safe pair of hands with a fragile witness.

'Jezza? Sorry to disturb your day off. I know you're on the

rota for tomorrow and I need you for something of a special op, to do with a protected witness. Ideally, I could do with you staying with her overnight tomorrow if you can possibly sort something for Tommy. I'm sorry it's short notice, and I'll understand if you can't, but it's only just come up.'

'There's no problem over Tom, boss. This is strictly between us two, please. I haven't told the others yet, especially not Maurice, because you know what a jealous sod he can be. But Nat's moved in with me now. He and Tommy get on really well, most of the time, so it shouldn't be a problem. And Nat knows he can always call Steve if he's having difficulty. Just as long as I'm able to phone Tom when it's his bedtime, it should work out fine.'

Ted hesitated. He was paranoid about anything to do with this operation. He'd had far more experience of such things than Jezza and he knew the risks involved if any other special operatives were interested in their witness. Jezza was sharp, though. She correctly interpreted his pause.

'I take it you want me to do that from a burner phone and make sure location is turned off on my work one? This is going to be that kind of special op, is it?'

'You'll have an armed escort at all times, and I'll be carrying. I don't want to put you under any risk ...'

'Boss, I've known you long enough to know that if you've risk assessed this, it will be safe. I'll check with Nat and Tommy but it should be fine. Count me in.'

It was later than Ted had hoped before he finally got home and put the car away. Trev was, as ever, sprawled in front of the TV, covered in cats, watching a classic film. Only little Adam sat slightly apart from the others, his eyes riveted on the door. There was none of the usual trail of dirty plates and cutlery everywhere so Trev must have been trying hard to be tidier, as he'd promised. That put the onus on Ted to open up more about his thoughts and feelings, something he always found hard to do, even with Trev.

'Oh, look, cats, there's a strange intruder in the house,' Trev told his feline companions. 'I vaguely recognise him, though, so he's probably not a burglar.'

Adam jumped down from his perch and trotted up to greet Ted, meowing noisily.

'Adam still loves me,' Ted replied, scooping the kitten up and sinking down next to his partner. 'I'm sorry you've not seen much of me this weekend. It's been a bit full on, and I'm going to have to be out again all day tomorrow. I'll make it up to you, though.'

'That's what you say every time. I am chalking them up, you know. But it's been on the local news about police divers up at Reddish Vale. Was that for your missing woman, and did you find her or anything else related to the case?'

'Nothing. She's still missing. It looks like it might have been a hoax call.'

'That's a bit sick, if it was. Why do people do that? As if you're not under enough pressure with resources without anything like that. Oh, and Shewee phoned to say sorry.'

'What's she done now?' Ted's tone was immediately suspicious.

'Had the ritual blazing row with The Olds about bunking off school and coming here. She got so angry she blurted out that we'd got married.'

'Well, that's not so terrible. They were bound to find out eventually, I suppose.'

'It is terrible. It is to me. I didn't want them to know. We agreed to keep it to close family only knowing about it.'

Just for a moment, Ted saw the hurt and betrayed fifteen-year-old boy, not the adult man he loved. The Trev whose parents had thrown him out unceremoniously when he'd come out to them. He'd gone to live with an aunt and had only found out after she'd been killed in a road accident that his parents had paid towards his keep and his education ever since he'd left home, although refusing any further contact with him. He dismissed it as nothing more than a feeling of obligation on their part, rather than any genuine interest in or affection for their son.

Ted put out a hand and took hold of one of Trev's, squeezing it gently.

'Sorry, I shouldn't have said that, it was an insensitive thing to say.'

He paused for a minute, thinking about the best way to phrase what he was going to say next. Trying to be open as Trev had asked him to, but not sure of his reaction. 'I'll need to be carrying for tomorrow. It's a bit of a special op.'

Trev turned to look at him, his expression concerned, all sign of his earlier anger evaporated as quickly as it had flared up.

'Is it something dangerous? You know I don't like you doing the armed stuff. I worry about you.'

'It's just a precaution. And I told you because you want me to be more open with you.'

Trev leaned over to kiss him on the cheek.

'That's true, I did. You know how fickle I am. But thank you for telling me. I'm pleased you're being more open. Have you had anything to eat? Do you want me to make you something?'

'I can't remember, to be honest. I think I might have had a bacon barm at some point. But I've gone beyond the point of being hungry now. I just need to unwind a bit, then shower and sleep.'

Trev was looking at him with a twinkle in his blue eyes which Ted knew well.

'You'll need to sort your shoulder holster out, then. Try it on to make sure it still fits you. You know what the sight of you in a shoulder holster does to me. How tired are you?'

Ted smiled indulgently.

'I thought I was tired when I got in. It seems I might have

been mistaken.'

The dive team were on site at first light. Different officers from the day before, with the advantage of being fresh and eager. Ted met Jo up at the reservoir. He had his own service vehicle with him so he was ready to head straight for the safe house once he got word that Green was on his way there. Jezza would make her own way as soon as he gave her the address. Ted had asked that the AFOs arrive at the house in an unmarked vehicle and plain clothes, only changing into uniform once inside. If for any reason anyone was watching the house, the sight of armed police going inside would be a giveaway that something was going on.

Ted had opted for casual clothes rather than his usual work suit. His cotton field jacket would conceal the weapon in its holster much more easily than his suit would. He'd signed the firearm out first thing, so he didn't need to go back for it if Mr Green should turn up sooner than anticipated. He would keep it on his person the whole time until he signed it back in. But he didn't want it to be obvious to any casual observer that he was armed.

Ted let Jo do most of the briefing of the dive team and the uniformed officers present. There were few people about at such an early hour on a Sunday morning but neither of them wanted any inquisitive onlookers. Since the station's mole had been outed and was being dealt with, there were far fewer early tip-offs to the press. They wanted to keep the lid on this one for as long as they could, especially if they had another fruitless mission.

'I don't suppose your caller said which lake?' the sergeant in charge of the team asked hopefully.

'We don't have much to go on at all, I'm afraid,' Jo told her. 'Just a vehicle up here last night and a splash of something going in the water. We can get Uniform looking round the banks to see if there's any sign of where anything might have gone in. We also need to keep in mind that this could be another hoax, like yesterday's effort.'

'Well, they're not big areas of water and we're starting in fresh, so we'll do our best and see what, if anything, we can find for you. If we start with the smaller lake while Uniform have a scout around everywhere else to see what they can find. I can't see at a glance where anyone could easily get a vehicle up close enough for body-dumping, but you never know.'

Ted was on pins, waiting for the call from Green which would take him away from the action. Hoping there was something to show for the search before he had to leave. Not a body. He wanted to hold onto the faint hope that Tara MacNamee was still alive and safe somewhere, just unable to get herself home.

Bang on ten o'clock, there was a call to Ted's mobile which he knew would be Mr Green. Instinctively he moved away from all ears, even Jo's, before he answered the call. He trusted Jo implicitly but this op was on a strictly need to know basis for security reasons.

Green was, as usual, economical, with words. No form of greeting.

'Address?' was all he said.

Ted told him and his only response was, 'ETA two hours.'

That meant Ted would need to be away from the reservoir site in an hour to allow himself enough time to get to the safe house and make sure everything there was in order. Right on cue, the dive team's sergeant came looking for Ted and Jo.

'One of the lads has found something. We're just about to recover it to shore then we can have a proper look at what it is.'

It was a delicate operation, not something which could be hurried. Ted kept glancing anxiously at the time display on his mobile phone, itching to see what the team had found, not wanting to leave himself short of time on the other operation.

Finally, he and Jo stood next to the sergeant looking down at what the water had given up. If it wasn't a body, it was certainly giving a good impression of one. It was thoroughly wrapped and trussed in some sort of plastic covering, neatly tied in several places. The wrapping was in good condition. It seemed clear that whatever it was, it hadn't been in the water all that long. The sergeant spoke first. Ali, she'd told them to call her.

'Well, it's up to you clever detectives to say for sure, of course. But I'd hazard a guess that if that is a body, we're not looking at a case of suicide.'

Chapter Ten

'Looks like we have ourselves a murder case, boss,' Jo said ironically. He was being formal in front of the dive team sergeant. 'I'd better call in the cavalry.'

He and Ted turned to move away a short distance after Ted had, as usual, thanked the sergeant for the team's work. She looked at him in surprise. She wasn't used to seeing a DCI on site, let alone one polite enough to say thank you for routine police work.

'I'm going to have to go shortly, for this other job,' Ted began. 'I've got Jezza tied up on it too for a day or so. It's a bit under the radar, this one, for now. So I'm sorry if that leaves you short.'

'We'll be fine, Ted. I have done this before,' Jo cut in with a grin which flashed his gold tooth.

'Yes, sorry, I didn't mean to sound as if I don't trust you. It's just ...'

'You're already under the microscope for the last case so you need to be all over this one from the start,' Jo finished for him. 'I understand that. We didn't slip up on the last one. It just had an unfortunate outcome. And we won't on this one. But I'll get video footage of everything so you'll still have eyes on, even if they're not first eyes. I'll get on to the coroner's office now to report it and summon up a pathologist.'

'Let's hope Professor Nelson is on duty. However the body met its end, this is a crime scene with the way it's been disposed of. So we could do with the big guns from the start. Why don't I go back to the nick now on my way to this other job? That saves you one job, at least. And I'll let the Super know. We'll need to put a statement out to avoid speculation. Who's in today? Is it Mike and Virgil? Who do you want out here and who left holding the fort?'

'Give me Mike here and we'll call up reinforcements if we need them. It's unlikely we'll find anyone who saw anything much of any use, I imagine, but between Mike and me, we should be able to get a statement or two.'

'Use the Uniform officers you have here to close everywhere off and get tapes up and I'll ask the Duty Inspector if they can spare any more bodies. The place is bound to fill up with gawkers as soon as word gets out, especially on a Sunday when it's not raining, for once.'

'Do you think the body is Tara?'

'I'd rather not speculate, until we know for sure. Whoever it is, it doesn't look as if they've been in the water all that long, judging by the state of the wrapping, so the timing would be consistent, if it is her. Right, I'll leave you to it. Mr Sulu, you have the conn.'

'Aye, Cap'n.' Jo had known Ted long enough by now to understand his fondness for quotes from vintage Star Trek, and from his favourite film, Blazing Saddles.

Once he'd done all he could to help Jo, Ted headed for the safe house. He parked his car in the next road and did a walk-past first, before he approached the front door. He'd messaged ahead to let the AFO know to expect him. He knew Jezza was already there. He'd spotted her car, also parked some way from the house, which impressed him.

It was Jezza who opened the door to him. The Firearms officer was standing further back in the hallway, covering the door. Ted decided he was getting old when he thought the constable looked as if he needed a note from his mam to be there on his own. Then he realised that was exactly the reaction people had to him; had done throughout his career.

He led them through to the kitchen to brief them both. He

was anxious to explain a few things about Mr Green before he descended on them. Otherwise it could get messy.

'Just a brief word about what we're all doing here. We're providing a temporary safe place for a witness in need of protection. All information is on a need to know basis but Jezza, I need you to get statements from her, so clearly you'll know her identity. It's not for sharing. With anyone. Is that clear? And for you, too ...' Ted looked to the AFO to identify himself.

'PC Neal, sir, Max.'

'Right, Max, well, I take a dim view of leaks. So anything you, or your colleagues when they relieve you, may become party to here goes no further. I'm sure I don't have to say that, but I just like to cover all bases.

'Now a few words about the person who is delivering the witness, in case he arrives early and unannounced. And he will arrive unannounced, Max, so don't make the mistake of pointing your weapon at him. You'll only make him angry. He's a Special Operative and is licensed to carry a firearm at all times.

'He's also special in other ways. He will, no doubt, immediately give each of you a nickname which you can choose to take as offensive. Ignore it. Otherwise it only encourages him. He has one for me. He's my Specialist Skills instructor. And my nickname goes no further than these four walls either. I hope that's clear?

'You call him Mr Green and you show him the respect he deserves. But you don't allow him to needle you, which is how he passes the time. And Jezza, whatever you do, don't be tempted to try your kickboxing skills on him. Not for any reason.'

Ted didn't for a minute think she would; he was just making a point. He knew she was a professional, good at her job. Even if the first time he'd met her she'd tried to pick a fight with him in the street because she was drunk. He knew that would never happen when she was on duty.

'He's the highest graded Krav Maga instructor in the country and he fights dirty. That's why he's very good at what he does. And that's all you need to know about him, or about this operation. Okay?'

They both nodded without comment.

'I've no reason to suspect at the moment that this operation is compromised or that you are in any danger. But please be vigilant at all times and if you have the slightest concern, you call for back-up immediately. Absolutely no heroics.'

Ted's finely-tuned senses heard or sensed something which the other two appeared unaware of, which worried him slightly. He motioned to Max to stand ready and to Jezza to move behind the PC for cover. She reluctantly did so. Ted palmed his handgun and melted into the shadows in a corner of the kitchen so he would be behind the back door when it opened.

The door did open and Green sauntered in, just ahead of a young woman. He eyed the AFO with barely concealed contempt and said, 'Don't point that thing at me, sonny. It might go off. And Gayboy, you should know better than to come at me from behind.'

Max Neal had the sense to keep his Heckler lowered slightly but his expression was indignant as he addressed Ted, who had stepped forward, putting his gun away.

'Sir, that door was locked. I checked it myself.'

'It's fine, Max, I know you would have done. Jezza, Max, this is Mr Green. And the entrance was his idea of a little joke.' He turned to the witness, who was looking bewildered. 'While you're here, it might be better if you didn't use your own name. Is there something we can call you? And do please take a seat.'

He pulled out one of the kitchen chairs and motioned for her to sit down. Green sat down opposite her and looked at Jezza.

'Mine's tea, NATO standard, *bokkie*,' he told her. 'Soon as you like.'

Ted had no idea what the word meant but he could guess that it was patronising, at best. He could sense Jezza's hackles rising. He needed to defuse the situation.

'Jezza, it would be really helpful if you could make a brew for everyone, please. Not you, Max, we need you somewhere in the hall, where you have clear line of sight to both entrances.'

Green made his trademark snort of derision and pointedly moved his chair well out of the way of the AFO's sight lines. Jezza hesitated but the boss shot her a look clearly asking for her cooperation, so she turned to the kettle, then started pulling mugs out of an overhead cupboard, setting them down loudly on the work surface to register her disapproval.

The witness sat down gratefully.

'Call me Susie, if you like. It's not my name but I've used it in the past. Him,' she said, nodding towards Green. 'He's a complete nutter.'

Green took absolutely no notice of her, sitting with his knees apart, forearms resting on the table-top. He looked harmless enough but Ted knew all too well the speed with which he could swing into action. He hoped he hadn't left casualties behind in getting the witness out but Green was a professional. Used to going in and out fast with no trail left.

'I'm assuming Mr Green will be on his way once he's had his brew,' Ted told her, looking to Green for confirmation.

'Don't be in too much of a hurry to get rid of me, Gayboy. I've done a lot of driving the last couple of days. I might just crash here for the night, take advantage of the doubtless luxurious accommodation. Sleeping soundly, safe in the knowledge that I'm protected by the might of the thin blue line.'

His tone was flippant, as it often was. Ted realised he must have been concerned at the lack of security. And that meant the situation may be worse than he'd feared. He would have liked to talk to him further, to find out how it had gone in London, getting the witness out. But there was nowhere they could ideally talk in private in the small, cramped house. Besides, he was itching to get back to the reservoir to find out what was going on there.

Jezza produced the teas. She put Green's mug down so hard the hot liquid almost sloshed out.

'Thanks, *bokkie*,' he told her, grinning.

Now she'd made the mistake of showing him the word annoyed her, although she may well not have known what it meant, he would use it all the time to get a rise out of her. It's what he did. Ted hoped it wouldn't get too heated between them and that Jezza would remain professional enough to rise above his deliberate baiting. He knew she would be Googling the word as soon as she got the chance.

Once he'd finished his tea, Ted stood up and asked Jezza to walk with him to the back gate so he could brief her further. He'd hoped he would have heard something from Harry by now but he'd still not been in contact. Which meant Ted still didn't know the plan to move the witness on.

'Don't let Mr Green get to you. It's what he does. Ignore him and he'll stop. Now, if she's happy to talk to you, I need you to sit down with Susie and record everything she's willing to tell you. It's just belt and braces, so as many as possible of us have details of her testimony.

'I need you to keep an eye on Max, too, and whoever relieves him. Green will needle them as well, just for his own amusement. Don't underestimate him, whatever you do. He's dangerous, especially when he's bored. But no one will get anywhere near the witness, or any of you, with him in the house. If you smile nicely at him, he may even cook you some supper. He's a surprisingly good cook, when he's in the right mood.

'Now I'm going back up to the reservoir but if you have any concerns at all, call me. Any time, even in the middle of the night.'

'Okay, boss. Should I snog you or something before you go?'

'Why Jezza, I never knew you cared. But you must know I'm spoken for.'

'I'm thinking of our cover, in case anyone should be watching us. What would be most natural to an onlooker, so we don't look like a pair of coppers trying not to look like a pair of coppers?'

'Good thinking.'

He put a hand on her arm, leaned forward, lightly brushed his lips against her cheek, and spoke softly in her ear. 'And if the nickname Gayboy ever leaks out into public knowledge, your next Personal Development Review is going to be your worst ever.'

It certainly looked different up at the reservoir when Ted returned. The crime scene wheels had rolled into action. There was tape everywhere to preserve any evidence, a tent had gone up over where the body was still lying and Crime Scene Investigators in white suits were going meticulously over every inch.

Ted was pleased to see that Professor Nelson's big estate car was parked nearby. He liked Bizzie. Got on well with her, both in the work setting and socially. It would save time and messing about if their body did turn out to be a murder victim as it would need to be a Home Office Forensic Pathologist who did the post-mortem for a murder case.

There was a small crowd of onlookers now and one or two members of the press he recognised by sight.

'Is it a body, Ted? The missing woman?' one of them called out.

Penny was there too, a camera slung round her neck.

'Have you got a statement for us, Chief Inspector?'

Ted was tempted to ignore them all but he thought he better say something. He turned back and said, 'As soon as we have anything to tell you, you'll be told. That's all I can say for now.'

He put a Fisherman's Friend lozenge in his mouth in preparation, signed in, donned full cover-alls and headed for the tent. Doug was Crime Scene Manager so Ted knew nothing would be missed. Jo was also inside the tent, covered up, as Ted was. He asked briefly about the other operation. Ted gave him the barest details.

Bizzie Nelson was working away at the body on the ground and barely looked up when Ted entered. She was, as usual, formal in company.

'Afternoon, Chief Inspector. As you can see, we are just in the process of unwrapping your parcel for you. It's taken some time as we've been photographing and filming at each and every stage. You've arrived at the most interesting moment, when we finally get to see what it is we are dealing with here.'

As she spoke, she was busy peeling the plastic covering back, slowly and carefully, from a centre incision. The bindings used to fasten the wrapping would have been photographed and any knots preserved intact in case they might provide valuable evidence. As she spoke, the Professor was also recording notes of everything she saw so that no detail was overlooked or forgotten.

'And there you have her. The Lady in the Lake. My initial observations tell me that this body has been in the water for less than forty-eight hours, but I can give you a more precise timing once I get her back to my lair and can examine her more thoroughly.

'You're observant enough to notice that whoever put her in the water obligingly left a ligature tied round her neck. At first glance it appears to be a pair of tights. They might even have been her own, as she doesn't appear to be wearing any.

'What I can tell you is that I doubt very much that this is your missing woman. As you can see, this one has long blonde hair and I think your lady has short grey hair, doesn't she? Also

I would put this one at slightly taller than yours and also more generously built. Probably younger, too. I will need to check all my findings back at the mortuary. But based on my experience of such things, I am fairly certain that this is not the body of Tara MacNamee.'

Chapter Eleven

Jo voiced what Ted was already thinking.

'So if this isn't Tara, where is she, and who is this?'

'No personal effects anywhere?' Ted checked, although he knew he would have been told if anything had been found.

'Nothing so far. Uniform are still searching, and they and Mike are questioning any onlookers. I'll phone Virgil, get him to start the ball rolling back at the nick. Any CCTV for a start, from anywhere roundabout here. Someone must have parked fairly close to dump a body in the reservoir. We'll need to do house-to-house all round, too. Let's hope for nosy neighbours, maybe even someone videoing anything strange going on. You know how fired up people get about fly-tipping. We're more likely to get a tip-off about that these days than about a body.'

'I'm waiting on a phone call for the next stage of my other op but what would I be most useful doing to help out while I'm here?' Ted asked him.

He was certainly the easiest senior officer Jo had ever worked with. Even when he couldn't resist taking over, he always apologised for it afterwards.

'Why not take a scout round and see if you can spot anything we might miss?' Jo suggested. 'You've got more experience than most of us with murder scenes. You might see something to give us a steer.'

'Just don't trample all over my crime scene, boss,' Doug warned him, only half in jest. 'We've not done a great deal out there yet.'

Bizzie Nelson joined in, without looking up from her work.

'And before you ask, Chief Inspector, no, I can't tell you when we can do the PM on your victim. All I can promise is that we will try to get you what we can, as soon as we can.'

Ted turned to Jo, about to speak.

'Missing Persons,' Jo cut in before he could. 'I know, I'll get Virgil onto that as well. With a bit of luck, we'll be able to find out who this is, if it isn't Tara.'

Feeling slightly redundant, Ted left the tent, keeping his coveralls on. He started to make his way carefully to the edge of the water. Doug already had markers and stepping plates in place for any areas with potential evidence. It was clear that he and his team had begun where the body was found and were fanning their way out from there.

The dive team had packed up and left the scene, their work done. They'd send through a written report later but their sergeant had told Jo that given the weather and water conditions, they'd probably found the body quite close to where it had gone into the reservoir. Bizzie Nelson had discovered large stones tucked inside the top layer of the plastic sheeting which enveloped the body. They would be tested for their origin but on initial inspection it looked as if they may have been picked up at the reservoir rather than brought from outside the area. That meant that whoever dumped the body must have been on site for longer than it would take just to drop their burden into the water. Hopefully someone would have noticed their presence.

Ted moved around carefully, not wanting to disturb the scene. He found the nearest place a car could have parked. It wasn't all that far. But it would still have needed someone strong to carry a body from there to the water's edge. Or possibly more than one person. From experience, Ted knew that, depending on how soon after death the body had been moved, there might have been issues with rigor mortis, making it more difficult to handle.

He wandered about, occasionally crouching down to look at the ground more closely, feeling like someone from an old western film or TV series, like The Lone Ranger. It wasn't long before Doug came out of the tent and walked over towards him.

'I hope you've been careful of where you've put your feet, boss. At least yours are not size elevens.'

Doug was a bit of a strange character, always more formal with Ted than he needed to be, but he and Ted got on well enough. Doug bred cats, spent his spare time taking them to shows and doing quite a lot of winning. It was he who had persuaded Ted to take the kitten, Adam, when despite a glowing pedigree, it had turned out as a chimera.

'Have you had a look round out here yet, Doug?'

'Only quickly to decide on set-up. Why? Have you spotted something?'

'Tell me your first impressions before I say any more.'

'What is this? I'll show you mine if you show me yours? All right, then. My first impressions are that this is a very clean site. No clear footprints, for one thing. That tells me that whoever brought the body up here was being very careful not to leave any traces of themselves. So I wouldn't be surprised if we found diddly-squat in the way of any identifying evidence, no matter how carefully we search. How does that fit with your own thoughts on the scene?'

'Spot on. I don't think we're going to get lucky. I can't even see any clear footprints. Those I have found all looked blurred round the edges. Does that remind you of anything?'

Doug was staring at him now, hard.

'Boss, I know you don't drink, and I don't think you do drugs, so it can't be that. Are you overtired? Stressed out about the inquiry? You're surely not suggesting ...'

'When was the last time you saw a crime scene as clean as this, Doug? Honestly? One where it looked as if the perpetrators may have been wearing forensic coveralls?'

'Boss, you're putting the cart ten yards in front of the horse. We've not even started searching out here. There could be all sorts of traces that we haven't even looked for yet, let alone found.'

'When, Doug?' Ted repeated patiently.

Doug sighed before he continued.

'Don't quote me on this because I'm just humouring you. In case you're losing your marbles and you may turn nasty if I disagree with you. But if there really are as few traces as you think, and if there are signs of Noddy suits and shoe coverings being worn, then the Derek Waldren case. Up in the woods near Roman Lakes. The one you couldn't nick anyone for. You're surely not suggesting there's a connection between the two cases, are you? Is this just you getting paranoid?'

'I don't know what I'm suggesting. I'm just observing similarities. For a start, what does the plastic she's wrapped in remind you of? First thought off the top of your head?'

'You're putting words in my mouth now. Leading the witness. But all right. This is me still humouring you because I think you really might have lost the plot. It's not dissimilar to what you might find used in the building trade. Heavy duty polythene, used for masking areas against dust doing a knock-through, that type of thing. Or protecting concrete after it's been poured but hasn't yet gone off. But it also has lots of other uses and applications. It could be from anywhere.'

'But we came across building trade items on the Waldren case. I do know that someone is definitely playing games with us. First the tip-off which prompted a search in completely the wrong place. Then when we'd been made to look like fools, a call to send us here. And it looks, on the face of it, as if this case has nothing at all to do with Tara MacNamee, so we're back to square one on that one.'

Ted wasn't even going to waste his breath running his idea past Jo yet. It was far too soon and he knew Jo would be even more convinced than Doug that the boss was being fanciful. Ted wasn't sure himself on that score. The previous unsolved case continued to weigh heavily on his mind and he realised it could be clouding his judgement. Making him see similarities where none existed. But the similarities could be coincidences. And Ted hated those.

There was no point in him hanging around, getting under everyone's feet. He was still deciding on what would be the best use of his time when his phone rang. An unknown number.

'Ted? Harry. With luck, I should be on my way up there later today by train. I'm having to do a bit of ducking and diving to make absolutely sure I'm not being followed, but I'm hoping to be with you by seven o'clock. Can you give me the address?'

'I'd rather not, just in case. I'll come and pick you up; that might be safer. Let me know if the timings change. Delivery was made successfully and our mutual friend is there and staying put for tonight, at least. I'll see you later.'

He ended the call. It was going to mean another late night for him. Assuming Harry made the train he was hoping for, and that, by some miracle, it was on time, Ted still needed to take him to the safe house and sort out arrangements there. Then he'd need to go and sign his weapon back in, which would add nearly another hour's travelling time at the end of the day.

He decided to phone Trev to do some more grovelling, while he had five minutes. He knew his partner had planned to go riding with Willow and Rupert earlier in the day but hoped he might be back by now, or at least somewhere he could talk.

'Did you have a nice time?'

'I'm still with Rupe and Willow. We're having a cream tea. And we had a billirant time, thank you. Are you home yet?'

'No, sorry, I was phoning to say I'm going to be late. Again. And I will make it up to you. Promise.'

Trev laughed.

'You are so deeply in debt to me now you'll never catch up with yourself. I feel a massive shopping spree coming on. You might even have to take me to London. Or Paris. If you really want to be forgiven.'

He broke off and Ted could hear voices in the background, without being able to distinguish what was being said.

'That's a fabulous idea, darling. Ted, did you hear that? Willow says she's going to send me away with a cream tea for you. I was just getting ready to leave. Can you at least sneak away for a tea break to eat it? You're entitled to a bit of a break, surely?'

Ted hesitated. It sounded tempting, especially as he'd not eaten much so far that day. But there was the problem of timings, and his firearm. He wouldn't take it home with him.

'Or better still, why don't I call round to the station? It must be quiet there. I don't suppose the Ice Queen or the Chief Super are in on a Sunday, are they?'

'I was just on my way back there. I'm at Sykes reservoir at the moment.'

'Even better! A picnic! Wait for me there and I'll come and find you. We can sit on a park bench and eat our scones. What larks, Pip!'

Ted didn't respond immediately. He was always acutely aware of being on show when working. Knowing that there would be press photographers lurking, or even bystanders looking to see their byline in a newspaper, if they could snap a photo which might be used. He was reluctant to be seen sitting picnicking at a murder scene. The station would be the safer option, although he still felt awkward at the idea.

'I have to get back to the station. Come there. Ring me from the car park and I'll come and find you. I'll need to sign you in with a visitor's pass.'

'I do wish you wouldn't tie my hands behind me when you go out, Bunny. I get such terrible cramps,' she began, as soon as he removed the gag from her mouth. 'Please hurry up and free them then I can stretch again.'

She'd taken to sending him out more often to the shops. Anything to get him out for even a short time so she could work on her plan. When he presented her with more strawberry yoghurt, she pulled a face.

'I don't really fancy strawberry today, dear. I'd like something much more exotic. Mango, perhaps? Or maybe papaya. You want me to eat more, don't you? So could you be very sweet and pop out for something different? I promise to show my gratitude.'

She was still managing to keep him at bay, though it was getting increasingly difficult. All she could do was to be clever, use her brains and try to beat him at his own game. Now each time he released her, she stretched her arms high above her head, striking a provocative pose which sent a shiver through his body and made a small sound, like a whimper, escape from his lips. As she lowered her hands, which he always retied at the wrists but in front of her, she let the backs of her fingers brush softly against his face, caress the side of his neck.

'There's no need to tie me up when you go out, dearest. I promise to be good.'

His look of cunning returned in an instant.

'But I can't trust you. Not yet. Not until you give yourself to me fully.'

She forced a look of sadness onto her face as she lifted her hands to stroke his face again.

'But I can't give myself to a man who so clearly doesn't trust me, dearest. Surely you can see that?'

Virgil was the only one in the office when Ted got back. Jo and Mike would go straight home from the crime scene at whatever time Jo decided to call a halt and wrap it up for the day. Ted headed for his kettle, in need of some green tea, offering to make a brew for Virgil at the same time. Then the two of them sat together by Virgil's desk while Ted brought him up to date with everything he knew so far from the reservoir site. Again, he made no mention of his earlier thoughts.

'If the person you found has blonde hair, then there's a possible match, boss. Helen Reading, aged thirty-two. Her boyfriend reported her missing this afternoon. He'd been away, doing some lads' thing. Wild camping, male bonding or something, so he was out of contact. He got back this morning, expecting to find her at the flat they share but there was no sign of her. No message, nothing.

'He's rung round all her family and friends. No one's heard from her and that's out of character, so he came in and reported it. I've got a full description here. Is it too soon to think about getting him to look at the body?'

'There's nobody else on the database who matches the description Jo gave you earlier?'

'No one, boss. Helen Reading is the nearest we have to that profile. Is the body on its way to the mortuary yet? Do you want me to arrange for him to view it? He's effectively her next of kin. The parents live abroad.'

Ted's phone was ringing. A glance at the screen told him it was Trev.

'Liaise with Jo, please, see what he wants you to do. Once you do that, you might as well knock off for today, if Jo is happy with that. I have to go and see about this call.'

It felt wrong on so many levels to be bringing Trev into the office which would be empty as soon as Virgil left. He hoped he could persuade Trev to behave himself. It would be just Ted's luck if he was caught enjoying a sly cream tea with his partner if either of his bosses decided to pay a quick visit in to work, to profit from it being quiet to get on with some work of their own.

But he needed a bit of down time before he went to pick Harry up and deal with whatever situation faced him on the other case. He still didn't know what the plans were for onward delivery of the witness. With everything else he had going on at the moment, he would be relieved when she was off his hands and outside his patch.

Chapter Twelve

Ted was taking no chances, going to collect Harry. The first time the two of them had worked together investigating paedophile rings in high places, it had cost Ted the life of one of his cats and put Harry on the run, in fear for his life.

Ted was glad of the once-familiar weight of the Glock against his side, hidden by his loose jacket. He hoped he wouldn't have to produce it, certainly not in a public space. If Harry's witness was half as strong as he said, there were people in high places who would stop at nothing to prevent her from testifying. They'd already proved that by having her thrown in prison on a dubious charge.

Parking his car a good walk away from the station, Ted made his way to the platform opposite to the one where the London trains came in. As he'd hoped, Harry phoned him shortly before his train pulled in. It was a brief call, just enough for Ted to give him instructions. He didn't want to be seen in public meeting up with him. He made sure Harry clocked him as he got off the train, then walked to the exit, pacing it so that Harry would be able to keep him in sight all the time.

When Ted got back to his car, his hand went instinctively inside his jacket while he waited to see who would open the passenger door and slide in alongside him.

It was Harry, and he appeared to be alone. Ted started the car as soon as he got in and pulled away. First he needed to make sure they were not being tailed before he went anywhere near the safe house.

'It's good to see you again, Ted. You're a sight for sore

eyes, I can tell you. I seem to have been running and hiding continuously since our last meeting. It would be good to find somewhere I could at least get one decent night's sleep without thinking it might be my last.'

'Well, with Mr Green in residence, at least for the time being, and an AFO on duty, you should be all right for one night, hopefully.'

'An AFO?' Harry queried immediately. 'Only one? Your top brass do realise what's at stake here, do they? Is that why Mr Green is staying the night? He's not happy with the lack of cover? Who's employing him for this?'

'You could say he's doing a foreigner. Theoretically he can exact his fee from my miserable hide any time he chooses to. But it'll be worth it, if we manage to pull this off.'

'We can do it this time, Ted, I'm sure of it. For the first time, I can see light at the end of the tunnel. I've finally found someone in the Met I know I can trust a hundred per cent. The wheels are in motion. I'll tell you all about the plans for onward delivery when we get to where we're going. It's only fair I fill our witness in on it all too as it involves her.'

Only when he was completely convinced they were not being followed did Ted drive anywhere near the safe house. As before, he parked his car some distance away and they walked the rest of the way. He'd phoned ahead to let Jezza know he was approaching the house with Harry, so once again it was Jezza who opened the door, then led the way down the narrow hallway to the kitchen.

The AFO had changed. It was now a sergeant Ted knew, by sight at least. He felt more reassured to have someone more experienced on for the evening shift. If anyone was thinking of making a move on them, they would almost certainly choose the hours of darkness.

'How's it going, Ken? All quiet?'

'Bloody ridiculous, with just one of us,' the sergeant replied. 'You know as well as I do it's impossible to cover all weak points here single-handed.'

'I know and I did try for more but the decision came from on high,' Ted sympathised with him. 'You've got Mr Green, for tonight at least, and Harry, here, and I are hoping to get our witness moved on as soon as we possibly can.'

There were appetising smells coming from the kitchen and Ted realised how hungry he was. The earlier scone was a distant memory. Green was working away at the cooker, a tea towel slung over one shoulder. He was looking completely relaxed, though Ted knew he never was, even when he seemed to be sleeping. Once on a training exercise with him, Ted had tried to take his car keys back from him while he slept and had almost got himself seriously hurt in the process.

All seemed perfectly harmonious in the house. The witness, Susie, was sitting at the table with a glass of wine. Green had a can of lager close to where he was working. Ted knew it would be all he drank. Never more than one can a day. Jezza had a soft drink in front of her as she sat back down at the table.

'I knew the smell of my *bobotie* cooking would soon bring you running back, Gayboy. Plenty for you too, Snowy, if you're hungry.'

Ted winced at the nickname Green threw over his shoulder, but Harry had met Mr Green before so he knew what he was like and had probably been given the nickname on their first encounter. He was probably used to worse than that, being an ex-police officer from a force once publicly accused of institutional racism. Green put his dish into the oven and turned to face them.

'Are you staying to eat or not, Gayboy? If you are, take your coat off and sit down. We need a briefing anyway so it may as well be over some decent food. I made plenty, just in case.'

It was tempting, but Ted hesitated. He felt strangely reticent about letting Jezza see he was carrying a firearm yet there was no point having it if he took it off to eat. He also felt sorry for Ken, standing out in the hallway while they all ate. He knew how good Mr Green's *bobotie* was. He'd had it before, cobbled together over camp-fires in a way which should have been impossible but hadn't been. He was already going to be late home, especially by the time he'd had to drive up to Openshaw to sign his firearm back in. He might as well stay and eat first.

Harry was already sitting down at the table with the air of a man looking forward to his first meal in some time without constantly having to check his surroundings to see if it would be safe to eat it. Ted weakened, took off his jacket and sat down. This was definitely going to cost him an expensive shopping trip for Trev, somewhere exotic, but he wanted to be sure that plans were in place to see the witness taken somewhere safe so that she could testify. It would mean a lot to Ted, and to the others, to see justice done for all the children who had suffered at the hand of paedophiles over the years.

Trev and the cats were dozing in front of the television when Ted finally got home, later even than he had intended. At least he felt satisfied he'd done all he could for the witness and he shared Harry's optimism that this time, finally, pigeons would be coming home to roost. There had been too many cover-ups along the way.

Jezza had made a start on recording Susie's testimony but still had more to get on tape before she was moved on to her next destination. Harry's contact was sending a team to collect her late the following morning, which should allow Jezza time to finish the job.

Trev opened sleepy blue eyes when Ted sank gratefully onto the sofa next to him, Adam immediately climbing all over him, purring ecstatically.

'Hey you, you're very late. Have you eaten anything since your illicit cream tea or do you want me to make you something?'

'Mr Green has been helping out with this witness. He made *bobotie* for us.'

'Yum, sounds good. I hope you've remembered that next weekend I'm going to this street festival in town, and I shall exact my revenge for all these late nights of yours by drinking far too much and behaving so outrageously you might have to arrest me.'

'I was hoping to join you for that. Not the getting drunk part, clearly, but I quite fancied going. The way things are looking at work, I can't see it being very likely.'

'When is the inquiry likely to finish, do you know yet? Because let's make a date now that as soon as that's over and everything's back to how it should be, we'll go out for a slap-up meal to celebrate. But you have to promise me that this will be one occasion when you don't phone to stand me up at the last minute. Switch your phone off, take some leave. Do whatever it takes, but for once I want to be able to celebrate by having your undivided attention the whole evening.'

'Even with my arms tied in front of me I've got terrible cramps in my back again, Bunny,' she told him the minute he'd removed the gag. 'Please can you hurry up and free me from the radiator so I can have a good stretch to ease it?'

She'd managed to persuade him, at last, to tie her hands in front of her before attaching them to the radiator. It had actually made it harder to get hold of the nail because she was now turned round at right angles to her tethering point which made it awkward to get her feet under the cupboard.

She'd bought herself as much time as she possibly could by asking specifically for the most exotic yoghurt flavour she could think of. She wasn't sure any manufacturer actually produced one made of pineapple, papaya and coconut, but she claimed to have had one before. She told him the specific supermarket which stocked it, further away than his usual venue. Her promises of showing her gratitude had sent him hurrying out of the flat, once he had secured her to his satisfaction.

He probably hadn't even made it to his car before she had kicked free of the hated shoes and squirmed about until she could get first one then the other bare foot under the cupboard.

It was painstakingly difficult to tease the nail out from its hiding place where it had remained undetected since she'd found it. Several times she almost cried with frustration when she thought she would never succeed. But finally, there it was, nestled in the palm of her hand.

She kept her thumb firmly on the head of the nail, to prevent it slipping through her grasp, and used the other hand, wrapped round the one which held it, to help conceal it.

'Thank you, dearest,' she told him as he freed her, retying her hands in front of her as always. 'Just let me stand up so I can stretch properly. I know how much you like to watch me stretch.'

He licked his lips as she began the movement, his breathing rate rising.

'So graceful, so elegant. I can't wait until you are truly mine, my darling.'

He was used to her hands coming down to touch his face and neck. Even the fact that they moved far more quickly than ever before didn't appear to make him suspicious. Not until the sharp point of the nail bit deep into the side of his neck and the blood started to spurt from the wound as she yanked it back out. Then his eyes opened wide in surprise and pain. His hands went instinctively to his neck, trying to stop the blood spraying from a damaged artery.

'Why did you do that? Why did you hurt Bunny when he's only ever loved you?'

'Because you've held me here against my will, you perverted creep!' she screamed at him. 'Because I want to get out of here and never see you again.'

The blood was going everywhere. She couldn't ever

remember having seen so much at one time. She started to panic. She'd only meant to hurt him, to buy herself some time with the element of surprise to find a way out of the flat. A way to freedom. She realised he could well be about to die in front of her eyes if she couldn't get this bleed under control quickly. And much as she hated him for all that he had done to her, she didn't want that to happen.

'Oh, god, lie down. Come on, lie down on the floor. I'll get a towel. I'll try to help you. But you've got to promise me that if I do, you'll let me go. Promise me, Gordon. Come on, lie down. Look, I'll press a towel against it. That should stop the bleeding. But lie on the floor. I can get better pressure on it that way.'

He was looking confused now. And there was so much blood. Meekly, like a child, he let her help him to lie down. She knew where the clean tea-towels were. She'd seen him take one from the drawer often enough. She grabbed a handful of them.

'Here, try to help me. You press on it as well. We can do this, Gordon, we can stop the bleeding. Then you're going to let me go and neither of us will ever speak of this again. Please, just try.'

He was visibly weaker already. How much blood did an adult human contain? And how fast was it pumping out of him? He was going pale. She tried to dredge up memories of a long-distant first aid course she'd done. Spurting. So that was an arterial bleed. The most serious kind. The side of the neck. So that must be the carotid artery. Supplying the brain with oxygenated blood to keep it alive and functioning. Was that right?

'Gordon, please try to help. We need to get some pressure on this to stop the bleeding.'

How long could the brain survive only getting oxygen from one side? She needed help. She'd only wanted to injure him so she could make her getaway. She had never intended to kill him. But was he now going to die? What would that mean for her?

'Gordon? Bunny? I need to phone an ambulance for you. Where's the phone, Gordy? Do you have a landline? Or a mobile somewhere? Bunny? I need to get help.'

If she dialled 999 would they automatically send the police as well as an ambulance? Would she be charged with wounding him? With murder, if he died? This wasn't meant to happen. She'd only wanted to hurt him enough to get away. She'd never intended to kill him. Why wasn't he responding to her?

'Gordon? Where's the phone? We need help. Or the keys to the door, so I can go and find someone. Please try to press on this towel. I'm going to try to find the phone. Just keep pressing here. It's going to be fine. You'll see.'

Should she try to tie some sort of tourniquet to stem the bleeding while she was looking round the flat to find a phone? Or a way out so she could go and get help. But might that not stop the oxygen flow as much as the bleeding was doing?

Phone. Phone. That was the thing. Find the phone. Call for help. Paramedics could save him and she could explain it all to the police if they came. With luck, someone would have reported her missing. And her hands were still tied at the wrists so they'd know she'd been held prisoner.

She raced from room to room of the small flat. She'd only ever seen the kitchen, the bathroom and the bedroom she'd been forced to share with him. Now she discovered a small sitting room and a minuscule second bedroom with a single bed. There was no sign of a landline telephone anywhere.

She tore round the confined space, rummaging frantically everywhere in her search. She was desperately looking for something to help. A mobile phone. The keys to the doors. She tried frantically to open a window. They too seemed to be locked and she couldn't see any keys anywhere.

'Gordon! Can you hear me?' He seemed to be unresponsive now and there was so much blood. She bent over him, shaking him by the shoulders as she spoke to him. She remembered that part from the first aid course. Shake and shout.

She shook again. Shouted his name again. Over and over.

No response.

Trembling with fear now, blood all over her hands and her clothes, she felt for a pulse at the throat, feeling for the steady thud signalling a still-beating heart.

Nothing.

She tried each wrist in turn. She remembered their instructor from the St John Ambulance telling them all it was always harder to find a pulse at the wrist with any accuracy.

There was none.

She felt again at the throat. Laid her ear close to his mouth to listen and feel for breath.

Nothing.

Gordon was dead.

And she had killed him.

Chapter Thirteen

'Keys, Tara. Stop panicking and focus on finding the keys. Whatever happens, you need to find a way of getting out of here,' she told herself firmly.

Logically, the keys would be in his pocket. She hadn't found them anywhere else and the front door had been securely locked when she'd tried it. Perhaps he also had a mobile phone in his pockets somewhere, although she'd never seen him with one.

She had to steel herself to touch him again. His body was already starting to feel colder to her hand, although that might have been her imagination playing tricks on her. There was so much blood it was hard to avoid standing or kneeling in it as she positioned herself to search. The only alternative she could see to the task which repelled her was to first try to make someone hear her.

What had he said about the neighbours? One was elderly and deaf, the others spoke no English. Was that it? Well, surely someone hammering on the walls and shouting loudly was enough of an international distress signal. And hadn't she read or heard somewhere that even deaf people could sometimes detect vibration. Pounding away at the wall might just get through to someone.

She thumped until her fists hurt, against each wall in turn. There was absolutely no response. She had no way of knowing if anyone was in next door either side, nor which was the more likely side to have someone who could hear and understand her. She seized a wooden kitchen chair and tried hammering away with that. But it was flimsy and quickly fell apart in her hands.

She went into the bedroom where the window overlooked the street outside. With clenched hands, she beat against the unyielding double glazing. It looked quite new and was certainly sturdy. She could see people walking past. Two youths, hoodies up, heads down, eyes glued to the screens of their phones. She might as well not have existed.

Next came a youngish woman, looking harassed, pushing a baby buggy with two small toddlers, one either side, clutching at her coat.

Tara beat against the glass with all her might, screaming at the top of her voice.

'Please help me! Please help me. Please!'

For the briefest moment, the young woman turned her head as if she had heard or sensed something. It seemed to Tara as if their eyes locked, just for an instant. Then the woman lowered her head again, speeding up, forcing the little ones to break into a jog to keep up with her. Perhaps the sight of a woman screaming for help from inside one of these flats was so commonplace as not to warrant any attention.

There was nothing else for it. She would have to force herself to go through Gordon's pockets. Nothing was easy to accomplish with her hands still bound at the wrists but she was more desperate to get out of there than to waste time trying to free herself. She would simply have to manage, even if it was a struggle.

Alive, she'd detested him. Found his every word and action repugnant. Spent all her waking hours thinking of ways to get away from him. Seeing him dead, by her hands, made her feel a strange sympathy for him, a desire to be at least polite when she spoke to him.

'I'm sorry about this, Gordon, but I'm going to have to go through your pockets to find the keys. I have to get out of here somehow and I promise I'll do something about you. I can't just leave you lying here, whatever you've done to me. But I need a way to get help, so excuse me while I just feel round in your pockets.'

She was frantically trying to remember what his routine had been, whenever he'd been out having left her alone in the flat. Where had he gone between coming in through the front door and moving into the kitchen to untie her? The flat was small. There were so few places to hide anything. The keys must be here somewhere.

There was nothing in his pockets. No key, no phone. She'd never seen him with keys in his hand in either the kitchen or the bathroom. She rushed into the small sitting room, pulling cushions off the sofa, wrenching open drawers on the sideboard, tipping everything in a heap on the floor. She was frantic now, forcing herself to stay calm, to think.

His old bedroom! Of course. He'd told her that the room he'd made her share with him had been his mother's room. Perhaps he would keep anything important in the bedroom which had been his. She dashed in there. There was a small bedside cupboard with a drawer. She fell on it, wrenching the drawer open, willing it to contain something of use to her.

A mobile phone. Tears sprang from her eyes with the relief as she grabbed it, pressed buttons, willed it into life, praying the battery wasn't flat.

It was a basic calls and texts model. It cranked into action. The battery indicator was three-quarters full. Because of her bound hands, she had to put it on the cupboard to hit the three precious digits accurately – 9, 9, 9.

As soon as she heard the voice, she scooped it up to her ear, sobbing now in relief.

'Police! Please send the police. This is Tara MacNamee. I was kidnapped. I've been held captive for more than a week, I think. I don't even know what day it is.'

A calm, measured voice asked her to slow down and clearly state her location. She screamed in panic. She'd been there so long she couldn't remember the name of the road she was on.

'I don't know, I don't know. Oh god, please help me. The man who kidnapped me is dead. There's blood everywhere.'

'Tara, did you say your name was? I need you to calm down for me, please, Tara. Are you in a house? Can you go outside and look for some road signs or other indications? I'm trying to get a trace on your position now.'

'You can't, you won't be able to. This phone's an old thing, ancient. I can't get out. The door's locked and I can't find the keys. Please help me.'

'Okay, Tara, we're going to help you but I just need a bit more information from you so I can send someone to find you.' The operator's voice stayed calm and patient. 'Can you tell me what area you're in?'

'Brinnington.' The relief of knowing something, at least, threatened to overwhelm her.

'That's great, Tara, you're doing brilliantly. Can you remember the name of the road?'

'I walked up Northumberland Road, I remember that. Then I turned off into one of those closes off there. I can't remember which one.'

She started crying again, unable to stop herself.

'Don't worry, Tara, we're going to find you. I just need you to stay calm and work with me. Can you get to a window? Can you see out at all?'

'Yes, yes, I'm at a window now. I can see out. I can see a tower block, a little way in the distance. There's a street name too, but I can't read all of it. Oh god, I can't see it properly. He took my glasses away and I can't focus without them.'

'Okay, Tara, just stay calm for me and tell me what you can read.'

'It's an avenue, and it ends in a D, I think.'

'That's fantastic. We're going to find you, Tara, we're sending cars out now to start looking. Now, can you tell me whereabouts you can see the tower block? In relation to you? And does it look far away or quite close?'

'It's to my left.'

She was trying not to gabble. Could they really find her, without a trace on the phone? Why hadn't Gordon got something useful like a smartphone? They could have been with her by now.

'On a clock face it would be about ten o'clock. And I can see the top one, two, three – the top three storeys of it.'

'That's super, Tara, we're going to find you. Now, I need you to stay on the phone for me and to stay at the window, looking out towards that tower block. We've got cars heading to your area now. You should soon be able to hear their sirens. Stay in the window and as soon as you see any of our cars or officers, you do anything you can to attract their attention, okay? Can you open the window at all?'

She started to panic again for a moment at that.

'No, no I can't. They're all locked and I can't find the keys. Nor the key to the front door to get out of the flat.'

'It's a flat, not a house? That's fabulous, Tara, that's helped us even more. Hang on, love, someone's coming. You just stay in the window and wave. Perhaps wave something like a towel or a pillowcase, so our officers can see you more easily? Just hang in there. We're on our way.'

'All right, Tony?'

'All right, Ted.'

Ted and the inquiry sergeant passed again in the corridor on Monday morning, exchanging the same greeting. Ted would have loved to know how things were going but he knew it was pointless asking. He would be told when there was some news.

He phoned Jezza as soon as he got to his office for a sit-rep from the safe house.

'We're getting there with the recording. This is dynamite

stuff, boss. I can see why she's in need of witness protection.'

'Is Mr Green still there?'

'He is. Still needling, but I'm all right, I'm keeping out of his way. He says he's staying until he sees her safely delivered to whoever is coming to collect her, then Harry is going with them. She will be all right, won't she, boss? Only she's been through so much already. I'd hate to think we were shipping her out to somewhere she'll be in more danger. Maybe even disappear for ever more without ever getting to testify.'

'If Harry is happy with the arrangements, then she'll be all right. He knows what he's doing. Come and find me when you get back. I'd like to hear her testimony as soon as I can.'

Ted had a quiet half hour at his desk sorting out reports before Jo appeared and stuck his head round the door.

'How's it going up at the reservoir?' Ted asked, as Jo came in and sat down, shaking his head to Ted's offer of a brew.

'SOCO are still working on site. It probably struck you already but there's not much to see. I mean nothing to speak of. No clear footprints, nothing like that so far, so we don't know if we're dealing with one person or more.'

'So what's the plan?'

It was Jo's case. Ted didn't want to tread on his toes and he knew he would do a good job.

'We need a positive ID first, of course. I'll get someone round to talk to Helen Reading's boyfriend, suss him out at the same time, check his alibi. With any luck he might be able to tell us something more about her which could help with identification. If it's looking likely it is her, we'll get him to confirm.'

'And what's the plan about Tara, now it seems certain that it's not her in the water?'

'I'll talk to Kevin about more officers, try and get some more house-to-house done from the last sighting of her up in Brinnington. Trouble is, you know what it's like up there. CCTV cameras get knocked out all the time, so it won't be easy. And there's a lot of places where no one will talk to us on principle.'

'We need to find her, Jo. The longer it is, the less hopeful the outcome.'

Now she knew help was potentially on the way, Tara could barely contain herself. She had her face pressed to the glass of the window, craning her neck from side to side, trying to spot a police car. Willing them to come and find her.

The operator stayed on the phone with her, constantly reassuring her that they were looking for her. She repeatedly asked if there were any more details Tara could give. Anything else she could see from the window which might help guide the police to her.

'Even if you see any passing vehicles, tell me what they look like, what colour they are, anything. If I pass that info to the area cars, it might help them to narrow the search down if they spot the same vehicle. They're using the sirens in short bursts so you might be able to hear them soon.'

'There's no traffic passing by where I am. Nothing. I can see a corner and the odd car going past there but nothing distinctive.'

'You need to stay near the window so our officers have a chance of spotting you. But is there anything you can see lying about which might have the address of the property on it? Any letters, any bills, anything like that?'

'I'm in the bedroom. I could quickly run into the lounge and see if there's anything there?'

She was running as she spoke, praying that the police car would not pick exactly the moment she disappeared from the window to drive past. She was still clutching the pillow case she'd grabbed from Gordon's room to wave if she saw them. Now she was kicking herself that she hadn't thought for herself to try to find an address. She'd been in too much of a state of panic.

She'd dumped everything from the drawers of the sideboard in a heap. She was straining with every fibre to hear the sirens, keeping an eye on the window as she scrabbled frantically at the pile on the floor.

'I can hear them!' she shouted into the phone. 'They're not far away. I heard a siren.'

'Stay near to the window, then you stand a chance of spotting them and let me know immediately you do, so I can tell them to look out for someone waving from a window.'

She could tell from the siren that they were not yet in the same road so she risked a glance and a rummage at the jumble on the floor.

'Oh my god!' she exclaimed. 'I've found something. With an address. And this must be his name. Gordon's. Gordon Wright.'

She read out the address on the envelope she'd picked up in her still-bound hands and heard the operator relay it.

'Our officers are on their way, Tara. Are you still unable to open the door to them?'

'Yes, I still can't find the keys.'

The sound of a siren was getting louder now as the vehicles approached.

'Stay on the line until the officers arrive and get one of them to speak to me before you ring off. When you hear them at the door, make sure you stand well back as they'll need to break in if you can't open the door to them. We don't want any risk of you being hurt.'

Tara was sobbing in relief now at the prospect of imminent rescue. She ran into the small hallway. She noticed for the first time that there was a shelf above the door on which stood a hideous jug with a handle. A piece of tourist tat, emblazoned with the word Pwllheli.

She had to jump to grab it and haul it down off the shelf. Inside was an assortment of keys, including car keys. She grabbed the largest bunch, screeching into the phone, 'I've found some keys. Tell them I've found the keys.'

The siren was loud now and obviously close by. She could hear footsteps in the stairwell as she fumbled, finally finding the right key to insert into the lock with trembling hands.

When the first responding officers arrived on the landing, they saw a door opening and a blood-soaked woman with her hands tied in front of her, her face streaked with tears, her voice thick with sobs.

'I'm Tara MacNamee. Thank god you've found me.'

Chapter Fourteen

'Honestly, boss, it was an amazing sight,' Jezza told Ted as he put mugs of green tea in front of them both and sat back down behind his desk to hear her report on the handover. 'Like a fairly bad TV cop drama, only real.

'The Met sent up two AFOs and a driver in a black van. Then there was a car with two plain-clothes goons who were straight out of a film. All buzz-cut hair, mirror shades and sharp suits. The testosterone levels nearly knocked me and Susie out. But I think she'll be pretty safe with them, and Harry's gone with her. He seemed to know and trust the suits so hopefully all will be well.

'Mr Green disappeared into thin air straight after they left. He never even said goodbye, and I'd grown rather fond of him and his strange ways.'

'He does that. He's a man of few words. And he doesn't do goodbyes.'

'Do you want me to transcribe the interview or just make you a copy?'

'A copy is fine. I'm hoping to find a bit of desk time today so I can go through it all. It's not our patch but I'd like to hear it anyway. I have something of a vested interest in the case.'

'Possibly more than something of, boss. Susie told me of one private party she and some of the children she was with were taken to, when she was living in the West Midlands. The things which happened to them that night were so bad that she and another girl decided to go to the police about it a few days later. Once they'd recovered enough physically and plucked up the courage to do so.

'Things are pretty clearly imprinted on her mind, and she has a good memory for detail. She'll make an excellent witness, I think, when she gets her moment in court. They went to their nearest police station, spoke to someone on the desk, then they were taken to see the Duty Inspector. They were fourteen at the time, she and the other girl, so he, quite wisely, opted to have a female PC with him while they spoke to him.

'Susie described him well. Short, stocky, a full moustache. A bit up himself, she said. Face as smooth as a baby's bum but with a broken nose. And she remembered his name, too. Marston, she said it was. Wasn't that ... ?'

Ted sighed, put an elbow on the desk and his head to his hand for an instant, closing his eyes. What Jezza had told him so far was good news for Susie but less so for him, if the case involved his old adversary, Roy Marston, now a Chief Superintendent. To say they didn't get on was putting it mildly. He was glad he wouldn't have any direct involvement in the case.

At the same time, he was surprised. Marston was many things. Arrogant, homophobic, a right bastard to work with, if your face didn't fit. But despite all his faults, Ted had never had him down as a bent copper. Quite the reverse, if anything. He was meticulous over detail. If he'd been the first point of contact for such serious allegations, Ted wondered why the case hadn't gone any further.

'Did she give you details of who this other girl was? Can she be traced? Asked to testify?'

Jezza shook her head. 'Sadly not, boss. She committed suicide less than a year after what happened to her. Susie said she never got over it. She took it especially hard that no one did anything, after the two of them had been to the police. They never heard anything more. She felt badly let down. Totally abandoned. She started drinking heavily and doing serious amounts of drugs. Jumped off the top of a multi-storey car park with all kinds of crap in her bloodstream.

'And Susie's no longer in touch with anyone else from those days. She had difficulty coping with it herself. She went off the rails big time for a while. In and out of juvenile detention centres, then prison, for quite a few years. While she was in prison, she met a prison officer who helped her turn her life around and made her determined to get justice for herself and the others.

'Then when she did go and start trying to get someone to take notice of her, she found herself in prison on a charge of assaulting a police officer. She swears she didn't do it, although she has got form for assault. And the way she's been treated, I wouldn't blame her if she had.

'Anyway, I'll sort you out a copy of everything, boss, but now I best go and get caught up.'

Ted snatched a late lunch at his desk in between sorting out paperwork and listening to the recording of Susie's testimony. He had to put his sandwich to one side for that. She spoke in a calm, detached manner but it was still graphic, harrowing.

Ted really hoped that this time, finally, she was going to get justice for herself and all the others who had been damaged, some beyond repair, by the activities of the paedophile rings. He had a bad feeling that the girl Jezza had mentioned, the one who'd jumped to her death, would not be the only one to have taken that way out.

It was mid afternoon when Kevin Turner strode into Ted's office, looking pleased with himself. Ted looked up expectantly. He was in the mood for some good news.

'The good news is, we've found your Tara MacNamee and she's alive,' he began.

'And the bad news?' Ted sensed there was some, from his tone.

'Is potentially very bad. She's killed the man whose flat she was found in.'

Again, Ted leaned his forehead against one hand for a moment.

'Why did we have to get a case like this when the Grim Guardsman's already in the building, looking into our last one? Who's there?'

'Alex and Greg were first responders, so we're definitely going to need a grown-up on site. It's way above their level.'

Ted made a point of knowing every officer in the station, at least by name. He knew the two PCs in question were young, keen, but with nothing like the required experience for a case that could be complex from the outset.

'And apparently, according to Alex, things might not be all that simple. Tara had phoned in and said she couldn't get out because she was locked in and didn't have access to any keys. But when my lads got there, she opened the door to them, cool as a cucumber, just some tears and sobs, which could have been put on. She had a big bunch of all the flat keys in her hand. And, Alex's words, not mine, she was dressed like a tart and had her hands tied in front of her with a pair of tights. So he's thinking kinky sex games that might have got out of hand.'

Ted frowned as he replied, 'I hope you're going to suggest strongly that neither of them puts words like that into any report which is likely to land on my desk.'

'Don't worry, I'm going to kick both their arses for them when they get back in for saying it to me. But he does have a point, Ted. You know this is going to have to be thoroughly investigated. And you know as well as I do that we're probably going to have to arrest her on suspicion of GBH at least, if not murder. There's a paramedic on site and he's examined her and says she's fit to be interviewed, but we should get a doctor to confirm that. The press are also there in force plus there's a large and fairly hostile crowd of onlookers forming already. So I'm happily passing the buck over to your team and I'd respectfully suggest that either you or Jo get over there yourselves before word of this gets out all over the media. It needs a senior CID officer on site, and soon.'

Kevin left Ted's office with the smug look of someone who had just passed a hot potato to someone else. He was right. The public always got up in arms when someone they perceived to be the underdog was arrested. And they'd almost certainly have to arrest Tara, at least on suspicion.

He was tempted to go himself but he knew he would have to liaise with the Ice Queen and their Chief Super. He decided he'd better call Jo and sort something out between them.

'Any news on the Lady in the Lake?'

'I was just about to call you. Yes, a significant development. Helen Reading had a distinctive scar from an emergency operation, according to the boyfriend, which matches one on our body. Virgil's gone with him to the hospital to make a formal identification, but it looks like a match. I've got Steve checking the boyfriend's alibi for the weekend but so far it's looking solid.'

'Well, we definitely have a significant development with Tara.' He went on to tell Jo all he knew to date. 'So we clearly need a senior officer there asap, and the only question is should it be you or me?'

'Well, that's a poisoned chalice, for sure,' Jo laughed good naturedly. 'I'm assuming that whichever of us doesn't take it has to deal with liaising with Her Majesty, the Chief and the press? In which case, I'm more than happy to go and play the big bad wolf arresting the poor little lady victim, if you like.'

'Who do you want with you? Bearing in mind we need to keep someone who hasn't visited the scene to interview Tara when she's brought in, just in case it does turn into a full murder enquiry.'

If they finished up having to charge Tara, no one who had been to the scene of crime could be in contact with her because of the risk of forensic contamination. At this stage, they had no idea whether or not Tara had been kidnapped and had killed the man holding her in self-defence, or if there was more to the case than met the eye.

'I'm guessing you'd like to have Maurice and Jezza to question Tara, when she's brought in? I can take Steve along with me, in that case. Sounds like this will be a great case for his portfolio. Mike can manage things up at the reservoir for now and Virgil can join him once he's back with the boyfriend. At least we'll hopefully have an ID on that case very shortly.'

'Well, it's certainly a relief to hear that Tara is alive and unharmed. But I agree, this is potentially a very tricky situation. What's the state of play like up in Brinnington?'

'Jo's on his way there now to evaluate and to decide on what action to take over an arrest on suspicion. I'll have a better idea once I get his sit rep.'

'I'd better have a press release drawn up and get it cleared by the Chief Super, one to cover either eventuality. There's bound to be a lot of interest in this case, with the amount of publicity there's been for Tara being missing. It might not go down too well if we do have to arrest her. I think I'll pass the dubious privilege over to you, Chief Inspector, to make the announcement to the press, whichever way it goes.'

Ted wasn't best pleased but her turning formal and using his rank let him know that any protest on his part would be pointless. He went back to his office hoping that Jo was going to ring him to say it was a clear-cut case of self-defence in the heat of the moment.

He trusted Jo. His DI had more than enough experience to handle a tricky case and Ted knew he would only call his boss in if he had any doubts.

'Boss, sorry, but I agree with the first responders,' Jo told him when he did phone. 'There is something a bit strange here. I haven't started to interview Tara or anything but she does seem very calm, and some parts of her story don't quite tally with what I'm seeing. I hate to be a pain, but I'd welcome second eyes on it. At the moment I can't see any alternative but to arrest her on suspicion, and there's already a bit of a lynch mob outside who've got wind of what's going on and aren't looking happy.'

'I'm on my way. Have you got enough Uniform officers to help if things turn ugly?'

'I wouldn't say no to a few more, if Kevin can spare any. CSI have arrived and are setting up. I think we should probably get Tara out of here as soon as possible, and the paramedic has cleared her to be brought straight to the station. It's just a question of whether we do it under arrest or not.'

To save time, Ted updated the Ice Queen by phone as he hurried out of the station to his service vehicle, before heading off up to Brinnington.

Jo was right about the mob rule in the street. There were a lot of people hanging round in the narrow avenue, being held back so far by uniformed officers. The press were there, too. Cameras and microphones turned in Ted's direction as soon as he approached the house.

'Is it a body, Ted?'

'Is it Tara MacNamee, Chief Inspector?'

'Have you arrested anyone yet?'

'Have you got a statement for us?'

Ted paused only to address a few words. He always spoke quietly. It meant that people had to shut up and listen to him. Despite his short stature, he was a commanding presence.

'I have no comment to make at this stage. As soon as I have anything to tell you, there will be a statement. Now please keep back, all of you, and let the teams do their jobs.'

'Not surprised if he's killed someone,' a woman in the crowd called out. 'Right weirdo, he is. What happened to that mother of his? That's what we all want to know.'

Ted signed himself in and pulled on coveralls before going to find Jo, who came out to talk to him on the landing outside the flat.

'Sorry to drag you out, boss, I just wanted a second opinion. Like I said, I haven't spoken to Tara yet but the first responders questioned her and there are a few things which appear strange on the face of it. She told them she'd been here ever since she disappeared over a week ago, being held against her will. She said she'd found a nail and stabbed him in the neck with that to make him let her go. But it hit the carotid artery so he bled out before she could get help for him. She couldn't call for help because she said she couldn't find the phone. But she did phone for help, although only after he'd died.

'There are also no defensive wounds of any sort on her. It looks as if all the blood on her was the victim's. So her attack on him doesn't seem to have happened in the heat of him going for her in any way. The paramedic couldn't find any injuries on her at all. So if she's going to claim self-defence … well, it doesn't quite add up at the moment.'

'Arrest her. On suspicion of unlawful killing. We'll have to. Then let's get her back to the station and let Maurice and Jezza interview her and see if that straightens out any anomalies. For the moment, I don't see we have any alternative.

'I'll clear it with the Super then make a statement to the press outside.'

Jo went back into the flat and Ted heard the familiar words of the caution as he took his phone out to call the Ice Queen.

'Tara MacNamee, I am arresting you on suspicion of the murder of Gordon Wright. You do not have to say anything. But it may harm your defence if you do not mention when questioned something which you later rely on in court. Anything you do say may be given in evidence. Do you understand what I've told you?'

Chapter Fifteen

'For the tape, can you please state your full name and address,' Maurice told Tara as he began the interview. Once she'd done so, he and Jezza gave their names and ranks.

They'd gone over with the boss, whilst they were waiting for Tara to arrive at the station and be checked over by a doctor, how he wanted the interview to go. Everything would be recorded and filmed but Ted wouldn't be watching them. He was busy in conference with the Ice Queen and the Chief Super, bringing them both up to date on the two potential murder enquiries they were now handling, then talking to the CPS about possible charges for Tara MacNamee, depending on what either the interview or the search of the flat revealed.

Professor Nelson wasn't available but had sent out another pathologist to the scene. Once again, if they did decide to go ahead with pursuing the murder charge, she would have to carry out the post-mortem, as the senior Home Office pathologist.

'Before we start, are you absolutely certain you don't want a solicitor to be present?' Maurice asked Tara. 'You're facing the possibility of a serious charge, depending on what you're able to tell us about what happened. You're entitled to a solicitor, and if you don't have one to call on, we can arrange one for you.'

'I just want to get it all over with. To get home to my own house and my little cat. Do you happen to know how she is, please? I've been so worried that she might be starving.'

'She's fine,' Jezza reassured her. 'I went to your house

after your market research supervisor reported you missing. I saw your cat, gave her a little cuddle and arranged with your neighbour to keep an eye on her and feed her until you were found.'

Tears sprang to Tara's eyes at the news. She smiled gratefully at Jezza.

'I also can't wait to get back home so I can have a long soak in a hot bath, without Gordon leering at me and pawing me. And to get into my own clothes instead of the tarty rubbish he bought and made me wear.'

The blood-soaked clothes and shoes she'd been wearing when she'd been found had been taken away for analysis and she was wearing an anonymous white coverall.

'Can you begin by telling us how you came to be in the flat with Gordon Wright, please, Tara?' Maurice went on.

'I was doing market research. For a cereal bar. I had to find people fulfilling different demographics, get them to taste it, then interview them with a list of questions. I found plenty of people who were unemployed but I also needed someone in employment, preferably middle-earning. Gordon had the advantage of being at home and he said he was an office manager, so that was going to be okay for what I needed.'

'And when was this?'

'A Friday. Just over a week ago, I imagine. I'm not sure what day it is today.'

'Monday,' Jezza told her. 'Did it not worry you, going into the homes of people you didn't know, on your own? You didn't even have a phone with you.'

'It worried me a bit, of course. And I would normally have had my phone, for safety. I'd put it on charge then completely forgotten to take it with me.'

Jezza had found the phone, still plugged in on charge, when she'd been to Tara's house following the report that she was missing. That part of her story checked out, at least.

'Even with a phone, isn't it quite a risky thing to do? Is it up to you to choose which area you go to? Because, not wishing to sound judgemental here, but the area where you were found doesn't have the best of reputations.'

'That was partly the reason. I was trying to find somewhere I'd not covered before. Somewhere I might find people at home during the day, so that usually means an area with fairly high unemployment. But yes, I'm always a bit wary. That why I always carry a pepper spray. Am I allowed to say that? Perhaps they're illegal to carry? I bought it online. It said it was legal.'

'So if you were carrying a spray, how did Gordon manage to take you prisoner, as you told the officers at the flat that he had done?' Jezza was pouncing on any inconsistency in her story.

'Honestly?' Tara asked her. 'I have no idea. I kept asking myself that, all the time I was there. I don't know if he somehow smothered me, if I fainted, or what happened. I'd had a bad migraine the day before. I can sometimes get dizzy spells with them.

'All I can remember is that he sounded ideal for the profile I needed and he seemed harmless enough. He was a gentleman, I do remember thinking that. He invited me to go through to the kitchen and he stood aside to let me go first. That's why I'm not entirely sure what happened because he was behind me so I didn't see what he did.

'The next thing I knew, I was tied up to a radiator with a pair of tights round my wrists. He kept my wrists tied together the whole time I was there. The only time he separated them was when I needed to use the loo so I could at least wipe myself. At least he allowed me that much dignity.'

She shuddered at the memory as she spoke.

Ted didn't approve of his officers playing 'good cop, bad cop.' But they had agreed between them in the planning of this interview that Jezza would go in hard after every minor detail, Maurice would take his usual sympathetic role of Daddy Hen.

It often proved an effective combination.

'So where was your bag all the time you were there? You said you had a pepper spray in it. Could you not get access to it to spray him and make your escape?'

'He hid my bag at some point. I didn't see it again for ages. I asked him for it but when he gave it back, he'd taken the spray out so I didn't have a weapon to defend myself with. And I was kept tied up, all the time I was there, like I said. Except for using the loo.'

'And he held you there without your consent?'

'Definitely without my consent!' Tara sounded indignant at this point. 'He repulsed me. He was creepy. He'd convinced himself he loved me and that I was in love with him and I'd tracked him down after seeing him in a supermarket one time. I didn't even remember having seen him.'

'Was he violent towards you at any time? Did he rape you, or attempt to rape you?'

'No, that was the weird thing. It was like he really did think we had some sort of beautiful romance going on. He kept saying he'd wait to have full sex with me, until I felt ready. Which I never would have done, not in a million years.

'He did sexually assault me, though. Often. He kept touching me all over, without my consent. And he'd rub himself against me until he, you know, until he climaxed, which was definitely not what I wanted him to do. So that's indecent assault, isn't it?

And one time he sort of smothered me with his hand so I passed out. That was really scary. I woke up to him spanking me with a slipper. There's probably not a mark to show for that, because I hardly ever bruise. But he did do it.'

Maurice cut in at this point. 'Tara, I think you could probably do with a refreshment break here so I'm going to stop the tape. You're not free to leave at this point, and there will be an officer outside the door at all times while DC Vine and I go and find us all a nice brew. What would you like to drink, and do you want something to eat?'

'Tea, no sugar, please. And I could murder a biscuit.' She didn't seem to see the irony in her choice of word. 'I'm suddenly hungry. I think it's the relief of being out of there at last.'

'No problem at all. Any particular type of biscuit?'

'Anything, thank you.'

'Interview suspended for refreshments. DCs Brown and Vine leaving the room,' Maurice announced, reaching out to stop the recording.

'It must have been a tough experience for you, Tara. You must have been in fear for your life most of the time,' Maurice told her. He was leaning forward, his arms resting on the table between them, making direct eye contact with her.

She opened her mouth to speak, thought better of it, closed it again then, after a pause, said, 'Yes. Yes, I was. I think it's only just starting to hit me now. Now that the initial shock has passed.'

Jezza kicked Maurice, hard, under the table. He winced, but carried on regardless.

'And you're sure you don't want a solicitor? It's your right, and you don't need to say anything until you get one.'

She was looking from one to the other of them now, starting to look tired and drawn.

'No, thank you. I just want to go home.'

As soon as they got outside the door, Jezza threw a punch which hit Maurice solidly on the arm. She was a kickboxer, a good one, with a highly effective punch.

'Maurice Brown, you big soft bugger. The boss will have you filing paperwork for the rest of your working life if he finds out you led a murder suspect like that.' Then her expression softened and she leaned closer to plant a kiss on his cheek. 'But I love you for it, you soppy great Daddy Hen. Go and get us that brew. I'll stand guard over her. But no more leading her, or you're definitely on your own.'

Tara thanked them politely for the tea and biscuits. As if they were at a social function rather than sitting in a police station where she could be facing a murder charge.

'I was starting to get increasingly afraid of Gordon and his sexual demands on me. I kept stalling for as long as I could. But we'd reached a bit of a Mexican stand-off and I could tell his patience was starting to run out. His expression had a way of changing if he thought I'd been playing games with him, as he called it.

'Of course I was playing games. I didn't want to be there. I didn't like him at all. I certainly didn't fancy him. And I definitely didn't want to have sex with him. Not until the moment I thought my life might depend on it. I did think about doing it then, in the hopes that he would then trust me enough to leave me untied so I could find a way to get out of there. But he was clearly an obsessive type and I was worried he might become even more so if I did.

'I kept sending him out to buy me different types of yoghurt, just to get him out of there. Then when he was out, I managed to find a nail, under the kitchen cupboards.'

Jezza pounced instantly. 'When did you find the nail, Tara? Was that on the day he died?'

Maurice suppressed a grin. Even Jezza was doing her best to guide Tara now.

'I'm not too sure. It's all very confused at the moment. I just know I found it by taking my shoes off and wriggling my foot about under the cupboards to see if there was anything there. My hands were still tied together and to the radiator, but I managed to get hold of it and conceal it in my hands.'

She paused to take another swallow of her tea.

'When he came back from the shops, it was clear he thought he deserved a special reward for going out to find the right yoghurts for me. Then I was really afraid. Scared he might finally try to rape me. Terrified of what he might do to me if I tried to fight him off. When he came at me, I hit him with the nail. I thought if I hurt him he might just back right off and let me go. I hadn't planned on killing him. I think it was just bad luck I hit an artery. I wasn't aiming for it. I don't know enough about human anatomy to be that accurate.

'And then, of course, I couldn't find a phone to call for help, or find the keys to get out. Not even to open a window to shout for help. I banged on the walls and shouted, hoping the neighbours might hear and come and do something. Gordon said the old lady one side was deaf and the people on the other side didn't speak any English. But they might have heard something. They might be able to confirm that I did try to call for help, even if they didn't do anything about it.'

'We couldn't shake her, no matter how we tried, boss,' Maurice told Ted as he and Jezza stood in his office to give their report of the interview. 'She's adamant she didn't mean to hurt him seriously, let alone kill him. She was terrified he was about to rape her, or worse, so she was just defending herself the only way she could.'

Ted was eyeing Maurice suspiciously. He knew what a sucker he was for anyone in distress. He hoped he could trust his professionalism to have conducted the interview by the book. He turned to Jezza and asked her opinion. She was less of a soft touch and he could usually rely on her for blunt speaking.

'What Maurice said, boss. I think any woman finding herself in that situation, especially for a prolonged period of time, would be at her wits' end wondering what was about to happen to her next. I know we can't clear her yet, until we have all the forensic evidence, but is there any way we can at least bail her and send her home? I think she's probably suffered enough for now, don't you?'

'You know that's not my decision alone, Jezza. I'll need to consult with the Super and the CPS, for sure. I'm inclined to agree, though. She needs to be at home, even if it's on pre-charge bail. Otherwise we'll get an angry mob down here camped on our doorstep, for one thing, as long as she remains in the station.

'Right, you two, get your notes up to date then you might as well knock off. There's no point in all of us being here until silly o'clock. Have you sorted refreshments for Tara and left someone with her to keep an eye on her?'

Maurice nodded. 'We're hoping she can stay in the interview room for now, unless it's suddenly needed. I think probably the last thing she needs right now is locking up in a police cell. We'll need to sort clothes for her to go home in, too. We won't want her being seen sent back in a white suit.'

Ted took a sneaky five minutes to phone Trev before he went to see the Ice Queen to discuss what to do with Tara, to warn him of another potentially late night.

'Have you found your missing woman?'

'We have, but it's complicated. We've had to arrest her. Hence the late night. We have a lot to sort out. I'm sorry, again. And I honestly will make it up to you – one day.'

'At this rate, a quick shopping trip isn't going to cut it. You might need to take me to Milano for fashion week,' Trev laughed.

The mere threat was enough to make Ted determined to wind things up and get home before too much longer, whatever it took.

He sat with the Ice Queen on a conference call to the CPS to discuss a way forward. At the moment, they had nothing like enough evidence to hold Tara for more than twenty-four hours and the Super, like him, was against even that from a PR point of view, as much as anything.

'If we bail her, and keep a discreet eye on her, we can always bring her back if we do find anything we could charge her with. I know you don't like going off gut feelings, Ted, any more than I do. But what's yours on this?'

'I think it's more likely than not that it's exactly as she

says. He kidnapped her, held her captive, subjected her to abuse and put her in fear of her life.'

'I agree. I think, despite what's happened, we need to be seen to be treating her as the victim in this, not the villain. Let's get her bailed and send her home with a babysitter to keep an eye on her. I doubt I can track down a Liaison Officer before tomorrow, so I'll find a woman PC to go with her. I don't think it would be appropriate to send her with a male minder, after all she's been through already, do you?'

Chapter Sixteen

Ted found his partner in the back garden when he finally got back home from work. Trev had clearly been dealing with something less than desirable from one of the cats.

'Brian again,' he told him as Ted walked over to kiss him. 'Puking up macerated mouse indoors once more. He really is gross.'

The cat in question was taking no notice, sitting on the grass nearby, washing himself. Adam, the kitten, had been sniffing at the older cat but immediately abandoned him and trotted over to Ted.

'I saw you on the early evening news. Looking all stern and policeman-like giving that statement. Not to mention incredibly sexy. Are you hungry? There's food available, and don't worry, I will wash my hands after dealing with vomiting cats.'

Ted followed him back into the kitchen, taking off his jacket. He usually preferred to shower and change as soon as he got home but he was afraid that if he did he might be too tired to eat. It was another long day after a run of them with no break. He yanked off the tie he hated wearing without even untying it, and opened the collar button of his shirt.

'You had to arrest your missing person, then? That seems a bit harsh,' Trev commented, making a start on sorting out some supper for them both. Ted knew he'd probably already eaten but could always eat more. He never put on an ounce, despite his appetite.

'Standard procedure. We have a suspicious death, until we can work out exactly what happened. She's been arrested while the investigation is ongoing but not charged and there's a good chance she won't be. Contrary to what you might read in some crime fiction books or see on the telly, we can't just accept someone saying a killing was self-defence and let it go at that.'

'You'd better not be working on Sunday. At least not all day. I spoke to Willow and she said she and Rupe are free in the afternoon and she'd be delighted to thrash you at squash at her club. She's rather good, as you might well imagine. And remember I'm going to that event on Saturday, so I'll expect to spend Sunday afternoon with my favourite policeman, at least.'

'I'm not sure my morale needs any more thrashing. And I don't know yet whether or not I'll have to work.' He saw the look Trev threw his way and hurried on, 'But I promise to be there if I possibly can. It's just a bit full-on at the moment with two potential murder cases. Not to mention the ongoing inquiry.'

'How's that coming on?' Trev was dishing up already. It smelled good and Ted realised how hungry he was.

'I'm in the dark at the moment. I won't hear anything until I'm interviewed and until it's all over. I pass Gerry's DS occasionally and we exchange a greeting, but that's about all.'

'And will you be interviewed by the Grim Guardsman in person? I imagine he could be very intimidating, although I've only met him at Jim's parties. I flirted with him outrageously, just for fun. He seemed to take it in good part, but I certainly wouldn't want to get on the wrong side of him for any reason.'

'I'm not sure yet how Gerry wants to run things. If he decides to make it all formal and on the record, it will have to be him as I'm entitled to be interviewed by someone one rank senior to me, and that would be him. And you do realise that one of these days someone is going to take your flirting completely the wrong way, don't you?'

'You're not worried about the inquiry though, are you?' Trev sounded concerned, planting a kiss on top of Ted's head as he put laden plates on the table, ignoring the comment about his flirting.

'At the end of any case, inevitably, there's always that doubt if you could, or should, have done something differently. It's worse, of course, when you don't get a result and there's a death you didn't anticipate.'

Trev put his fork down and laid a hand over Ted's. 'It'll be all right, you know. Because I know you. No one does more to make sure every case is handled properly from start to finish. That's why I try not to complain when I hardly get to see anything of you. But just promise me you will try to make it to the club on Sunday afternoon.'

Jo and Ted were having a catch-up before the full team briefing. They were in Ted's office, although it was smaller and more cramped than Jo's, which he shared with Mike Hallam. Even with two of them in there, it was bigger than Ted's broom cupboard. Ted was brewing up for them both; green tea for himself, strong black coffee for Jo.

Jo took out a packet of nicotine chewing gum and put a piece in his mouth.

'Sorry about this disgusting habit. *Mi mujer* discovered I hadn't actually given up smoking as I'd told her I had, all those years ago. So now I'm under orders to do so or face dire consequences. And believe me, when *la madre de mis hijos* speaks like that, you don't argue. And I really miss a smoke after my morning coffee.'

Seeing Ted's expression, he laughed. 'Oh sorry, Ted, have you not covered that vocabulary yet in your Spanish lessons with Trev?'

Ted grinned in his turn then abruptly, the two of them switched into work mode. The banter was always there, not far under the surface. It was what most of the emergency services used to get themselves through the harder aspects of their work.

'Priorities for the day?' Ted asked, to start the ball rolling.

'You can't easily run two suspicious death cases side by side yourself, no matter how good you are. Why don't you put Mike or Rob onto one of them and I can oversee it, if they need help?'

'Mike, for sure. I'll stick with the Gordon Wright case, then, as I've already been involved in that one and leave him with Helen Reading.

'I'm a bit worried about Rob at the moment, to be honest. Have you noticed he's not himself? I know he's worried about the inquiry, but he's also getting obsessed over this bishop and the historical abuse allegations. I've told him it will have to go on the back burner for now, with these other two cases, but he's working on it in every spare hour he's got, a lot of it in his own time. He keeps saying he doesn't want the bishop to die before he can bring a case against him.'

'He does have a point,' Ted said mildly. He was the only one on the team who knew why the case was significant to Rob in particular.

'He wants to visit Peter Spencer in prison to get statements from him as a victim of the bishop, then go and confront His Lordship with them.'

Spencer had been arrested for kidnapping and torturing young men. When he'd confessed, he'd mentioned having been abused by the bishop when he was a child.

'He's spoken to him a couple of times and says at times he appears lucid but clever enough to "forget" anything he doesn't want to answer. The home are protective of him but even they admit he does seem sharper sometimes than others.

'The problem is, we need to wrap up the Tara MacNamee case as soon as we possibly can, surely? It's not fair to keep that woman hanging on to know whether or not she's going to face charges. Not after all she's been through already. Always assuming her story of kidnap is true, of course, and she's not very cleverly stringing us all along. And we're short enough of bodies without putting Rob onto something else. Not to mention the fact that there will be two PMs, hopefully this week, which someone needs to attend.'

Ted sighed. It always came down to a lack of enough officers to do the job as they would like it to be done.

'I'll talk to the Super about bringing in a few extra officers from somewhere. It will mean pulling them off their own cases, of course, but it's better than nothing. It might help.'

'I think we should find someone from outside our team because there's somewhere else I think we need to be this week. It's Nigel Denby's funeral on Friday and I think someone should attend it as an observer. And that should be someone who didn't interview any of the football team members during the initial investigation, as they're bound to be there and I don't want them alerted to a police presence. I'd like them watched carefully without them knowing they're being studied as well.'

Nigel Denby was the young man whose death was the main reason an entire case was being looked into by Superintendent Gerry Fletcher and his team.

'Well, that rules out all of us, plus Charlie and Leona, I think,' Ted told him. 'We could ask Kevin for one of his officers, in plain clothes. Or I could bring Graham Winters in. He wasn't on the original enquiry and he shows a lot of promise. Leave it with me. I'll also phone Professor Nelson and see if there's any remote chance that both our PMs could happen on the same day, which might be easier for us in terms of hours. She'll need to do both anyway, if Gordon's death really was a murder, but perhaps she could at least give us her preliminary findings at the same time.'

They could both hear the rest of the team arriving and heading for their desks. Jo stood up, put his gum back into its wrapper and put it in his pocket.

'Right team,' Jo began, as he and Ted between them had agreed he would lead. 'To pinch the boss's phrase, settle down. We have a lot to get through.

'We need to sort out the Tara case as soon as we can. It's not fair to leave her in suspense, not knowing whether she's going to face charges or not. Rob, I need you liaising with Forensics on that. Anything and everything from the scene needs feeding back as soon as it happens.

'We also need a thorough background check on Tara and on the deceased, Gordon Wright. Maurice, you and Jezza on that one.'

'Find out what happened to his mother, please,' Ted put in. 'Something someone in the crowd shouted out when I got there yesterday makes me think there might be a bit of back-story there which we need to know about.'

'Is someone suggesting his mam is boarded up under the bath or something?' Maurice asked. 'When did she die? Wouldn't she be stinking, and wouldn't SOCO have found her if so?'

'That's your job, Maurice,' Ted told him. 'Find out if and when a death was registered at that address. Chase up a death certificate, find out what the cause of death was. It could be relevant. And when you've done that, find the doctor who signed the certificate, ask them for more detail. Of course, if you can't turn up a certificate, we need to find out what did happen to the mother.'

'Next, the Helen Reading case. Virgil, what did you make of the boyfriend?' Jo went on.

'Devastated. Genuinely, I would say. And blaming himself. They've lived together a couple of years and this was the first time he'd gone away without her. Steve's been contacting the people he says he was with and it seems to check out. Steve?'

'So far they all give him a strong alibi. But they were wild camping, so it's probable that no one else saw them, only the group of three friends he was with. And, sir,' Steve looked directly at Ted as he spoke, rather than to Jo, 'haven't we been here before? A bunch of friends all alibiing one another and no independent verification? It was the boyfriend, Eddie's, car they went away in so I've started trying to pick up any sightings for it to see if we can tell how many occupants there were.'

Jo was looking towards Ted now, too.

'It has to be said, boss, and we have both commented on it. The crime scene up at the reservoir appears to be one of the cleanest we've ever seen – bar one.'

'You're surely not suggesting there's some sort of a connection between the killing of Helen Reading and the death of Derek Waldren in the last case, are you?' Jezza's tone was scornful.

'Not a connection necessarily, Jezza,' Ted told her. 'Similarities.'

'That sounds like bollocks to me,' she scoffed, never reticent about voicing her opinion. 'What's the link between this Helen Reading and the other case?'

'That's what we're going to try to find out, Jezza,' Ted told her patiently. 'Maybe nothing at all. But Steve's right and so is Jo. There are some possibly superficial similarities which we should look at, without wasting too much time on it.'

When they'd finished, Ted went back to his office to phone Bizzie Nelson.

'Good morning, Edwin,' she greeted him breezily. She sounded to be in a good mood. 'You're going to ask me about your two bodies, I assume? I'm just trying to sort out my work schedule to see which of us can do which one and when. Which is the most urgent for you?'

'Both of them. But if I had to choose, I'd like the Gordon Wright one first because I'm anxious to know if I need to charge Tara for that or not.'

'If it wouldn't be too tedious for you, or your charming DI with the gold tooth if he's the one who comes, I have a gaggle of young ghouls wanting to go into pathology who are coming to see what we do here, tomorrow morning. A nice juicy PM on a possible murder case might be right up their street. Then I could crack on with your Lady in the Lake straight after that, once they've gone. Does that help?'

'Thanks, Bizzie, much appreciated.'

Ted had no idea where the rest of the day had gone. He was astonished by the time showing on his mobile when he answered a call from Trev, sounding forlorn. He had genuinely meant to make an effort to get home at a decent time for once.

'Hello, I don't know if you remember me, but I'm your husband. I'm wondering if you might grace me with your presence at some point. Only there's a parcel for us and I'm dying to open it.'

'Sorry,' Ted said apologetically. 'I honestly hadn't realised how late it had got. Give me half an hour and I'll be there. Go ahead and open the parcel, though.'

'I couldn't possibly. It's addressed to both of us. Mr Ted Darling and Mr Trevor Armstrong. And it's from Harrods, if you please. Mrs Adams kindly took it in for us and I think she's as excited as I am. So hurry back.'

Ted did hurry, as much as he could. Trev was like a small child, smiling with delight at the Harrods box on the kitchen table, fending off the cats who were as intrigued as he was.

'I'll let you be the one to open it,' Ted told him.

Trev needed no encouragement, falling on the box and tearing it open, pulling out the tissue paper-wrapped contents.

'Oh my days, did you ever see anything so pricelessly camp in your life? His and His monogrammed silk dressing gowns? They must have cost a fortune.'

He handed one to Ted who slipped it on, aware of the fact it was likely to be the most expensive item of clothing he had ever worn. Ted rummaged in the box, looking for a card to say who they were from, as Trev tried his on. He read aloud from the printed card.

'Thank you for taking care of our daughter. Congratulations on your marriage. Gethin and … what's this name, Ay-oh ...'

'Aoife,' Trev spat bitterly, perfectly pronouncing the Irish name as Ee-fa. He snatched off the robe and hurled it onto the floor as he added, 'My toxic parents. Take it off, Ted. I want nothing from them. Nothing. Send them back. Throw them away. I don't care which.'

Wordlessly, Ted slipped his off and went to put his arms round Trev, who was bristling with anger.

'Hey, they were making a gesture, that's all.'

'Because it's the correct thing to do, in their social circle. Do you want to know the true irony behind this? Shewee told me my father's secretary is gay and outrageously camp. It will be him who was taxed with choosing something suitable. It's fine to have a gay secretary. Just not a gay son. Even if he lost his virginity to a friend of yours who abused that friendship and trust under your roof. Get them out of my sight.'

Ted kept him folded in his arms. He put his face close to Trev's ear and spoke quietly.

'They must have cost an absolute fortune. It would be such a shame simply to throw them away. Just imagine how much could be raised by donating these to a LGBT charity, for instance.'

He felt his partner's tension leave him. Heard the start of warm laughter. When Trev bent to look him in the face, the familiar sparkle was back in his eyes as he said, 'Ted Darling, you devious little detective! You've just reminded me of yet another reason why I love you.'

Chapter Seventeen

Ted wasn't sure whether he'd drawn the long or the short straw in agreeing to attend the hospital for the post-mortems, leaving Jo free to be at the helm back at the station. It was going to take longer than usual with the Professor in a teaching role for her students. But she was right. It wasn't every day they'd have the opportunity to observe the post-mortem for a possible murder case, let alone two potential ones on the same day.

At least the students would be confined to the viewing gallery, out of harm's way. Ted was in coveralls and closer to the action, so he could discuss things with Bizzie more easily. He was interested to know what sort of a teacher she was. He knew she had a fondness for telling racy stories so he suspected she might be a popular speaker with younger people. He remembered one time when he and Trev had been invited to dinner and she had them both in stitches with a tale of being humped by a randy young Rottweiler while she attempted to examine its dead owner.

She began by introducing him. 'This is Detective Chief Inspector Darling from Greater Manchester Police. He's here because this gentleman in front of us has met a sudden death and it will be his job, and his team's, to find out what it's all about. My role here is to tell him all I can about the fatal wound and how it might have been inflicted on the deceased. In other words was this a defensive blow, struck in self-preservation? Or could it be some sort of a dastardly attempt to try to disguise a cold-blooded murder as something else?

'Whilst I am working, my lovely assistant James, over

there, will be beginning the preliminaries on our Lady in the Lake, who is another potential murder victim. She was found dead in a reservoir but we can't assume the cause of death was drowning until we examine her. It's unusual for us to have two seemingly separate cases, both resulting in possible murder most foul, at the same time. So, young ladies and gentlemen, you are here on a good day.

'Now, we are all going to be rather busy so I'd be obliged if you could all refrain from fainting or puking during the process. Or if you must do either, at least have the decency to go outside the gallery to do so. The lavatories are conveniently close by.'

Ted glanced at the eager young faces behind the screen. She already had them eating out of the palm of her hand. He doubted any of them would find the time to be unwell. Bizzie was a true professional. Whilst maintaining a respect for the bodies she was handling and talking to him, as well as recording all her findings, she still found the time to recount amusing anecdotes about her work to her audience. Ted was relieved that they were slightly watered down from what he knew she was capable of.

She began with all the routine basics but she didn't give the name of either victim in front of the students. After a brief but thorough examination of Gordon Wright's body, she turned to the watching audience. There was an intercom system to the viewing gallery so she could ask them detailed questions.

'From my initial observations, this appears to be the fatal wound,' she indicated the side of the neck. 'It has punctured a major blood vessel here, which is …?'

A studious-looking girl with long hair tied back and tortoiseshell-framed glasses hit the intercom button before any of the other students could move.

'The carotid artery, Professor.'

Bizzie praised her before asking more questions, deliberately ignoring her when she tried to answer everything, teasing answers out of more hesitant students instead. She was good, Ted acknowledged to himself. It was a different role to the one he knew her in best and he was impressed at this different side to her.

'Now we come to the part that the Chief Inspector is dying for me to get on with, although he's far too polite to say so. And in order that I can dazzle you all with my brilliance, I'm going to ask him not to tell me what weapon was used, if indeed he knows. I am, hopefully, going to tell him. The weapon was not present in the wound when the body was first examined and I personally haven't seen it.'

The nail which Tara had admitted using to wound Gordon Wright had been bagged at the scene and sent for forensic examination. Bizzie was already right in her conclusions. It had not been left in the wound. Had it been left in place there was a slight possibility the resulting bleeding would not have been as catastrophic.

Bizzie peered closer, bringing her overhead light down to help her to see more clearly. With her gloved hands, she manipulated the wound, checking for the angle of penetration and any distinguishing marks she might find.

'I'm going to stick my neck out and opt for a wire joinery nail, quite probably a round-head.' She looked at Ted who gave a brief nod. Bizzie looked back towards the students. 'Would anyone like to hazard a guess at why I'm specifying a round-head rather than an oval or a lost-head?'

The studious girl spoke again. 'Without knowing how the nail was driven in, but taking an educated guess, with enough force behind it anything other than a round-head might have penetrated more deeply and possibly remained in place?'

'Your deductive skills are good. But it's important to remember that in the world of forensic pathology, there are no guesses, educated or otherwise. The DCI wants detailed, scientific conclusions he can work with. I leave the guesswork up to him and his team.

'Now comes the fun bit, although not as much fun as James and I are going to have later on, I'm afraid, as that would take too much time to set up for you. I'm going to attempt to replicate the angle of the blow in order to assess where the person delivering it was positioned at the time and how much force there was behind it. Because from my first observations I'm reasonably sure that this wound was made from above the victim rather than from the side.

'James and I will play about on donated cadavers later on but for now I'm going to ask the DCI for his cooperation. I'd also ask him to forget that he holds black belts in four martial arts and not to attempt to defend himself, as our victim has no visible defence wounds.'

There was a ripple of reaction from the students, no doubt impressed to hear her say that about the small and seemingly insignificant policeman they had been mostly ignoring, whilst hanging on to Bizzie's every word.

It went against all of Ted's martial arts training to stand passively whilst Bizzie simulated attacking him with an imaginary nail in her hand. He told her quietly, out of earshot of the students, the details he knew about the nail and the way in which Tara had been found, with her hands bound together in front of her.

Bizzie tried various different approaches, finally getting Ted to crouch down as she stood over him, arms raised, before plunging them downwards, stopping only when the side of her hand touched his neck over his carotid artery.

'All of this is subject to confirmation, and as I've explained, James and I will play about later on to test the theory. But based on my initial conclusions, I would say that this man received a fatal blow with a nail, delivered by someone standing above him and bringing their hands down with some degree of force.'

All of which was useful to Ted to work from, but not good news for Tara MacNamee. If the blow happened as Bizzie

Nelson had suggested, it was harder to envisage it as a self defence reaction by someone in fear for their life.

Ted's phone had been switched off whilst he was in Bizzie's autopsy suite. He turned it on again as he walked back to his car, then scrolled through to see what calls he had missed. There was one from Jim Baker, still on sick leave and still climbing the walls with the inactivity. It was a thinly disguised plea for Ted to call him back, with lots of apologies for bothering him.

Ted immediately felt guilty. Jim was someone else he'd been neglecting, as well as Trev. They both understood the demands of the job, but Ted would welcome discussing the current cases with Jim, even if only in a brief phone call. He decided to pick up a sandwich and a coffee somewhere and park up while he ate them and talked to Jim at the same time. Ted hardly ever ate in the local café which some officers favoured. He could seldom justify to himself the time for a sit-down meal there. He also found the food it served a bit too much like school dinners for his taste. He knew he was spoiled rotten by Trev's cooking.

'Ted!' There was a note of relief in Jim's gruff voice. His fiancée Bella had been fussing over him non-stop ever since his collapse. She'd started back to work in the mornings which was why Jim had tried calling him as soon as he was alone, Ted suspected. 'Tell me how it's going. I saw your piece to camera. It sounds like an interesting one. What have you got?'

Ted filled him in on all the details he knew so far, trying to take small enough bites of his lunch so as not to be talking with his mouth full. He didn't fool Jim, though.

'Ted, that better not be a bacon barm you're scoffing while Bella left me with nowt but a bowl of rabbit food for my dinner,' he growled. 'I don't know how you can stomach it anyway after a morning at a PM.'

'It's beansprouts and grated carrot,' Ted lied shamelessly.

'And breakfast was a long time ago.'

Jim grunted, unconvinced, then asked Ted what his next move would be on the Gordon Wright case.

Ted gulped coffee to wash down the last of the barm before he spoke.

'We'll need to interview Tara under caution again, I think, but with a strong recommendation she gets a solicitor. I'll put someone other than Maurice onto questioning her this time, though. You know what a great soft a'porth he is. I haven't had the time to go over the first interview tapes yet but I don't want him coaching a potential suspect. It's a tricky enough case, without that.'

'Do you think she killed him deliberately, then, rather than in self-defence?'

'I honestly don't know yet, Jim. I just don't want to get another one wrong. Certainly not with Gerry and his team still in the building.'

'Shut up, you silly sod. You didn't get the last one wrong. Shit happens, Ted. It comes to all of us in time. And thanks very much, you bastard. Now I'm going to have to sneak out for a bacon barm before Bella gets back and it's all your fault.'

'Give me five minutes to catch up with Jo then you two come and join us,' Ted told Maurice and Jezza, working away at their desks, as he strode across the main office in search of Jo. 'And Maurice, I want some answers from you.'

'Yes, boss,' Maurice said meekly at Ted's retreating back, while Jezza grinned at him and said, 'Ooh, you're heading for detention, bonny lad.'

Ted told Jo all that the post-mortems had revealed so far. As well as the information she'd given him on Gordon Wright, Bizzie had also told him that based on their initial findings, Helen Reading had been strangled from behind with the pair of tights which had been found round her neck, and that she had been dead when she entered the water. She'd examined and photographed them still in place at the scene then they'd been sent straight off for further forensic examination, with an urgent plea for them to be examined as soon as possible for DNA or anything else of use to them. The wrapping she had been found in, together with the cord used to tie it, would also be examined but Ted wasn't hopeful either would tell them very much, especially after their immersion in water.

'Is the type of ligature significant here, do you think, Ted?' Jo asked him. 'You don't think our Gordon could have killed Helen Reading? Maybe even boasted about doing it to Tara, which is what panicked her into killing him in case she was next on his agenda?'

'It's a possible theory. Strange that Tara never mentioned it if that was the case, though. Once we've heard what Maurice and Jezza have dug up this morning, I'd like Tara brought in for further questioning under caution. And I'd like you to do it, Jo. I'm not entirely sure I trust Maurice to be impartial. You know what a sucker he is for a sob story. Give her plenty of warning and tell her to sort out a solicitor. Another thing which bothers me slightly, from the post-mortem, is why she jabbed an artery then pulled the nail back out. That made him bleed far more than if she'd left it in, of course, and might even have been the difference between him living and dying.

'I don't want to take the chance of this case going tits-up on us because Maurice was being soppy, taking everything she said at face value. Make sure you go over the recordings before you speak to her and let me know if you pick up on anything out of order. And we'd better wait for Professor Nelson's written report, which should be prompt, as usual. Then we can make disclosure. That alone might make Tara see that the implications are serious if she doesn't get proper legal advice before we talk to her next.'

Jo was eyeing Ted shrewdly as he spoke.

'You're still thinking about a possible link between the Helen Reading case and Derek Waldren, aren't you?'

'It's the timings that are niggling at me. If this was a crime series on the telly, they'd make something of those phone tip-offs about bodies. Following on from all the publicity that Tara was missing. First a call getting us to look in completely the wrong place, and probably at a time when Helen Reading was already dead and at the bottom of Sykes Reservoir. That's somebody playing mind games with us. Who? Was that Gordon? Teasing us about what he was capable of? Or someone else entirely, rubbing our noses in our lack of progress and emphasising it by leaving the Sykes crime scene as clean as the one in Roman Lakes. I want to find out about those phone calls. We need to trace whoever made them. Find out what their game is.'

'Boss, stating the obvious, we're struggling with not enough available officers as it is. I know it's very likely that whoever made those calls is the same person who put the body in the water, or at least knows who did. Can't we just stick to tried and trusted policing methods of looking at the evidence and going from there? Are you sure you're not getting just a tad paranoid, with the inquiry going on?'

It was about to get heated. Ted knew Jo was probably right. He was reading too much into things. He opened his mouth to reply but there was a brief knock on Jo's office door and Maurice and Jezza trooped in. Ted took a few calming breaths before he addressed them.

'Tell me what you found out about Gordon and Tara.'

Maurice spoke first.

'Gordon's mam died a couple of months ago, boss. Death certificate says natural causes. I got to speak to the doctor who signed it because she's off work sick herself at the moment.

'Mrs Wright was elderly, getting a bit forgetful, but not Alzheimer's or anything. She had a heart condition and she was on medication for that. The doctor had been to see her a couple of days before she died because Gordon was having trouble getting her to take her pills. The doc is one who still does house calls when necessary, so she went round to examine her and change her prescription to something she might find easier to take.

'She said she was surprised to hear she'd died so soon after. She didn't expect her to go so quickly. But there was nothing to suggest it was a suspicious death so she signed off on it and there was no post-mortem.

'She also said Gordon rather fell apart at the seams with his mam gone. They were very close. She had to sign him off sick from his job because he wasn't coping at all. I spoke to one of the lads doing house-to-house up there and he said some of the neighbours were muttering about Gordon having done away with his mam because she was a nuisance and a bit of a burden to him, stopping him having a life of his own. But another one told a different story altogether. She said Gordon was very possessive, very smothering of his mam. She didn't mean he might have put a pillow over her face or anything. She used a strange phrase. She said it was like he loved her too much.'

'And I haven't turned up anything at all on Tara,' Jezza put in. 'Just that one mention that she was at a private party where some dope was being smoked. Big deal. That could apply to any of us, I imagine. So it looks likely that she was held prisoner by a bloke who was creepy and obsessive at best, and that she reacted in self-defence.'

'But as you both know perfectly well, it's not up to us to decide that. You write up your notes factually and we leave it up to CPS to decide whether or not we charge Tara. You leave nothing out and you put nothing extra in. Is that clear enough for you both? Maurice?'

'Clear as the waters of Kinder Downfall, boss.'

Chapter Eighteen

Ted looked a little shame-faced as he went in to see Jo later in the afternoon. He'd been on the brink of a rare flash of temper before Maurice and Jezza had interrupted them. He'd spent most of his time since then in his office, wading through the accumulated stacks of reports on his desk. He'd had a brief call from Harry, sounding positive, saying that they now had their witness in a secret location, safe and under full round-the-clock armed protection. He was also staying with her as it kept him safer.

Officers working on the case had continued to interview her and her testimony was being taken seriously, for the first time since the offences had happened. There was a positive feeling about the whole thing.

'I wanted to keep you in the loop and to thank you for your help all along in this, Ted. Without you, and certainly without our mutual friend, we'd never have got this far. I finally feel we might be close to getting some justice.'

'The Duty Inspector she mentions, in the West Midlands allegations. Marston. I know him. I've worked with him a couple of times and frankly, I'm surprised. He's a prick and a bigot and he likes to throw his weight around. But the one thing I wouldn't have believed of him was that he would brush any case under the carpet. Quite the reverse, in fact. I'd like to hear how it pans out, his involvement in it.'

'We've got a team working on that already, talking to him. His story is that he took statements from Susie and her friend, wrote everything up and passed the file on to the station's

Detective Superintendent to decide on the appropriate course of action. Marston left there, shortly afterwards. Nothing suspicious, it was all planned. He was surprised not to hear anything more but then he rather lost touch. He was busy furthering his career and as you know, he's climbed quite high up.

'We've also got a team up in the West Midlands going over everything. It's one of those towns where the old nick where this happened is no longer there and some files seem to have been mislaid in the transfer to the new building. We're chasing up the Super, who's long since retired and now lives in sunny Spain. So we're not short of eager volunteers to go and interview him but we've not yet tracked him down. Apparently he's gone off to some ancient old coppers' reunion do on the Costa Plenty or wherever, so we might have to wait until he gets back.'

'And what about the constable Susie said sat in on the interview with her?'

'At the moment we can't trace her, either. Married, divorced, remarried, emigrated. Heaven alone knows where she is at the moment or what she's called now. Your friend, the now Chief Superintendent Marston, is sticking adamantly to his story that he followed procedure and passed the files on to the Det Sup at the time and he's no idea what happened after that.'

'He doesn't do backing down, that's for sure. But much as I can't stand the pompous bastard, it seems to go against what I know of him that he would have either fudged a case or deliberately lost files in something like this. Too much glory for him to lose, for one thing.'

Jo looked up from his own pile of documents, his expression neutral, as Ted entered his office.

'Sorry, Jo, I was being a bit arsey earlier. I just can't shake the notion from my head that all this messing us about could be Antoine and his cronies, rubbing our noses in it that we couldn't get them for the killing of Derek Waldren.'

'The same thought has crossed my mind, of course,' Jo told him as Ted sat down opposite him. 'But we didn't have a shred of evidence for the Badger case, and we've got nothing at all to suggest he or any of them are linked to the current case.'

He used Derek Waldren's nickname, acquired because of his involvement in the St John Ambulance Brigade and its junior members, The Badgers.

'You know as well as I do that if we start sniffing round Antoine again, with no apparent justification to do so, this current inquiry won't be the last we'll hear of it. We just need one lead, one tiny little piece of evidence, that would give us the green light to start digging. We can't go simply off the note Nigel left behind, without anything independent to corroborate that. We couldn't then and we still can't now.

'Something might show itself at Nigel's funeral on Friday, of course. And by the way, speaking of that, I heard while you were at the hospital that Graham Winters is on board with us from tomorrow, so we'll need to brief him on what to look out for there.'

'Don't forget there is the tiniest gleam of hope on the horizon where the lovely Antoine is concerned and we may yet be able to prove something, from what Sal told us. With both Drugs and Fraud now sniffing around them both, if there's anything to uncover, they might very well do so.'

'Drugs and Fraud together should certainly bring some more weight to bear.'

'Interesting that Fraud think that young Antoine's seeming success with this supposed online currency trading he does is simply a front to launder the money his dad is making from the coke. Makes sense, when you think about it. Sal's keeping me posted on when the joint raid might be. Which is why all of this needs to stay within the team, for now. You never know who's into the white powder these days. People who would stop at nothing to keep a good reliable supplier from going down.

Even some police officers, for sure.'

'Goes without saying, boss. And don't worry about me, Ted. A sneaky cigar and a good Irish whiskey when the wife's not about is the worst of my vices. That and serial flirting. Though with no intention of following it up.'

'I could phone Sal again and see what the chances are of getting one of us on the teams that go in for the raid. If they're searching Antoine's part of the house and have a warrant for all his property, you never know what one of us might find to link him to a lot more than money laundering.'

'Like it,' Jo said appreciatively.

'I'll give Sal a quick call now. Then I might push off at something like my official finishing time, if you're happy with that. I've been neglecting Trev something shocking lately so I thought I might surprise him by turning up for the junior self-defence class and then our judo session afterwards. I'm always in a better mood after some hard physical training with Trev.'

'Way too much information, Ted,' Jo laughed, ignoring Ted's protestations of, 'Judo, Jo, I was talking about martial arts.'

'Anyway, it's not up to me what time you come and go. You're the boss, boss.'

Sal gave Ted the number of a DI from Drugs who was coordinating the planned raid on the home of Louis and Antoine Martin, involving officers from both Drugs and Fraud units. His name was Adrian Jacobs and he listened in polite silence as Ted set out his cases and his interest in Antoine. He may have stayed quiet but his scepticism was palpable through his silence.

'I have to say, Ted, that if I saw that in a TV show, I'd be throwing the remote at the set and saying it was a load of old bollocks. We've been working on this case for a while now. In fact, one of my officers clocked your lot's interest in the property earlier on and flagged it up as of possible concern if you started trampling all over our case. But then you had to back off when your lad went under the train, so we said no more.

'But do you really think young Antoine is a killer, twice over now? And if you do, if you had no forensic evidence at all against him for your first case, what makes you think he might have obligingly left you any trace to the second killing? Always assuming he was involved in it at all, that is.'

'Because our theory on the Derek Waldren case was that Antoine and the others were wearing coveralls and gloves which they then handed to Nigel, the lad who died in the train incident. Nigel worked as a cleaner at the hospital so he had access to its incinerator for disposing of clinical waste. That would explain why we found nothing at all. But now Nigel is dead, we don't know if they would have equally effective means of getting rid of anything they used. All of that is if, and I grant you it's a big if, Antoine or any of the others were involved in the killing of Helen Reading, our body in the reservoir.

'If I could get even one single officer in there when you go in with warrants, they could have a look for anything which might help us with either case. All my officers are well behaved, house-trained. They wouldn't get under your feet. But they would be looking for specific items which probably wouldn't be of any interest to either Drugs or Fraud so your teams might just overlook them. If we found anything we could use to arrest Antoine, even on suspicion of unlawful killing, it might be helpful for you if he was tucked safely away in custody for twenty-four hours or possibly more, if we got an extension.'

'It's not up to me, of course. I'll have to run it past my gaffer, and Fraud too. I'm sure they would say they'll only agree if you understand this is our joint operation, we have the say about everything and our cases take priority.'

'Well, if we really have to play poker on this, my double

murder trumps even a serious drug dealing offence. But I'll promise to give you my most experienced officer which will be my DI, Jo Rodriguez, so he definitely won't get under your feet.'

Jacobs laughed. 'Oh, I know Jo. I know all his secrets and he knows way too many of mine. We can work together. I'll still have to check with the gaffer but I'll keep you posted.'

Ted couldn't resist a silent air punch as he ended the call.

It was a toss-up as to who was more pleased and excited at Ted's unscheduled appearance at the dojo, on time, by the skin of his teeth, for the start of the juniors. Trev beamed his delight as his partner came in and slipped out of his shoes at the door. But Ted's biggest admirer amongst the juniors, Flip, forgot all the rules of etiquette and rushed up to him, grinning all over his face.

'Ted! Great! Trev said you wasn't coming and it's been ages since I've seen you.'

Ted returned his smile while quietly reminding him that he should be kneeling on the mat with the others, waiting to begin the session. Then he went over to take his place next to Trev who gave him a sly wink.

The evening was exactly what Ted needed. Time away from the station, which felt almost like nicking off school. Being with Trev, doing things together which they both enjoyed. Above all, Ted loved working with the youngsters, watching their self-confidence grow with every new defensive move they learned.

He was particularly pleased to see how well Flip was doing since he'd joined the junior judo club as well as the self-defence one. It was nice to see him developing a sense of pride in himself, a new assurance in the way he carried himself. As soon as the junior session had finished, Flip hurried over to ask his waiting foster mother if he could stay to watch the seniors. Ted was his idol and he loved to see him in action on the mat, especially when he sparred with Trev.

Trev had walked down as usual. As they drove back together in Ted's car, Trev was grinning from ear to ear.

'Well, that was a lovely surprise. I wasn't expecting you at all. I didn't think I'd see you until much later this evening. So as neither of us has showered yet, I'm hoping you may have a few more surprises for me when we get home.'

Jo noticed how much chirpier Ted was for morning briefing the following day but hid a smile and didn't comment. He respected the boss's right to keep his private life exactly that. He was just pleased that he appeared more focused and less tetchy than he had been the day before.

'Have we got anything further on Helen Reading?' Ted asked the team.

'All the boyfriend knows is that when he left on Friday afternoon she was planning to go round to see a friend of hers that evening. She would usually walk there so they could have a few glasses of wine together and sometimes she might stay over for the night. I've traced the friend and spoken to her. Helen never arrived. She tried to phone her, got no reply, but didn't think any more of it as she sometimes got called in to cover shifts if anyone else was off for some reason,' Mike Hallam replied. 'She worked at the hospital, a nurse in A&E. I checked there and she hadn't been called in. She wasn't due to work over the weekend but she should have been in on Monday. When she wasn't, they tried to contact her but there was no answer on her mobile.'

'Where is the phone?' Ted asked. 'Have we found it or traced it yet?'

'It wasn't found at the scene. Not by the divers, nor by the search teams around the reservoir. Steve's been working on trying to get a trace on its whereabouts but there's nothing. It must be switched off. Maybe even had the SIM card taken out and destroyed.'

'So we don't even know where she disappeared from? But there's a possibility that it was between her home and wherever this friend lived? More door-to-door, then?' Ted looked to Jo who sighed.

'We're stretched thin as it is, boss, but we'll have to do what we can. We've also been looking for any possible link between her and Gordon Wright, just in case this was him. The only reason to even think that at the moment is that tights were used on both Helen and Tara. I'm arranging for tests to see if there's any similarity in the tights. Geographically there's no connection, Helen lived right the other side of town from Gordon.'

'Was he ever treated in A&E? Could they perhaps have met there?' Ted suggested.

'Perhaps he had to take his mother there sometimes?' Jezza added. 'If she was elderly and frail, maybe she had falls or other injuries. Shall I check that out?'

'Thanks Jezza.'

Ted turned to Graham Winters, an officer from South Manchester who'd worked successfully with them before and had been drafted in specifically with the funeral in mind.

'Graham, welcome back. Jo can find you plenty to do today, and you'll have a fair bit of reading up for background, for a start. But what we mainly need from you is to be our eyes and ears at this funeral tomorrow. Nigel Denby went under a train as we were investigating a murder case with an entire former youth football team as potential suspects, as you no doubt already know. The ex-captain is a controlling type called Antoine Martin who is a definite suspect in the murder of Derek Waldren, although we haven't a shred of evidence against him to date.

'Antoine and the team staged a very theatrical show at a recent benefit match and there's a good possibility that he might lead something similar at the funeral tomorrow. We need someone there who wasn't involved in that case so won't be recognised by anyone, to see what happens and to note anything and everything which might help. Someone who can just blend in and look like a mourner at a young former football player's funeral, but who won't stand out as a plain clothes copper.'

'I know the offside rule, at least, if that helps, boss?'

'Perfect. You know a lot more than I do.'

Chapter Nineteen

'So we need the public's help again on this one. We need to try to narrow down where Helen Reading disappeared, which means posters, an appeal for information. Maybe even a reconstruction,' Ted summed up to the Ice Queen as he caught up with her later that day. 'Trying to do it all on the knock is just going to eat up what resources and budget we have. And we could waste a lot of time on door-to-door if we start in entirely the wrong area.'

'I agree. If we could at least narrow down where she was last seen it would be a start. And presumably you want to focus also on where her body was found? I take it nothing's emerged from house-to-house near to the reservoir?'

'Nothing of any substance, no. Nothing on any cameras, either, but there are some significant blind-spots round there which anyone with any kind of local knowledge would probably know about. I'm still waiting for the full PM results and anything at all from forensics, so we're at that frustrating stage of not really knowing what direction to start in.'

'Would it be wise at this point, do you think, to avoid any suggestion of a link between the two cases? We don't want any sensational press headlines.'

'Absolutely not. In all probability there is no connection. The only common denominator is that Tara's hands were tied with a pair of tights and Helen was strangled with a pair. But they're not exactly unusual or hard to come by. We'll know better when we get the forensic reports, of course. Hopefully there might be some trace of DNA on either or both pairs which should tell us one way or another. Forensics know we need a result as soon as possible on Helen Reading, and Professor Nelson also knows we need to crack on with the Gordon Wright case. We don't want to keep Tara MacNamee hanging on any longer than we have to before she knows if she's facing charges. A cleverly worded statement should help rather than hinder us.'

'You can safely leave that to me. I'll talk to the Press Office to see if we can get something out in time for the early evening news today. They can also put something on the website, and release it on social media. You know we've had good results that way before now.'

Ted was still a self-confessed Luddite about such things, but he did grudgingly concede that it often brought faster results than older methods like flyers on trees and lamp-posts. Just as long as no one expected him to spend his time sitting at his desk and tweeting, or whatever they called it.

His first bit of news came later in the day in the shape of an email from the forensic team working on the pair of tights which had been knotted round Helen Reading's throat when her body was recovered from the reservoir. The information wasn't what he was hoping for. Further tests were needed in confirmation but early examination had suggested that the tights were brand new, unworn, so there were no traces to be found on them except those of the victim. None from whoever put it there, so they were in all likelihood wearing gloves. The report stressed that there was no initial evidence of DNA in the foot region in particular, on either side of the material, to indicate that they had ever been worn.

Tara had told the first responders that Gordon kept her hands tied the whole time she was held in the flat, changing and washing them obsessively. But according to her, they had always come out of a drawer in his mother's bedroom, so she had assumed they'd belonged to her. She had spoken of them as being of a less flattering type than would normally have been worn by someone younger. Thicker, more stretchy, like support tights, so harder to escape from.

Did this latest information rule out the likelihood of a connection between the two cases? Or was it too soon to be making that assumption? Ted would need to discuss it with Jo and the rest of the team to see if anyone might have any ideas on the subject. Ted called a second team meeting for the end of the afternoon to go over any new information which had come in during the course of the day.

'Someone on the road where Helen Reading lived reported hearing what sounded like a van stop briefly, a door bang, then it drove off again fast,' Mike Hallam told them. 'The woman told the officers on house-to-house that she looked out of the bedroom window as she was expecting a mail order delivery and it was late. All she could say was that she saw a white van, something like a Transit, but she wasn't sure, pulling out of the end of her road pretty sharpish and driving away. It didn't have a logo, she didn't take notice of the reg number and she's no idea who was driving it. When she realised it wasn't her delivery, she went to find her phone to get straight onto the vendor to ask where her order was. This was Friday evening, around the time Helen would probably have been setting off to walk to her friend's house.'

'Oh good, a white Tranny van. That will certainly narrow things down – not,' Jezza put in.

'It's more than we had before, DC Vine,' Ted told her dryly. He didn't mind her flippant remarks too much. He just needed to remind her to focus on the positives. It would be easy to get dispirited with as little to go on as they had.

Mike ignored her and carried on.

'I'm getting all cameras checked and double-checked in the vicinity. Liaising with Traffic and Uniform to see if anyone was logged for any offence or any other reason whilst driving a white van similar to a Transit in that area or nearby at any time which might be relevant. Nothing so far.

'I've also arranged for Gordon Wright's little car to be gone over in detail. In case there's the slightest trace of Helen Reading ever having been in it, given the tenuous link of the tights. No results back yet, and again, they know we need them urgently.

'It will also be useful to see if there's any trace of Tara ever having been in his car. She claims to have been held in the flat the whole time without going out, and of not having known him prior to going there. But any evidence of her having been in Gordon's car at any point would potentially blow both claims right out of the water.'

'I've arranged with the Super to get a press release out and get it up on the website and social media. So stand by for the floodgates opening with endless helpful and less than helpful calls and messages from the public,' Ted warned them. 'I'm planning on working lateish tonight so I can field some of them.'

Trev would be off to his karate club for the evening and had planned the postponed meal out with his friends from there, which he'd had to sacrifice when Shewee had turned up out of the blue.

'I've been talking to the boyfriend again,' Virgil put in. 'He's devastated. Apparently genuinely so. He has no idea who would have wanted to harm Helen in any way. There's no jealous, obsessive ex in her past. In fact they both still sometimes have a drink with her last boyfriend and his new partner.'

'Is that normal or a bit weird?' Maurice asked. 'I certainly don't go out for cosy drinks with my ex. Could it be the ex-boyfriend stringing them along and all the time holding a burning grudge against her for dumping him?'

'You're making assumptions, Maurice,' Ted warned him. 'We don't know who dumped who. So for that, you get the job of tracking down all of her exes and digging into them a bit more. Virgil, find out from the current boyfriend if he has details for any of them. He probably has if they were in contact and on good terms.'

He told them the initial news on the tights and asked Jo for full details of what Helen had been wearing.

'No tights. Jeans, bare feet, slip-on shoes. Knickers, a bra, a blouse and a jacket. There was no handbag or any other personal effects found. Not so far, anyway, but something might yet turn up.'

'So where did the tights come from?' Ted mused aloud. 'Might she have been carrying a new pair with her for some reason? The boyfriend said she sometimes stayed the night with the friend she was planning on visiting, so did she have a bag with her with a change of clothes in it?'

Jezza answered his queries.

'She'd be unlikely to want to put on a pair of tights under jeans unless the weather was much colder than it has been. If she had a change of clothes with a brand new pair of tights, where is the clothing? It must be somewhere and we need to find it. She could have had a dress, perhaps, different shoes. Have we checked with the friend whether they were planning on going out somewhere together? Somewhere they might get dressed up for?'

'You get that one then, Jezza, first thing tomorrow. See when you can talk to the friend and ask her what their plans were and if Helen would usually bring a change of clothes with her. And if she did, you're right. Where are the rest of them? I'll talk to Uniform again, make sure they know that's what we might be looking for. Perhaps get a dog team to help with finding any missing personal effects. She must surely have had a bag of some sort, so we need to find it.'

'Would the boyfriend know if anything was missing from her wardrobe?' Rob suggested.

'A lot of blokes wouldn't notice. I'm ashamed to say I might not. Would you know if something of Sally's wasn't there?' Virgil asked him.

'I might. It would depend on what it was. She's got one dress I love seeing her in. I'd know if that wasn't with the rest of her things.'

'Okay, I'll talk to the boyfriend again, see if he can help. He certainly wants to. He does seem genuinely to be in a bad state. He can't imagine who might have done this or why.'

Ted hesitated before he put an idea to them, well aware that it might sound fanciful.

'The Professor has confirmed her early findings that Helen was strangled from behind with the tights, which were then left knotted round her neck. Just suppose for a moment that Helen wasn't necessarily a targeted victim. That this was an opportunistic crime.'

The team members were looking at him with various expressions. At least they were listening to him. He knew it was all going to sound crazy. He wasn't entirely sure he believed his own theory.

'Let's say, for some reason, that our killer wanted a body. Any body. To make a point. Either something to draw our attention away from looking for Tara. Or maybe just to make us look stupid. Let's imagine that this was simply a drive-by snatch. Grab the first suitable female they see, in a place where they might not be noticed.'

'So something like a white delivery type of van would be ideal, if it had a sliding side door. There are so many about they become anonymous, especially without a logo. Someone driving it, someone in the back to slide the door open, drag Helen inside. The driver gets them out of there, fast, while the second one is in the back, probably already strangling her,' Jo suggested.

'That would pretty much rule out Gordon as the killer, wouldn't it?' Rob asked. 'Unless we can find out if he had access to a van, perhaps through his work. Isn't his car a little Astra? Not the ideal vehicle to snatch someone. And who would have been his accomplice? Haven't the neighbours all said he was a loner?'

'Unless they did know each other,' Jezza put in. 'Gordon and Helen, I mean. I haven't yet found anything to link them, but that doesn't mean I won't. And if they did know one another, she might quite happily get in a car with him, accept a lift. The white van might not be connected to the case, after all.'

'How far did she have to walk, to get to this friend's house?'

Virgil replied, based on what he'd found out from the boyfriend.

'No more than a twenty-minute walk, but it was raining, on and off, that day, so she might have been glad of a lift with someone she knew, in case it started again.'

'Let's see what this evening brings in response to the appeal for witnesses,' Jo told them, to wind things up. Before they finished, Ted asked him where they were at with the next interview with Tara.

'It's arranged for Monday morning, boss. And she is attending with a solicitor. So we'll need to prepare disclosure documents of what we have so far. Even if it doesn't amount to much yet. She's starting back to work this weekend at the pub where she waits on. Then apparently she's going to start doing some more market research shifts from next week, but she's asked just to do places like shopping centres, with lots of people around. Understandably, she doesn't want to go house-to-house any more.'

'She's still a cool customer, though,' Jezza responded. 'Not everybody who'd been through what she says she has would be ready after just three days or so to bounce back to the point of being fit to go back to work.'

'Perhaps she's innocent of anything other than defending herself,' Maurice put in, as usual showing empathy for the person he perceived to be the victim. 'Perhaps she wants to keep herself busy and be around people while she gets back on her feet. And she probably needs the money, too. She wasn't earning anything while she was locked up in Gordon's flat.'

'We need some careful questioning of her to try to get at exactly what did happen to her. And that's why, Maurice, this time I want Jo doing the interview under caution. We all know you're inclined to be a soft touch, which is not a criticism. But I'd like something of a second opinion on what you found out in the first interview. I'd like Jo to see what he thinks of her. We've got more detail of how the blow was struck, so Jo, you can read up on that and ask for her explanation.'

Ted wasn't expecting a visit from Superintendent Gerry Fletcher any time soon. So when his office door opened abruptly the following morning, before even any of the team were in, and the Grim Guardsman strode in, Ted immediately shot to his feet.

'For god's sake, Ted, stop bobbing up and down like a Jack-in-a-box every time I come in. You're giving me a complex.'

Fletcher sat down in the spare chair opposite Ted.

'It's only because I get a crick in my neck looking up at you otherwise, sir.'

'And stop with the "sir" bollocks, too. You must be the only DCI who still does that in this day and age. Have you got the kettle on? I thought I might try some of this green tea of yours that everyone talks about, while I'm feeling adventurous.'

'I've just brewed up, so I can soon do you one. With or without mint?'

'Mint?' he said the word as if it were an indecent proposition. 'Aye, go on then, why not? As it's an adventure, I might as well go the whole hog. But don't you dare breathe a word. I have a certain reputation to live up to. There are those who are convinced my only drink is the blood of newborns and it suits me for them to think that.'

Ted made the tea and sat back down, putting Gerry Fletcher's mug in front of him. He picked it up and sniffed it suspiciously before taking a small swallow.

'It's not that bad, actually. Right, enough of the small-talk. Now to business. My team and I are close to having gone through all the paperwork. So early next week, we're going to need to start interviewing you and your team members.

'We have to do this and it needs to be done properly. But I know what your case-load's like at the moment and I don't want to pull any of you away from it any more than absolutely necessary. I'm going to put the same proposal to all your officers as to you, and that's what I'm here to discuss with you.

'Now we could do the full malarkey. You could have your Federation rep with you, plus a solicitor, if you want one. I'd have a second officer with me, possibly two. Everything recorded, a copy of the tape for you, blah-blah-blah. That's the by the book way, and that's what you're entitled to, if you want it. Or you and I could simply sit down together like grown-ups and talk. We could still record it on a phone so there was no question of a cover-up, but no reps and no extra officers. It's entirely up to you. You're not under suspicion of anything, but we do need this independent inquiry and it has to be seen to be impartial. Not us closing ranks to protect our own. You don't have to decide today. Think about it. Talk to Big Jim, perhaps, see what he says. But let me know how you want to play it.'

He drained his mug and stood up to leave. Ted resisted the temptation to leap to his feet again.

'This stuff isn't actually as crap as I thought it might be,' Fletcher said, as he put the mug back down on the desk. 'But if you mention that to anyone, you'll find out exactly why they call me the Grim Guardsman.'

Chapter Twenty

Ted and Jo had agreed not to take up time with a full briefing that morning. There was plenty to be getting on with and everyone knew what they needed to do. Instead they'd regroup at the end of the day for an update. Ted was particularly interested to hear what Graham would report from Nigel Denby's funeral. He and Jo had both spent time with Graham outlining their interests. He'd read the file, looked at all the faces of the football team so he would know who he was looking at.

Despite all their efforts to date, they didn't have a great deal to show for two weeks' hard work on Tara's case, and a week now since Helen Reading's body had been found. As a morale booster, Ted suggested they should all have a swift half in The Grapes to finish the day. He'd be in the chair for the first round, as was his custom.

Ted had plenty of work to keep him tethered to his desk for much of the day. Most of the team were out but Jo volunteered to do a sandwich run for the two of them. They'd both have to snatch eating time without breaking off, but it was better than nothing.

Ted hastily swallowed his mouthful when his desk phone rang and the switchboard operator told him, 'A call for you, Chief Inspector. An Inspector Maloney, from the Met. Will you take it?'

Ted's immediate thought was that something had happened to Harry. Or to their witness. He couldn't think of any other reason for an unknown DI from Scotland Yard to be calling him.

'Is that DCI Darling? This is DI Ray Maloney, from the Met. I want to know what the fuck you think you're playing at, pissing all over an op me and my team have been setting up for nearly three years now. And without the courtesy of liaising. Risking the whole bloody thing going tits-up.'

'I'm not sure I like your tone, DI Maloney,' Ted responded mildly.

That was another thing which singled Ted out as an old-fashioned sort. He genuinely didn't like a lot of swearing, although it was widespread in some forces. He was partly buying himself some time. He could work out immediately what had gone on. All hell would have broken loose as soon as Mr Green intervened to get the witness, Susie, away from the group who'd commissioned her release from prison. The undercover officer he knew only as Ian would at some point have been summoned by his controller, probably DI Maloney, by the sound of things, and he would have done what most officers would in his shoes – blamed everything on someone higher up the chain of command. He certainly wouldn't have admitted to having met with Ted to instigate the snatch.

'I take it you know your op was already compromised?'

'Never mind that crap. We were dealing with it. Who the fuck is this Lone Ranger bloke you sent in and why were we not consulted? And what's happened to the witness?'

'Even if I knew, you surely don't expect me to discuss it with someone I've never met, over the phone? And are you saying your op against the group has collapsed without her?'

'Not totally collapsed, no. But we'll have to move in sooner than planned so we'll get them on various terrorism charges. They're daft enough to have explosives around like it's play dough. But we can't now nail them on the blackmail and extortion side of it we were hoping for as well.'

He appeared to be calming down a bit, his tone and language more moderate. Ted could just imagine the DI's frustration at such a long and carefully-planned operation not turning out how he'd hoped. Ted was simply getting the brunt of it, the only person Maloney had identified to date.

'Who is the James Bond type with the big gun who lifted the witness, anyway? My officer said he scared them all shitless, him included. He did some digging around after the woman had gone and came up with your name from somewhere. So who is he?'

'If I told you that he'd have to kill you,' Ted said, only half joking. For the first time, Maloney laughed.

'What the hell is it all about? I know the group hoped that the witness could bring down half the government, which is all they're interested in. Does this mean she'll never get to testify? The nonce bastards get away with it yet again?'

'I'm not really involved in this case. Not officially. But if I was a politician, I'd be using phrases like "guardedly optimistic" about her chances of testifying.'

'So what's your involvement in all of this? Considering you're up north there somewhere? I thought most of this historic kiddy-fiddling stuff was centred down here on our patch?'

'It's pretty widespread. But yes, a lot of it happened on your manor. And you mentioned it was the Lone Ranger who snatched the witness. The Lone Ranger's sidekick was called Tonto. I'm Tonto, ke-mo sah-bee.

Maloney laughed again, louder this time.

'Fair enough. And let's hope both of us get the results we want out of the different cases. Sorry about earlier. It just gets a bit frustrating when a case you've been pissing blood over for years looks set to come crashing down round your ears.'

Ted knew exactly what he meant. He and his team had gone through the same feelings of frustration at the end of their last case which had come up against a brick wall.

'Good luck with it all, Ray. If you ever get brave enough to venture "oop north", feel free to look me up.'

Tara MacNamee was sitting nervously across the desk from her solicitor, occasionally nibbling the skin at the side of her thumbnail. It was a disgusting habit she'd broken years ago. Now it seemed to have crept back into her arsenal of comforting gestures. The lawyer's name was Wells, and she looked younger than Tara, whom she'd invited to call her Julia.

Tara hadn't wanted a solicitor. She didn't see why she needed one. Couldn't work out why she found herself in this stressful situation, after all she'd been through. All she'd done had been to find a way to finally escape from Gordon's clutches. She'd never intended to kill him. Just wound him enough to make him let her go. She'd certainly never meant to let him die. If she could have found the stupid phone sooner, she would have called help for him and perhaps saved him. Now she was facing this nightmare situation where the police seemed to think she'd deliberately murdered him.

Julia Wells had listened carefully and in seeming sympathy to everything Tara had told her, making notes and recording everything, with Tara's permission.

'I'm sorry that I'm going to need you to go over everything again with me, Tara. But I need to have a clear picture of everything which happened. I hope it was explained clearly to you, when you were arrested, that it is standard procedure in the case of a suspicious death. And that it doesn't necessarily mean you will be charged with anything. If you weren't told all of that, I will certainly be taking it up with the senior officer involved.'

'I honestly don't remember what was said. I was totally in shock. It was so awful. I do remember that the first policeman who interviewed me, at the station, was very kind. He made sure I had a break and a cup of tea. He seemed to understand what it had been like, not knowing if Gordon was planning to kill me after he'd raped me or not.'

The solicitor's lips twitched slightly at her client's words and she looked down at her notes to cover it. Occasionally, in her line of work, she'd come across decent police officers who went to great lengths not to bring the wrong person to court. It sounded as if Tara had been lucky enough to have encountered one of them.

'Now, please tell me, in your own words, exactly what happened to you from the moment you first met Gordon Wright. It's important that we're fully prepared for your next interview on Monday morning. We're going to sort all of this out, Tara. Trust me.'

'Graham, I'm hoping you'll take centre stage with news of Nigel's funeral,' Jo began, once all the team members were assembled at the end of the day. 'That death isn't directly linked to either of the current ones, as far as we know at the moment, but we have unfinished business on that previous case so we need information. For now, let's start with a round-up of what, hopefully something, we've achieved today between us.'

'I managed to speak to Helen's friend,' Jezza told them. 'She also works at the hospital. She's gutted by what happened. Blaming herself that she didn't do something when Helen didn't turn up, because it wasn't like her. But they'd both had a long, hard week, having to do extra shifts to cover, so she assumed she'd just decided on an early night instead and didn't call to cancel for some reason. It had happened like that once before.

'They weren't planning on going out. They were both too knackered. It was going to be a girlie night in with pizza and rom-coms, so no, Helen wouldn't normally have brought a change of clothes. If she did decide to stay the night, she kept the essentials there because she often did.

'The friend, Tricia, tried calling her the following day but her phone was switched off so she thought she was probably sleeping and decided she'd wait until she heard from her. It was only when the boyfriend got home and called her to see if she knew where Helen was that she started to get really concerned.

'After that I went up to Brinnington to see if house-to-house had turned anything up. It got interesting with Gordon's neighbours. The ones Tara told the first responders were supposedly illegal aliens. Long story short, they're not. It's an extended British Pakistani family. There were a few communication difficulties initially but luckily Nazir, from Uniform, was on shift so he was summoned and he translated.

'The grandmother of the man who lives in the flat, and who works as a warehouseman, was at home with her daughter-in-law and some other female members of the family. They did hear knocking on the wall and somebody shouting. They didn't react because they tend to keep to themselves. They've been the target of a lot of racist abuse so they prefer not to get involved.

'The best bit, from our point of view, is that they all remember exactly when they heard the knocking. They were settling down to watch a favourite TV programme they always watch at the same time every day and it was just starting. And that would mean that Tara was knocking on the wall more than five minutes before she placed the emergency call, which would pretty much tie in with what she's told us so far.'

'So it looks like she's telling the truth,' Maurice said, smiling his satisfaction.

Ted was going to leave the meeting to Jo but he stepped forward at this point.

'All right, everyone, let's not get ahead of ourselves here. You know it's not our remit to decide on her guilt or innocence. We just prepare the file and send it to CPS to decide. This is good, it's a start. But we're going to need a lot more than that before they can decide whether or not we need to charge her. And the interview on Monday will be pivotal. Jo, at some point, you and I need to discuss the Professor's theory on how the fatal wound was delivered, before you speak to Tara.'

'Right, boss. Okay Graham, over to you. Nigel's funeral.'

'First off, there were only a few people there, not many at all. Nigel's mam, of course, and a man with her who had his arm round her. They looked very alike so possibly her brother, but that will need checking out.

'And you were right about the old team putting on a spectacle. Some of them were pall-bearers, the rest marched behind the coffin as it came into church, with Antoine at the head of them. Same get-up as the reports say they wore for the benefit match. Dark track suits, black arm bands.

'It was Antoine who gave the eulogy. Now I know you've told me, and I've read it in the reports, that he has a tendency to be arrogant. Full of self-confidence. Well, not based on personal experience, I hasten to assure you all, but on training courses I've been on, I would say he was high as a kite on the nose candy.'

'You mean yayo, blud,' Virgil told him with his familiar irony. Virgil had interviewed Antoine and found his "rich kid pretending to be street-wise and talk the talk" act annoying. 'Our Antoine likes to make like a gansta, big man. So he'd most probably call coke yayo.'

'He is a cocky sod don't forget, Graham,' Jo told him. 'We all found that, all of us who spoke to him.'

'This was more than that, though, I'd swear. He was flying. So much confidence. It was like he believed himself completely untouchable.'

'So you're thinking our Antoine might be dealing a bit of coke, as well as all his other habits?' Rob asked. 'Do we need to start looking into that?'

Ted and Jo exchanged a look and Ted stepped in again.

'Right, this is on a strictly need to know basis and it goes no further than this room, please. Everybody clear?'

He waited until he had a nod or murmur of confirmation

from every team member before he continued.

'I'm not proposing to go into the details at this moment. But none of us are going to look into this at all until further notice. Not just because of the ongoing inquiry into the case but because of further information from Sal following on from what Virgil told us earlier. About interest in Antoine's father Louis, from both Drugs and Fraud.'

'So you're saying Drugs are planning a raid, boss?' Jezza asked him, astute as ever.

'I'm not saying anything of the sort.'

'But we're detectives. That's what we do. We detect. And if you're being all mysterious at the mention of Antoine and cocaine in the same breath, then that's what's going on.'

Ted tried to look and sound stern as he told her, 'For that, DC Vine, you can go halves with me on the first round when we adjourn to The Grapes, which I suggest we do now.'

It was always good to spend some down time with the team, especially as a morale-booster. Ted had no intentions of staying long. He wanted to get home at a decent time if he could.

The Grapes was starting to get busy as some of the officers from Uniform were knocking off for the evening and making their way for a drink together before the weekend. Ted spotted the two young first responders, Alex and Greg, in the bar as he and Jo collected their drinks and headed for a quiet corner, leaving the rest of the team to find their own places. He was still waiting on their full reports from the crime scene. Although he had their initial notes, they didn't have anything like the amount of detail he wanted from them. They looked guilty as they saw the DCI looking at them and both remembered a sudden urgent appointment in the gents to avoid him.

Ted wanted to talk to Jo about weekend cover before they left work mode behind them and enjoyed a quiet chat.

'I'm planning on coming in myself tomorrow for much of the day. I'll need to get the disclosure docs sorted for the solicitor, for one thing. Trev will be at this festival and with any luck I might find some quiet time to finally see what the top of my desk looks like underneath the piles of paper. It's been so long I've forgotten. I'd quite like to be off on Sunday though, if you could cover?

'Like I keep saying, Ted, you're the boss. Fine by me. Although that leaves me without a valid excuse to get out of shopping with the wife, if you're at the helm tomorrow.'

Jo moved off to talk to one of the Uniform officers and his place was taken by Rob.

'Boss, I'm not on the rota for tomorrow so this is in my own time and I just wanted to check with you that you were okay with it. I've got a visiting order to go and see Peter Spencer in prison. He's agreed to talk to me, on the record, about what happened to him at the hands of the bishop. I've been digging into the file and I've found quite a lot of allegations against the bishop where the complainant is still alive and some have agreed to talk to me.

'I really think there's a chance we can make a case against him. Once I've got all the victims' statements, I want to talk to him again and possibly arrest him, if you agree. I'm hoping we might have him. That he won't get away with what he's done.'

Ted was looking at him searchingly.

'Rob, just make sure this doesn't take over your life. I agree, it would be good to see justice done. But don't let it take its toll on you. Why not get off home to Sally? Spend some time with her. Don't become another statistic of a copper who let work ruin his home life.'

Ted stopped off to say good night to Dave, the landlord, before he left.

'I don't know, Ted. Your team are a dead loss to me. Look at them all. One swift half and that's their limit before they're all off back to their homes and partners. Even your young lad there, what's his name, Steve? He's in a hurry to get off. Has he got a steady girlfriend, then?'

Ted laughed. 'He has, but I think the attraction for Steve at the moment is a very rude parrot who swears a lot.'

Chapter Twenty-one

Bizzie Nelson was certainly a night owl. Ted knew she often didn't sleep at all and when she did it was only for a few hours at a time. So he was not surprised, when he booted up his computer on Saturday morning, to find that she'd sent through her full reports on the post-mortem examinations of both Gordon Wright and Helen Reading shortly after midnight. The one on Gordon gave him something else he could disclose to Tara and her solicitor.

Both reports confirmed her initial findings. Gordon Wright died from catastrophic blood loss from a punctured carotid artery. There were no defensive wounds on his body, no signs of any kind of a struggle. Bizzie had noted that an analysis of the deceased's blood had shown that he was on medication which could have resulted in blood thinning and delayed clotting, but there was nothing else of any significance.

Bizzie's experiments on cadavers, after Ted had left, had confirmed the exact angle of penetration of the wound, which clearly indicated that Tara had been positioned above Gordon at the time. The blow with the nail had also been delivered with some degree of force.

That part of the report bothered Ted. Without hearing Tara's explanation, which Jo would hopefully get from her in the second interview on Monday, it was hard to envisage a situation where Tara would feel threatened to the point of being in fear for her life if she had held the superior position, standing above her supposed captor. He was trying to imagine the scene, based on his martial arts training. At the moment, he was having difficulty picturing why Gordon would have remained passively still while she brought down her hands with sufficient force to penetrate his carotid artery with a nail. And he couldn't dismiss the fact that she'd pulled it out, rather than leaving it in the wound, plugging the bleed to some extent. Was that an understandable action in the heat of the moment?

He would need to try the moves himself to see how it played out. He decided he'd better ask Trev to go through the scenario with him. He wasn't sure he was comfortable with role-playing anything like it with one of his officers. It wouldn't be the first time he'd asked Jezza if she minded being tied up for a reconstruction. Asking her a second time might be pushing his luck.

The report on Helen Reading gave him less than he had hoped for. Death was confirmed as having been caused by strangulation from behind. There were no defensive injuries on her body either, although there was some slight bruising around the mouth. Bizzie's notes described them as being consistent with a hand being clamped over it, again from behind. There was a faint possibility of identifying whose hand it was but that would require further testing which would take more time. An absence of sweat and skin cells suggested a gloved hand, which wouldn't help them much.

Bizzie was never prone to speculation. Her reports were always meticulously factual, based on evidence she could produce to a court of law, if necessary, rather than even educated guesswork. She had made a note for Ted's benefit that there had been traces of fibres on Helen's clothing which she described as not dissimilar to those found on the type of coveralls routinely worn by CSIs. They had been sent off for detailed analysis, together with the victim's clothing. There were also fibre traces of other, dark, clothing, which were also being examined.

Ted didn't like the news. He didn't like it at all. It was yet another similarity, confirmed for him, between the death of

Helen Reading and the findings on the body of Derek Waldren, found dead in the woods near Roman Lakes. Ted didn't need to go through the reports on the Waldren case to know that the coveralls were exactly the same type found at that scene, although there had been no other clothing fibres on that occasion.

When he'd caught up on all his mail and messages, Ted went in search of Kevin Turner. He was still waiting on full reports from the first responders and getting annoyed by the delay. Time to get Kev to give them a prod. He finally tracked him down, sitting studying a bank of monitors covering several areas of the town. He could tell from Kev's body language and expression that he was not best pleased to be doing so.

'Is this a punishment for some wrong-doing?' Ted asked him. 'Or are you so short-staffed now there's no one else to do it?'

'Bloody powers that be. It has been decided that, as it's up to the Duty Inspector to decide how and where to deploy the hundreds of officers at our beck and call, it's productive use of our time to watch where the action is and decide on what units to deploy to where. And apparently we can best do that by sitting here on our bums in front of monitors half the day,' Kev grumbled, his tone sarcastic.

'You're not expecting any trouble at the festival though, are you? Music, dancing and foreign food tasting – it doesn't exactly sound like your typical rave.'

'And we both know that the real crime goes down where there are no cameras watching them anyway, so it's yet another bloody pointless box-ticking exercise.'

Kev broke off and leaned closer to one of the monitors. 'Hang on, is that your Trev?'

Ted bent over his shoulder to look. His tone was resigned as he replied, 'Yes, that's Trev. That's Trev all over.'

Trev was dancing in the street. He had on his favourite tight jeans, a brightly-coloured shirt open right down the front revealing his perfect six-pack. He held a bottle of lager in one hand, his other arm draped round the neck of a young man who was hanging onto him like a limpet as they both gyrated to the music.

Despite being a brilliant linguist, with an outstanding ear for language, Trev was utterly tone-deaf when it came to singing, although always full of enthusiasm. But he could certainly dance and he was throwing some impressive shapes.

'Who's the lad? They definitely look very pally.'

'No idea,' Ted said cheerfully. 'Trev gets very pally when he's had a drink or two. Especially when he starts on the beer. He's usually a wine drinker. I'm surprised he's not snogged you at a party before now.'

Ted laughed, seeing Kev's evident discomfort at the thought. Kev turned to look at him as he asked, 'And does it not bother you? Seeing him like that? With someone else?'

'I'm a rubbish dancer, so it's nice to see him doing something he enjoys. Besides, it's always me he comes home to. Though goodness knows why.'

'And have you ever, you know, cheated on him?'

Ted was smiling, watching Trev on the monitor, thoroughly enjoying himself, with no inhibitions. Ted knew he would actually be paying not the slightest attention to the young man he was with. It was all about living in the moment as far as Trev was concerned.

'Look at him. Where would I find better than that, and prepared to put up with being shackled to a boring middle-aged copper? What about you? Have you ever cheated on Sheila?'

'This is strictly between us, right? It's not going to be taken down and used in evidence against me at a future trial, officer?' When Ted nodded solemnly and traced a saltire over his heart with his thumb, Kevin went on, 'Once. At some drunken party in the nick. I can't even remember what it was for. I was a sergeant, newly promoted, she was a young PC. A very drunken bunk-up in the back of an area car in the garage. We so nearly got caught at it, too. A DI came down to get a vehicle, going on a shout. I was never able to look him in the eye again. Nor the PC. She put in for a transfer not long after, so I think she was as embarrassed as I was.'

Ted was still chuckling to himself as he went back upstairs, having secured Kev's promise to chase up the missing detailed reports he needed.

'I'm off out on the butty run, boss, if you want something.'

Ted looked up in surprise as Jezza put her head round his office door. He hadn't realised the morning had gone by already. He'd barely lifted his head from his desk since talking to Kevin. Jezza was the only one in the main office. The rest of the team members on duty were out working the case. She was in charge of handling any phone calls prompted by the various appeals.

'Only I'm not going near the deli so it can't be a bagel. You'll have to make do with a barm or a baguette.'

'Thanks, Jezza, but I think I'll go out. I fancy a mooch about where Helen Reading may have disappeared. If you've got any follow-ups that need doing out that way, give them to me. That will free Steve and Mike for any new ones.'

Jezza stepped into his office, looking at him intently.

'You do think Antoine and some of the others are mixed up in this, don't you? That's why you're taking a personal interest.'

'I don't think anything at the moment, Jezza, it's too soon to jump to any conclusions. And I know most DCIs seldom see the light of day, but I have been known to venture outside my office occasionally, you know.'

'You definitely think that, though. I can tell. Come on, boss, for training purposes at least, tell me your reasoning. How am I ever going to learn to be a top detective like you unless you share your thinking with me? It's about the lack of DNA at the scene and the possible fibres from a CSI suit again, isn't it? That same as in the Derek Waldren case.'

Ted had circulated the PM reports as soon as he'd received them and Jezza had clearly read them already. She was certainly keen.

'I thought you were going out for a sandwich?'

'Make me a cup of your green tea and I'll survive without for now.'

Jezza could be persuasive when she put her mind to it. Ted wasn't entirely sure he was ready to share his ideas, but she was always eager to learn, and she wasn't afraid to speak her mind. It wouldn't hurt to bounce some theories around over a cup of tea. Besides, he was supposed to maintain a mentoring role for his team members and this was a good opportunity to do so.

He brewed up, put the mugs on the table in front of them and sat down.

'All right, if you want this to be a training exercise, you tell me any similarities you see between the two cases.'

'No DNA at the crime scene and the possible fibres, like I said.'

'Now the differences.'

'Different cause of death in each case.'

'Very different. One a strangulation, which was probably relatively quick. The other was a protracted torture.'

'Different victim profile.'

Ted was about to respond when they heard a phone ringing in the main office. Ted picked up the call from his desk phone. He listened, made some notes, then hung up.

'Right, that's another one from near where Helen Reading lived and it sounds much more likely this time. A witness claiming to have seen someone bundling a woman into a van. So I'll take that one, and anything else that's outstanding out that way.'

'Mr Baines? Detective Chief Inspector Darling, Stockport

Police. You called to report a possible sighting of an incident, is that right?' Ted held his warrant card up towards the man who had opened the door in response to his knock, clearly caught in the middle of eating something as he was still chewing and there was tomato ketchup on his chin.

'A Chief Inspector? You don't look like one. Are you even tall enough to be a policeman?'

Ted thought, not for the first time, that if he'd had a fiver for every time he'd heard that, he could afford to treat Trev to a nice holiday somewhere expensive.

'There's been no height restriction for many years now, Mr Baines. And I am a Chief Inspector, you can see from my warrant card.'

'You'd better come in then, I suppose,' he said grudgingly, holding the door open then walking in front of Ted on his way back to the kitchen. 'I thought they'd just send a bobby.'

'I happened to be in the area when your call came in so you've got me.'

Baines nodded at a chair for Ted to sit down then retook his own seat, picking up a big, fat chip sandwich which reminded Ted he had yet to eat anything.

'You phoned in because you said you had some information regarding an incident after you saw an appeal on the news, is that it?'

'That's it, aye,' Baines spoke round a mouthful of chips.

'And when was this?'

'Friday of last week. I forgot all about it until I saw the recent appeal. I were out in the front garden. Bastard kids are always walking past and chucking their rubbish in the gardens. Drinks cans, chip packets, that kind of crap. And worse. Anyway, a white van was passing and it stopped where a woman was walking along the pavement, lower down, on this side. The side door slid open and a lad got out. He put his arms round her and said something, I'm not sure what. Something like, "here you are, come on then, get in", something like that.

Then he sort of bundled her into the van, the door slammed shut and the van went off.'

'And how did the woman react?'

'Well, she didn't really. She didn't shout or anything. But it all happened very quickly. She didn't really have much time to react. I'd forgotten all about it until we saw it on the telly, me and the wife, like. And it was the same woman in the photo they showed. I'm sure it was.'

'What time was this, Mr Baines?'

'The wife had just started watching one of her bloody soaps. That's half the reason I went outside. Friday, so it must have been Corrie. That would make it half seven, then.'

'Coronation Street's usually on twice on a Friday evening, Mr Baines. So was it the first one or the second. Half seven or half eight?'

'Ee, I'm not sure now. The first one, I reckon. We'd not all that long finished us tea and done the washing up and stuff.'

'And can you tell me anything about the man you saw? Age, height, anything about him?'

'Young. Well, youngish.'

'What sort of age?'

'You can't tell with kids these days, can you? Could be teens or twenties. Say between about sixteen and, say twenty-two, twenty three?'

'Anything else at all you can tell me about him? How was he dressed?'

'Like they all dress these days. Dark top with a hood, dark bottoms. I can't say more than that, sorry. I didn't get all that much of a look at him really, it were all very quick.'

'Would you know him if you saw him again?'

'I might. I'm not bad at faces. That's how I knew it were the same woman, when I saw her photo on the telly.'

'And did you see the driver at all? Could you give me any kind of a description of them?'

'No, I didn't really see who was driving, just the lad who

got out of the side door, and put the woman into the van. Then the van just drove off up the road, turned left at the top there. It was a white van, like a delivery van, but I'm not sure what model, unless I looked at a few. A sliding door at the side. Back doors with no windows. No name or writing or anything that I could see. Just a white van.'

No matter how hard Ted pressed him, Baines was adamant there was nothing else he could add. It hadn't amounted to much but it was more than they'd had before. He thanked the man, who showed him to the door, still munching on his sandwich.

Ted had almost gone out of the front gate when Baines called after him, 'Oh, the lad was black. Did I mention that?'

Ted made several more calls in the area from the details Jezza had supplied him with, but he didn't get much to add to the little he had already. He picked up something to eat and went back to the station to write up his notes before calling it a day. He phoned Trev to see if he needed a lift home. At least his partner never drove when he drank. He'd been planning on walking into town for the festival then either walking back or catching a bus.

'Are you having a good time?'

'Billirant!' Trev said enthusiastically. It had become one of their sayings, ever since Trev sent a drunken text message with the typo in it, as he always insisted on disabling the auto-correct on his phone.

'I'm just leaving, if you're ready and you want a lift?'

'I just started walking. I may have drunk slightly too much lager so I thought I'd better walk to sober up a bit. My husband is a policeman and he is very boring, especially if I roll home drunk.'

'I am your husband and I resent that remark. I'm not boring. Well, not very. I'll swing by and pick you up on the way. Oh, and I saw you on the monitors.'

'Oops! Was I being completely outrageous, officer?'

'Slightly, so we do need to talk about the young man you seemed to be wearing.'

Trev let out a shout of laughter.

'Being interrogated by my favourite detective sounds like the perfect end to the day.'

Chapter Twenty-two

'Are you sure you haven't been smoking some of Trev's whacky-baccy?'

Jim Baker stopped walking and turned to look at Ted. It was an open secret that Trev liked the odd spliff. Ted's house rules were that it was not his concern as long as he never did it at home or in his company.

'You're getting a bit obsessed with this Antoine lad, because you didn't nail him for the last one. And the reason you didn't nail him was because there was no evidence. None. Just the letter from the lad who jumped and that could be a load of old bollocks. His way of getting revenge. You've got nothing this time. Your witness saw a black lad. He can't give you the age or any other details. Have you any idea how many people that could apply to?'

'Keep walking, Jim,' Ted told him sternly. 'You're just using this as an excuse to stop. We can get a coffee after you've had some exercise. And Bella has already told me to make sure you stick to decaff, so don't think you're sneaking a double espresso or anything.'

They were in Lyme Park. It was quiet, on a Sunday morning when the weather forecast wasn't too promising for the day. They were walking up to The Cage, an old hunting lodge, for the views, but Jim was not a walker. He was supposed to be taking plenty of gentle exercise to help his recovery, Left to his own devices he would have preferred a stroll round the rose garden. It was on the flat, for one thing, but the route Ted was taking him on involved a long, steady gradient.

'You're nearly as much of a nag as Bella is,' Jim grumbled. 'I thought you wanted to talk shop? We could do that just as easily in the café.'

'We can do it better out here without the risk of being overheard. You know that exercise is good for you. It's what both the doctor and Bella ordered. And I'm not getting obsessed. I'm just keeping an open mind to the possibility that the Helen Reading case is somehow linked to that of Derek Waldren.'

'And the most likely link would be this Antoine lad and his mates. Like I said, it's starting to smack of obsession. I know that and you know it, too. You can't go after them, with the inquiry still ongoing. And I thought you said the Chief had warned you off? If he didn't, then I will and I'll make it a direct order.'

'You can't order me to do anything, Jim. You're on sick leave,' Ted reminded him, not for the first time. 'Anyway, we might just have got lucky. I spoke to Sal recently, in confidence. Drugs have got their beady eyes on Antoine's father, Louis, who's suspected of supplying coke to some of Greater Manchester's brightest and wealthiest types. Including a lot of lawyers, which is why he's so far never come under the spotlight. They watch his back for him and protect him fiercely.'

'So why are Sal and Fraud interested in a Drugs case?'

'Because Fraud think that young Antoine's seeming success with this supposed online currency trading he does is simply a front to launder the money his dad is making from the coke. Fraud and Drugs are planning a joint raid and Sal is going to give me the nod when it's happening. It won't be for a while yet. They have undercover officers on the ground who've told them Louis Martin is expecting a big new shipment some time this month. I can send an officer in when they search, to see if they can spot anything at all which might tie in with our cases. That could possibly give us something. There's just a chance we might find some clothing to link him to Helen Reading.'

'Case, Ted. Case. Singular. At the moment you only have one with even a tenuous link to Antoine. So pretend I'm not off sick. Imagine there isn't this other op getting started. You've come to me with a notion to pursue Antoine for both murders. Convince me you've got grounds to open an investigation, for starters, let alone take it forward. Something concrete which implicates Antoine in the deaths of either Derek Waldren or Helen Reading.'

Ted hesitated for the briefest moment, but Jim pounced, instantly.

'You can't, can you? You've got nothing, and you know it. On the strength of that letter, naming Antoine, if you called him in for an interview under caution, his daddy would immediately get him the best lawyer available who would want disclosure on both cases. If you showed the letter and then said "a witness saw a black youth in an unmarked white van abduct a woman believed to be Helen Reading" said lawyer would doubtless respond to your interview under caution request in two short words, one of which was *off*. Now you're relying totally on this search and that might reveal nothing at all. Which would leave you well and truly up the creek without a paddle.

'I know you're desperate to get a successful result, for you and the team. The last case not having a proper conclusion was a sickener for everyone, and I think that's what's affecting your usually reliable reasoning and judgement. Sometimes they just get away with it, Ted, and hard as it is to stomach, we just have to suck it up.'

Ted was quiet for a moment as they walked. The Big Boss was right and he did know it. It didn't make it any easier to accept. They'd reached The Cage now and stood side by side while Jim looked about him, with no great enthusiasm.

'Right, great, I've seen the view, honour is satisfied. Now can we go and get that coffee? And tell me more about the other case, your kidnap woman. You don't really think she deliberately killed him, do you? It's going to be a minefield if you finish up having to charge her.'

'I don't honestly know, Jim, is the short answer. Her version could be perfectly genuine. It's really the angle of the wound that bothers me a bit as it doesn't quite fit with the whole being held captive story.

'When Trev got back from the festival yesterday, I got him to help me with a re-enactment. We tried all kinds of different moves and positions ...'

'Have to stop you right there, Ted. This is getting into the realms of far too much information.'

Ted chuckled. Jim was his best friend but he still struggled a bit with anything to do with Ted's private life.

'I think it's your mucky mind that's at fault here, Jim. I was talking about moves Tara would have had to make to kill Gordon Wright as she did, if it really was in self-defence while she was in fear for her life.'

'What are CPS saying from the evidence you've given them so far?'

'Basically that we're miles off any burden of proof to show anything other than self-defence. I think, deep down, that it's exactly what it seems to be, on the face of it. But it will depend on her interview with Jo tomorrow morning.'

'Well, for the first time since I was signed off sick, I'm actually bloody glad not to be in on this case and having to decide the way forward. And again, ask yourself honestly if you're just desperate for a case you can wrap up. After all the PR on this one, the last thing in the world you need on it is a wrongful arrest. There'd be riots outside the nick, for one thing. Now, can we go and get that bloody coffee? And if I promise to drink that decaff muck like a good patient, don't tell Bella if I have a sticky bun with mine.'

'So we're back to the Antoine theory as a possibility?' Jo asked, after Ted told him about his visit to a potential witness the day before when he called in at the station.

'Well, I spoke to Big Jim this morning and he pointed out the obvious – that there are probably quite a few black youths in the area who would fit the description the witness was able to give me, such as it was. But yes. I would say nothing we've heard so far rules him out at this point. The trouble is, that doesn't get us very far. We can't move against him in any way before this raid happens or we risk screwing that op and we wouldn't be very popular if we did that.'

He was remembering his phone call from Ray Maloney in the Met and not relishing getting other similar ones from Fraud and Drugs.

'Professor Nelson does mention there were some dark fibres on Helen's clothing, as yet unidentified, and the witness said the person he saw get hold of the woman was wearing dark clothes. It is possible that if this was Antoine and he does use coke, he got careless. Didn't change into a CSI suit until he took Helen's body to dump it in the reservoir, and completely forgot he would leave traces on her before he put coveralls and gloves on. He may be clever, but coke could make him think he's invincible. Enough to make stupid mistakes.'

'But surely any clothes he wore at the time, if it was him, would have gone into the wash long since? They won't be lying round conveniently for us to find.'

'He's a spoiled little rich kid. Has his own wing of the house. He won't be short of clothes to wear. And living with Trev is like living with a teenager. He's only just mastered the art of putting his clothes in the laundry basket, although putting them in the washing machine defeats him. He does all the ironing, though,' he added hastily, in case he sounded as if he was criticising his partner, not wanting to be disloyal.

'So it's all riding on whether or not I spot anything incriminating during the raid, then? Particularly unwashed clothing. And is that going to cause conflict? Suppose I find something I think belongs to our case but either Fraud or Drugs want it as well? Do we arm wrestle over the exhibits? Rock, paper, scissors? Or do you engage in unarmed combat with their SIO? My bet would be on you.'

'I've already told Adrian Jacobs that we hold the winning poker hand if it comes to that. What would that be? A straight flush?'

Ted wasn't a gambler, nor a card player. It was clear Jo was by the look on his face as he replied, with a wistful note to his voice, 'Royal flush, boss. Ace, King, Queen, Jack and the ten, all the same suit. The dream of any poker player.'

'D'you play, then? I didn't have you down as a gambler.'

Jo gave him one of his most wolfish grins.

'I have many vices, boss. Not all of them known to *la madre de mis hijos,* and I try to keep it that way. Don't worry, though. It's a rare indulgence, rather than a serious habit. I'm not like Mickey.'

He was referring to Sergeant Mickey Wheeler who had been outed as the station mole, selling confidential information to any source to fund his out of control gambling habit. That discovery had been a major contributory factor in Jim Baker's heart attack.

'Right, well, excuse the weak pun, but I'm gambling on you being able to find out from your interview with Tara tomorrow whether there's any level of culpability there. Or if it really is just as she told us. The unfortunate outcome of a week of terror. We need to try to pin down exactly when she found the nail, so we can consider, or let CPS consider, the possibility that the killing was pre-meditated. Another thing you will need to do is get a detailed explanation from her for the apparent disparity in how the wound was inflicted. I spent some time last night with Trev, going through the moves ...'

'Whoa, boss, that's definitely too much information,' Jo laughed.

'Bloody coppers. Filthy minds, the lot of you,' Ted replied, though he was smiling as he said it. 'I got exactly the same reaction from Big Jim this morning. I mean the moves necessary to recreate the angle of the wound which killed Gordon Wright. We had to play about a bit ... Take that look off your face for a start, Jo. I'm being serious here.'

'Sorry, boss, I'm trying to, honestly. But my imagination is working overtime. And me a good Catholic boy, too. I shall have to go to confession.'

'Our height differential was all wrong. Gordon Wright was only a bit bigger than Tara whereas Trev is much taller than me. But the only way we could reproduce the same effect – and bear in mind this was just a very rough reconstruction, and Trev wasn't entirely sober so he kept falling about laughing – was if the Gordon role-player was kneeling down at the Tara substitute's feet.'

Jo became instantly serious. 'Now that is disturbing. Does it raise the possibility that this was all some sort of kinky role-play gone horribly wrong? Tara was some sort of dominatrix? So why were her hands tied, if that was the case?'

'That's what you need to find out tomorrow, Jo. I don't want to pile the pressure on, but we need to get this one right. You might possibly need to get Tara to act it out, to be certain. And make sure you record it. But that will depend on whether or not her solicitor would allow her to.

'I don't want to finish up with us charging her if her story is true. On the other hand, I don't want another possibly guilty party to walk free for lack of evidence.'

'No pressure, then, eh?'

'None at all. Just get me a result. And speaking of pressure, I'm about to love you and leave you and put myself under some. I have a burning ambition not to make a total prat of myself by getting thoroughly thrashed every time the Chief invites me for a game of squash. If I could even win the occasional point against him that would be something. So a friend of ours is going to give me a coaching session this afternoon.'

Jo laughed. 'Are you sure you aren't a closet Catholic, Ted? All this martyrdom and self-flagellation stuff is very reminiscent of the older-school teachings of Rome.'

'Atheist, me,' Ted told him with a grin. 'Had to be, with an ex-miner known to all as a bolshie commie bastard for my dad. My mam is Chapel. Used to take me along when I was little, but it never rubbed off on me. I liked the singing, though. But I stayed an unashamed heathen. Anyway, I'll see you tomorrow, if I survive this afternoon.'

Trev was as bright and chirpy as Tigger, despite his over-indulgence of the day before. He had the ability to bounce back quickly from anything and hardly ever suffered with hangovers. He'd made a light lunch for when Ted got back, not wanting them to be playing squash on a full stomach but knowing that Ted's breakfast, most working days, consisted of a round of wholemeal toast, with butter and honey, often eaten on the way from the kitchen to the garage to get his car.

'I've put you a set of clean clothes out on the bed. Something suitable to be seen in at Willow's club,' he told Ted.

Trev despaired of Ted's total disinterest in clothes, calling him a disgrace to gay men everywhere. He was always firmly in charge of all his wardrobe decisions.

'We should have come on the bike,' Ted said gloomily as he parked his small Renault amongst the Jags and Astons at Willow's club in Cheshire. 'At least that has some sex appeal. Now I feel inferior before I've even started.'

'Come on, it's going to be fun. Relax. You're in safe hands with Willow. You know she'll look after you.' He put a hand on one of Ted's and gave him a kiss on the cheek. 'You'll be fine, you know. You're much better at most things than you think you are. Especially at being a policeman. I may be biased, but I'm very proud of you.'

Ted knew his words were well meant but somehow they made him feel worse. More expectations to live up to and at the moment he wasn't sure if he could.

They found Willow and Rupert waiting for them in the bar, sipping iced mineral water. They paired off before going to find their allocated courts – Trev with Rupert, Ted with Willow, as planned. Ted began tentatively, thoroughly expecting Willow to wipe the floor with him, though determined to make his best effort not to let her. As he'd expected, she was an excellent player. He knew she'd played badminton competitively and did a lot of sports which helped keep her model's figure in perfect condition.

After a warm-up they played two hard, fast games, with Ted trailing but doing his best to hold his own. They'd decided to play three games, whatever the score, but took a short break before the third. Ted picked up his towel to wipe sweat from his face.

'Can I give you a bit of advice, Ted, on how to improve your play?'

'I'd welcome it. Anything at all you can suggest to help my technique so I don't always look like a complete idiot, playing the Chief and constantly losing points.'

She smiled at him fondly as she said, 'It's not your playing technique, Ted. It's your total lack of self-belief. You're a good player. You could be even better if you just believed in yourself a bit more. Not just at squash. I've seen the way you look at Trev when you're together and you're constantly worried, aren't you? Worried that you aren't good enough for him.'

Ted said nothing. She was spot on. He always doubted himself, in most things he did. But how could he explain, even to a friend, feelings he struggled to put into words to his therapist. And to his partner. The deep-seated feelings of a victim of sexual abuse as a child. That it had all somehow been his fault, that he was to blame.

'Trust him, Ted. Believe in yourself. He sees what a good man you are and he absolutely adores you for it. Rupe and I laugh at him sometimes when he's with us. He's always talking about you, all the time. "Ted would like this," "I think Ted could jump this now his riding's coming on".'

'Does he?' Ted was surprised.

'Believe in yourself, Ted. You can do more than you think you can. And start by winning this next game.'

He didn't quite win, but at least he ran her to ten-all before he finally conceded defeat to a far superior player. Willow always had to bend down to kiss Ted, which she did fondly at the end of the match.

'You see? Believe in yourself and you can do it.'

Chapter Twenty-three

'All right, Tony?

'All right, Ted,' Gerry Fletcher's sergeant replied as the two of them once again passed in a corridor. 'Gaffer says have you got some time when he can talk to you today?'

'We've got an interview to sort this morning, which will tie me up for a while. Would this afternoon be okay?'

'I'll let you know if it's not. He'll come and find you.'

The temptation to ask how things were going was almost unbearable, but Ted knew it would be a complete waste of time. He went on his way up to his office, wanting time for a discussion with Jo about the forthcoming interview before morning briefing.

The missing full reports were finally on Ted's desk, so Kevin Turner must have chased up his officers. Ted scan-read them, shaking his head in despair at some of the spelling in one of them in particular. He'd need to send them straight through to CPS for their advice on whether or not there should be charges. They weren't going to get a definitive answer until at least after Jo had finished the interview and put in his report.

'Boss, the search of Gordon's flat turned up a load of shopping receipts for the time that Tara says she was there, becoming daily up until Gordon died. I've got Steve and Jezza working through them and contacting the stores concerned to see if there's any CCTV available for the relevant times. If Gordon's the one shopping each time and he's alone, that probably adds weight to her saying he went out leaving her a prisoner in the flat.'

Ted sighed. 'I wish it really was like in fiction. That we could simply take her word for it. "Oh, you stabbed him through a vital artery in self-defence, did you? Well, that's fine then, off you go." Sadly, as you and I both know, it's not like that. So we're wasting all this time and all the resources we don't have just to make absolutely sure we're not letting a calculating murderer walk free.

'I'll be watching the interview and I'll tell you if I think of anything you've not asked her, but I don't suppose there will be. Depending on who her solicitor is, I doubt they'll let her say anything much anyway. Have you sorted out a female officer, for form's sake, if Jezza's tied up?'

'Kev is lending me Susan Heap. I don't know what the station would do without her if she ever asked for a transfer.'

'Very true. I might not be alive today if it wasn't for Susan.'

Almost unconsciously, his fingers traced the fading scar on his left wrist from a knife injury which had severed one of his arteries, involving surgery and a hospital stay to put right.

'At least as soon as CPS give their verdict, we'll be able to pull the team off the Gordon Wright case, hopefully, and put more onto Helen Reading. Nothing new on that one since I saw you yesterday, I take it?'

'No fresh leads, boss. Mike and Virgil have been checking cameras around where we had that sighting to see if they can pick up a white van which might be the one in question. Trouble is, white vans are hardly a rarity and we've not yet found one which might be ours. The likelihood is that whoever was driving it, if it was involved, knows perfectly well where most of the cameras are and was deliberately avoiding them.'

'Which suggests meticulous planning and someone clever, or who thinks they are. Which reminds us again of … ?'

'Our friend Antoine and his merry band. But in that case are you saying Helen was a deliberate target?'

‘Not necessarily. Maybe whoever it was simply cruised an area they knew well enough to know where the cameras were and just grabbed the first person they saw who might fit their purpose.’

‘Doesn’t Antoine drive some fancy sports car worth a fortune? Why don’t I get someone to dig around and see if he’s ever had a speeding ticket in it from being flashed by a camera? It won’t tell us all that much, but it would make it more probable that he might be the sort to be ultra careful of any type of camera.’

‘Anything’s worth a try, where that slippery customer is concerned, if it’s not taking up too much time which could be more productive elsewhere. It really would be good to get him behind bars, finally, if we’re right about him.’

‘Oh, I’m as sure as you are that we’re right, boss. We’ve just been unlucky enough not to be able to prove it. Yet. But once I get in there on the raid, we might be in with a sporting chance. If it is Antoine, who d’you think was his accomplice on this one? And do you think there were a few of them, like last time? Jerome, Marvin, Donal?’

‘Assuming it was them and that story wasn’t something Nigel made up to hide the real killer’s identity, of course. I doubt Antoine would risk it again with too many of them. The more there are, the more someone is likely to crack. Jerome was always his second in command for the team, wasn’t he? Him, perhaps. There must have been someone to drive, if it really was Antoine in the back of the van.’

‘Is it worth us digging around into those three, see what their movements are for the night in question?’

‘I’d say definitely not at this stage. The last thing we want to do is give Antoine any inkling that he’s in the frame, especially because of the planned raid. And he seems to have them all so far under his thumb they would certainly tip him off if we went anywhere near any of them.’

They could hear the team trooping into the main office, so

they both stood up to join them. Jo laid out who needed to do what for the day, then Ted stepped forward.

'Superintendent Fletcher and his team will be starting to question all of you as from today, I imagine, as I'm up first this afternoon. I just want to stress again that none of you are under suspicion of any misconduct and that if there is any blame flowing around, it's my name on this case as SIO so it will be coming my way. It goes with my job title.

'You all need to be open and honest in what you say. If it's the Super himself who interviews you, don't under any circumstances try to be economical with the truth for any reason. He will know, believe me.'

'Is he as bad as they say, then?' Jezza asked.

Graham Winters was still with the team, making up numbers while they were stretched. He gave a theatrical shudder at her question.

'Worse,' he said. He was the only one of them to have been interviewed by Fletcher, on an earlier case. 'He made me feel as guilty as sin, even though I knew I'd done nothing wrong. I'd second what the boss said, but I would add that as long as you answer him honestly he is very fair. Scary, but fair.'

Tara MacNamee and her solicitor were shown into an interview room and took their seats opposite Jo and Susan Heap. Jo, ever the gentleman, stood up as they entered the room. Once he had started the recorder running, he asked everyone present to identify themselves for the tape. The solicitor was in a combative mood right from the start.

'Julia Wells, solicitor, representing Ms MacNamee. And I must state for the record, in the strongest possible terms, that I consider your treatment of my client to be absolutely outrageous, after all she's been through. She should be treated as a victim, not a suspect, and I intend to pursue the matter rigorously, whatever the outcome.'

Jo doubted his charm-offensive smile would have any

effect on her but he tried it all the same.

'Your objection is noted, Ms Wells, and I assure you that we are doing all we possibly can to resolve this matter as soon as possible.'

He felt genuinely sorry for Tara who was looking as if she hadn't slept for days and probably hadn't eaten either. She was pale and drawn, looking from him to her solicitor and back, as if watching a rapid rally at a tennis match. He couldn't imagine how she was going to get over any of it easily. If she was completely innocent, she was going to feel badly let down by a system which had treated her as a potential murderer.

'And I should tell you at the outset, Inspector, that I have advised my client to say nothing at all at this stage.'

'I quite understand. Tara, that is your right, of course, as Ms Wells has said. Could I just add, though, that it really would help our investigation enormously if you were able to answer one or two questions which I would like to put to you, if that's all right? And is it all right if I call you Tara?'

She was looking at him intently, wide, frightened eyes with dark shadows under them. She looked, Jo thought, like a small rabbit must look at the weasel which was just about to devour it. She nodded a couple of times.

'Tara, could you tell me, please, when you found the nail? The one which you used on Gordon.'

'You don't have to answer that.'

Tara looked uncertain. Jo was trying to give her his most reassuring smile. The sympathetic father of six who understood fear and pain. Not the hard-bitten policeman going for the throat of a villain he knew was telling him a load of old fairy tales.

'I honestly can't say,' she said hesitantly, looking towards her solicitor to see if she was going to intervene. 'The day before he died, perhaps? I had no real sense of time.'

'Thank you, Tara. And what did you intend to do with the nail, when you found it?'

'Tara, you really don't have to answer any of these questions.'

'But if I just tell them exactly what happened, then perhaps I can go home and it will finally all be over.' There was desperation in her voice, a slight catch, as she replied to the solicitor, whilst all the time keeping her eyes on Jo, her look beseeching.

'Your solicitor is quite right, Tara. You don't have to answer. All I can say is that it would help us enormously if you did.'

'I thought I might be able to threaten him, perhaps. Or hurt him enough to make him let me go. I knew I couldn't use it to cut myself free. I couldn't angle it to get at the tights and they were thick and stretchy. The point of a nail would never have cut them.'

'Do you have any form of medical training, Tara? Have you ever done a first aid course, perhaps?'

'No, nothing like that. Well, just a bit of basic first aid in the Guides when I was young.'

'So how did you decide which bit of him to try to hurt?'

'I really would advise you not to answer any questions at this stage.'

'But then it will just go on. And on.' Her voice was going up in tone now, veering towards hysterical. 'If I tell them once and for all exactly what happened, they'll have to believe me. Won't they?'

The tight-lipped sceptical look on Julia Wells' face said it all. She clearly had considerably less confidence in the police than her client had.

'It wasn't a huge nail. I knew it wouldn't go in very deep so I didn't think it would do much harm. I thought about going for one of his eyes. But then I thought that would be dangerous. I didn't want to blind him, or worse. I just wanted to make him understand that all I wanted to do was to go home. And that if he would only let me go, I would promise not to say anything to anyone.'

'Can you tell me exactly where Gordon was positioned, in relation to you, when you struck him with the nail?'

'I knew I had to gain his trust if I was to have any success at all because I'd only get one try. If I failed, he'd take the nail away. He never left any knives or anything sharp about. He wouldn't even give me a hot drink, they were always lukewarm. He must have realised a hot one would have been a weapon if I'd thrown it into his face.

'I kept sending him out to get me different yoghurts. He always left me tied up. When he got back, he would crouch or even kneel in front of me to free me from the radiator. I told him I got cramp so he would let me stand up and stretch. He liked kneeling there looking up at me while I did that. I could see that it turned him on. I'd started bringing my hands down then stroking the side of his neck. He really liked that.

'So that final time, I did it but with the nail in my hands and I just stuck it in him. To hurt him, nothing more. But then I saw the blood. I tried to stop it. I used towels and pressure, whatever I could think of. But there was so much blood and it was coming out so fast. I didn't know what to do. I hammered on the walls, tried to find a phone. Looked for the keys to the house so I could go out and get help. But I couldn't. So he died. And I never meant him to.'

'Why did you aim for his neck with the nail, Tara? Why not his face? And what made you pull the nail back out?'

'He liked me touching his neck. He always wanted me to kiss his neck. I wouldn't kiss him on the mouth. Ever. He revolted me. I didn't want any physical contact with him but he kept insisting. He was becoming more demanding every day. I didn't know how long I could keep holding him off before he got nasty. And I didn't know what he might do to me after I slept with him, if I did. I didn't want to aim for his face because of his eyes. And it's bony, too. I didn't know if it would hurt him enough to make him let me go if I perhaps hit his cheekbone and just scratched him. I don't know why I didn't leave the nail in. I was just reacting by instinct.'

'And Gordon Wright was just kneeling passively at your feet while you did this to him?'

'Really, Inspector, I must object to your tone and to this line of questioning,' the solicitor cut in.

Jo ignored her completely and went on, 'Tara, did you go to the flat with Gordon of your own free will?'

'Inspector, this has gone too far. Your implications are absurd and offensive.'

Jo blanked the solicitor again and carried on with his questioning.

'Did you go there specifically to see Gordon?'

'No, I certainly did not.'

'Had you ever met him before?'

'No, I hadn't. If I had, I wouldn't have gone near his flat. He seemed harmless enough when he opened the door to me but as soon as he overpowered me and tied me up, there was something really creepy about him. About the way he kept looking at me.'

'There was no kind of a relationship between you? He hadn't asked if he could kneel at your feet while you hurt him?'

'Absolutely not.'

'Did you intend to kill him?'

'No, I did not. I just wanted to hurt him enough to make him allow me to leave.'

'Do you know if Gordon was on any kind of medication?'

That question seemed to surprise her. She frowned and shook her head.

'I never saw him take anything. He'd mentioned being off sick from work but he didn't take any tablets that I saw. Not in front of me, anyway.'

'Let it go, Jo,' Ted told him through the earpiece. 'You gave it your best shot but we aren't going to get any more out of her.'

Once Tara and her solicitor had left, with Jo promising to let them know as soon as possible what CPS's decision was, Jo went to find Ted.

'We've almost got premeditation there, rather than heat of the moment stuff. Especially when she mentions avoiding the cheekbone and going for a softer area. As if she knows more about anatomy than she's letting on.'

'You know what, Jo? It's in cases like this that I'm heartily relieved that it's up to the clever sods at CPS to decide if there's a case to answer or not, rather than humble coppers like us.'

Chapter Twenty-four

Ted was sweating cobs, as his dad would have said. Sweating like a pig, he thought to himself, and managed a smile at the irony, although like most coppers, he hated that nickname for them. He'd taken off his jacket and hung it up. Rolled up his sleeves and tugged his collar and tie loose. But nothing was working. He could feel damp patches spreading under his arms and a cold trickle running down his back. He just hoped his deodorant was up to the challenge.

He knew he was stressed and he was trying his best to control it. He'd gone through all the martial arts techniques he'd ever learned to slow his breathing, clear his mind, control his heart rate. But so far it wasn't doing any good. He was dreading his forthcoming meeting with Gerry Fletcher. That was because, rightly or wrongly, when anything happened within his team, he always blamed himself. He was the boss. It was his role to make sure mistakes didn't happen.

He hadn't had any lunch. His stomach was not in a receptive mood. He'd made do with green tea and honey. He just hoped Fletcher would not keep him waiting too long. If he was for the high jump, he'd sooner know as quickly as possible. Ted always preferred to face trouble head on.

He only just stopped himself from springing to his feet when the Grim Guardsman strode in, his expression impossible to read. Ted didn't bother offering him a brew. He knew that, informal or not, this was not going to be that sort of an encounter. Fletcher nodded a greeting then sat down opposite Ted, taking out his phone and putting it on the desk so he could record their conversation.

'Right, Ted, let's get this done, shall we? Can you confirm that you're happy to proceed without your Federation rep or anyone else present?'

'That's correct, sir.'

'Let me just start by saying that if more senior officers kept their own and their team's paperwork as tidy and up-to-date as you do, me and my team's work would be a lot easier. It's exemplary. But now we've been all over everything, there is one obvious question which I have to ask you first of all.'

Ted knew what it was going to be. It was the one he'd been asking himself, over and over, ever since the incident happened.

'You brought in this psychologist, this Anthony Hopkins...'

'Anthony, sir,' Ted corrected automatically, sounding the th together, which Fletcher had made a single T.

'Anthony, then. But did you at any point ask him the direct question of whether or not, in his professional opinion, he considered Nigel Denby to be a suicide risk?'

'I did not.'

He admitted it. Said the same thing he'd told himself over and over in the nights of broken sleep which had troubled him. He hadn't and he should have done.

Fletcher was looking at him hard. Ted held his gaze.

'But at no time did Hopkins volunteer that thought? He didn't flag up for you, either when you were talking or in his subsequent written report, that in his clinical opinion – the one he was being paid handsomely to give – the lad was a suicide risk? In fact, didn't he say to you, when he observed an interview with Denby in your presence, that putting pressure on him would probably result in him simply saying what he thought you wanted to hear?'

'He did say that. But I should have asked the specific question. In so many words.'

Fletcher raised his eyes to the ceiling. Sighed loudly. He

was trying to throw Ted a lifeline which he was obstinately refusing to take.

'That's easy to say with hindsight. But like I said, considering what Hopkins charges for his time, I don't think it's an unreasonable assumption to think that if he did consider the lad to be at risk, he would have come out and said so.

'Right, moving on. It's unfortunate that neither your DS nor your DC had eyes on the lad at the exact moment when he went off the platform and that the CCTV for that side of the station wasn't operational that day. Not much reliable eye witness testimony for the exact moment, either, not even from the train driver. So are you absolutely convinced the lad jumped and wasn't pushed by someone who then slipped away in the confusion? There was nothing in his note to suggest he planned to kill himself, after all.'

'I did consider the possibility. There was so much going on when it happened, of course. Everyone was looking at the train and the tracks when they realised what had happened, so it's not impossible that someone else was involved and they simply disappeared when everyone was distracted. We just don't have anything to indicate that there was. Nobody saw anything much.'

'Suicide is the most likely explanation, I grant you. But a coroner's court might just hesitate about bringing in that verdict without any indication of clear intent. I wouldn't be surprised if it ended up as an open verdict.

'Right, those are the only questions I had for you, based on having gone through the files. We'll obviously need to talk to your DS and DC, the ones who were on the platform. Your DI too, as he was running things from here, and all those who interviewed Denby at any point. I know your young DC, Ellis, is it, was one of them.'

'Steve Ellis, yes. He interviewed Nigel at one point.'

'We won't keep you hanging on for too long and I promise you'll get our findings as soon as possible. They'll go to your

Chief Super, of course, but I'll copy you in.'

He leaned forward and switched off his phone.

'Right, now, not on the record. Just two coppers talking shop together. How much weight do you give to the letter this lad Denby left? There's no way you can use it, clearly, now the writer is dead. But do you think it's true? The four lads he names as being the killers. Is that likely, in your opinion, from what you learned about them from the case? Denby must have known that if he came forward in person with those allegations, he was still facing a prison sentence for his part in the conspiracy to murder, if not the murder itself. So perhaps the fact that he admits his part in the letter is his way of saying he wasn't going to be around to face the consequences.'

'Antoine is definitely the leader. Arrogant, clever, something of a risk taker. I would say that it wouldn't surprise me if it was true. But like you said, we had no evidence on which to go after him and with the inquiry, we couldn't do so. The Chief made that clear.'

'And now? Once I put my report in, will you try to pursue him?'

Ted wasn't about to mention the upcoming raid. If Fletcher didn't know about it, it wasn't his place to tell him.

'None of us wants to see him walk free if he's guilty. We'll be keeping a very close eye on him. And if and when anything turns up which we can use, we'll be on to him.'

'Good, I'm glad to hear it. Right, that's it, then, Ted. That wasn't so bad, was it? If I were you, I'd put the kettle on now. Oh, and find a dry shirt from somewhere.'

Ted usually kept a full change of clothes in the back of his car for emergencies. He went out to have a look what he could find in it. There was a small group of people, mostly women, standing near to the station steps. One of them held a tatty poster, made from a bit of old cardboard, on which someone had scrawled with a black marker pen, in uneven capitals which bunched up too close to the right-hand edge, 'FREE

TARRA MCAMEE.'

At least there was no sign of a press presence taking notice of them, Ted thought as he ducked his head and prepared to hurry across the car park to his Renault. One of the women recognised him and shouted to the others, 'That's him. That's that inspector what was on the telly saying they'd arrested her. Oy, you! Not so fast. Why don't you let 'er go? She did nothing. It was that sick bastard what kidnapped her and tortured her.'

It was the last thing Ted needed after his interview with Fletcher. He would have to be extremely careful what he said to them as they would inevitably misquote him. But if he refused to say anything at all, it was only a matter of time before allegations of a police cover-up were appearing everywhere. There were already several phones pointing at him, probably filming his every move.

He stopped and turned to face them, keeping his tone and expression as neutral as he could manage.

'I'm Detective Chief Inspector Darling. I have no official statement to make at this time. All I can say is that Ms MacNamee is not being held here. She attended for interview, with her solicitor, this morning, but was allowed to go home. That's all I can tell you for now, I'm afraid. There will be an official statement as soon as there is anything we can release.'

'Well, you would say that,' one of them called to his retreating back as he headed for his car. 'But how do we know it's true?'

As luck would have it, when he got to his car, there was everything in there bar a fresh shirt. For a moment he considered nipping to the nearest supermarket and grabbing one, any one, but he decided his time would be better spent working on the cases. He knew Jo would have sent through his interview notes at the first opportunity, so there was a slim chance they might get at least a phone call from CPS later in the day, with a heads-up on their decision. They knew there was huge pressure on all of them for an early result.

Now he had run the gauntlet of the protesters in the car park, he ought to go straight to the Super to tell her what had happened. He wished he didn't look as if he had been hosed down and left to dry. Without a clean shirt, he couldn't do much to make himself more presentable. He sloshed a bit of aftershave around as a precautionary measure and went back to the station, dodging the small group who were still standing there as best he could.

He'd fully intended going back to his office for his jacket before he went to find the Ice Queen. As luck would have it, he met her coming out as he was going back in. She looked at him, raised her eyebrows but didn't comment on his dishevelled appearance.

'I was informed that there was something of a demonstration taking place. Is that so, and do I need to go out to deal with it? If not, you'd better come to my office and tell me about it. You look as if you could probably do with some coffee.'

Ted seldom drank proper coffee in the afternoon and she knew it. Her offer was probably a reflection on how bad she thought he looked. He followed her to her office, trying to surreptitiously sniff his armpits as he walked.

He sat down as the Ice Queen indicated and she put coffees in front of them, Ted's exactly how he liked it. He filled her in first on what had happened on the car park.

'It seems that you handled the situation exactly as I would have done, although no doubt someone will twist it out of all shape on social media before the day is out. But with any luck, we might hear something, even if it's informally, from CPS about their decision before the end of the day. Then at least we can put this whole affair behind us all. I imagine we want that almost as much as Ms MacNamee does. Is there anything else you wanted to discuss with me?'

It was her most tactful way of asking for an explanation of

his bedraggled appearance. He told her about his interview with Gerry Fletcher. She listened to all the details then said, 'You really shouldn't blame yourself, Ted. Nobody else does. This was a very unfortunate incident but not anything in which the outcome could have been altered, I suspect. If this young man's mind was made up to end his life, even if either DS O'Connell or DC Vine had been able to stop him on this occasion, he would undoubtedly have found a way at some time in the future to carry it through.

'I fully expect Superintendent Fletcher to rule that no one was culpable and all procedures were correctly followed. I know you well enough by now to be certain that would have been the case.'

Her words raised his spirits slightly. He was about to thank her when her phone rang.

'Yes, please put him through.'

She listened silently for a moment, then responded, 'Thank you for letting me know. That will be a source of relief all round.'

She spoke to Ted as she put the phone down.

'CPS. We'll have their full detailed report in the next day or two but they are saying they don't think it would be in the public interest to pursue any kind of prosecution against Tara MacNamee in relation to the death of Gordon Wright. So I suggest you get someone to tell her that as soon as possible. I would just caution that whoever does it should be extremely guarded in what they say. And it's imperative they don't apologise for our actions to date. The last thing we want is for her to try for a wrongful arrest claim or anything like that. I'll talk to the Press Office about a statement.'

'I'll send Jo. He was the one who arrested her and he can be charming and sympathetic when the occasion calls for it. I'll brief him on what to say and what not to say and I think we can trust him to get it right. I suspect the team will be almost as relieved as she is.'

It was almost knocking off time, so all of the team had drifted back in to write up notes and clear their desks at the end of the day. Ted walked into the main office, waited until he had everyone's attention, then announced, 'No further action against Tara, CPS have ruled. Jo, can you go round to see her, sooner rather than later. And I'm sure you don't need me to tell you, be careful what you say. No doubt Ms Wells will want retribution.'

A cheer went up from the team at the news. None of them had enjoyed working on a case they had grave doubts over.

'And of course this now means we can concentrate all our efforts and resources on the Helen Reading case as of tomorrow morning.'

'Oh deary dear, look what the cat dragged in,' Trev laughed at the sight of Ted when he got home, quoting a line from Ted's favourite film, Blazing Saddles. 'What happened to you, apart from a wardrobe malfunction and an aftershave overdose?'

'The Grim Guardsman happened to me. I had my interview with him today and I got a bit stressed waiting for it. Do I smell like a wrestler's jockstrap? I'll go straight up and get a shower if that's the case.'

Trev gave him a hug and a kiss on the cheek. 'Not too bad, but I imagine you'll feel more human after a nice shower. You've time, before supper's ready. Did he tell you anything or do you have to wait for his findings?'

'His team need to talk to the rest of mine first. I doubt I'll hear anything much before the end of the week at the earliest.'

'It's bound to be good news. Why don't we go out for a meal somewhere on Friday night to celebrate?'

Ted made a face. 'There may be nothing worth celebrating,' he said gloomily.

'Well, a meal to cheer ourselves up, in that case, although I don't believe that for a moment. It's ages since we've been out. I shouldn't need an excuse to get my husband to take me out to dinner. Let's do it, Ted. You book somewhere really nice, push the boat out a bit. And promise me you'll turn up on time to take me.'

'I've no idea how the week's going to pan out, or what time I'll be able to get away on Friday ...'

'No excuses, Ted. It's not often I ask for your undivided attention so unless you get a pile of bodies on Friday afternoon, promise me you'll book somewhere suitably extravagant and take me out.'

Ted never could refuse his partner anything. Hoping he wouldn't be putting himself in an impossible situation, he solemnly promised before he disappeared upstairs for the much-needed shower.

Chapter Twenty-five

Gerry Fletcher and his team did their best not to take Ted's team members away from the Helen Reading case any more than they had to. But they did need to speak to them as part of the inquiry. The Grim Guardsman himself opted to interview both Rob and Jezza as the officers who were tailing Nigel at the time of his death. Both had been honest enough to admit that for a few seconds, neither was looking directly at Nigel at the crucial moment.

Ted was relieved to hear that Fletcher had assigned his female sergeant, Chrissie, to speak to Steve. He dreaded to think how DC Ellis would have survived a grilling from the Grim Guardsman himself. Ted didn't want to be seen to be coaching Steve in any way, but he was worried about him, knowing how anxious he got even with Ted's calm approach and reasonable manner. He found time for a quick word with Bill Baxter, now a civilian manning the reception desk, who was also Steve's new landlord, to find out how he was doing.

'He'll be fine, Ted, don't fret. I've been helping him a bit. Reassuring him that no one would expect him to pick up on interviewing him that the lad was a suicide risk. Especially not when even your posh and expensive psych didn't raise it. Don't you worry about young Steve. I'll see him right. You'd do better to be concerned about Rob O'Connell. He's visibly coming apart at the seams, in case you hadn't noticed.'

Bill was right. Ted was concerned about Rob but trying not to fuss over him which would only serve to make him think he had something to be worried about. Rob was up first with Fletcher on Tuesday morning and Ted briefly reassured him, asking him to report back as soon as he was done. Fletcher hadn't kept him all that long. Ted put the kettle on when Rob came in, clearly relieved the ordeal was over.

'I should have kept my eyes on Nigel the whole time, boss. I let myself get distracted for an instant, looking at the stone train. I saw him go flying under it but there's no way I could swear whether he jumped or was pushed. It was just a blur of movement and it happened so quick.'

'It's fine, Rob. You did exactly the right thing. You told the truth. Didn't try to hide or colour anything, and that will always work in your favour. I'm sure you have nothing to worry about.'

Ted put a coffee in front of his DS and sat back down at his desk.

'Right, tell me where you're up to with the bishop. Has that case got legs, do you think?'

'A very good interview with Peter Spencer. Very frank and detailed. I taped it all and it's all there. Dates and places I can check out to see if the bishop was in the right area at the times Spencer gave me. I've also been tracking down some of the other surviving victims who made complaints at the time and getting their statements. What I want to do next, boss, is to go and see the bishop again, if the nursing home watchdogs will let me in, and put some of these allegations to him. Depending on what he says, I think there's a chance we might just have him.'

'Any defence lawyer is immediately going to bring his state of mind into question. Does he have a definitive diagnosis of dementia of any sort?'

'No, boss, that's the encouraging thing. They say he's confused, more so some days than others, and he has some mobility difficulties which mean he can't manage living alone. But not Alzheimer's, nothing like that. Not what I was led to believe at first. Nothing he could use as a real get out of jail card.'

'And the million dollar question CPS will want an answer to. Would a prosecution really be in the public interest?'

'Boss, you know as well as I do that Peter Spencer was emotionally scarred by what the bishop did to him. That he went on to kidnap and torture young men, one of whom died as a result.'

Ted opened his mouth to speak but Rob cut across him, 'Yes, I know what you're going to say. We can't know whether he would have done something like that whatever had happened to him in the past. But it won't have helped him. That kind of thing can change someone forever. It messes with your head. Makes you think you might have somehow been to blame for what happened to you. That you must somehow have deserved it.'

Ted knew Rob had been abused as a child. What Rob didn't know – very few people did – was that Ted was also a survivor. He understood all too well the feelings Rob was describing to him. They plagued Ted a lot of the time too, despite the counselling and Trev's unswerving support.

'Boss, I really want to see this case through. I think we should pursue it while the bishop is still alive and before he really does become unfit to plead. I don't think he's at that stage yet. Sometimes I think he's still as sharp as a knife and he's just playing games with everyone, me included. I'm happy to work on it in my own time, if you need me to.'

'You know I can't allow you to do that, Rob. Not if we want a successful prosecution out of it. Make sure you log all the hours you spend on it. I'll talk to Jo and get him to free you up from the Helen Reading case whenever he can. Then once we hear the outcome of the inquiry, we may be all systems go to start again with Antoine and the others. There may yet be things we've not uncovered so far, other angles we can explore.'

Rob went on his way looking happier than he had for a

while. Whatever the outcome of his interview with Gerry Fletcher might be, at least it was now over. The waiting was always the worst part, as Ted knew all too well.

Before they knocked off for the day, Ted went to catch up with Jo to tell him about Rob and the case on the bishop. They were interrupted by Jo's desk phone. He answered the call, listened, made a thumbs up gesture to Ted, then thanked the caller before he rang off.

'Green light on the raid on Antoine and his father for tomorrow morning. Sparrow's fart, when they'll both hopefully still be tucked up unawares in their beds. So let's just hope and pray Antoine's been cocky enough not to do his housekeeping properly and we finally get something to link him to at least one offence we can nail him for at long last.'

'Right, team, settle down.'

With Jo out on the raid, Ted wanted to brief everyone on what was happening and what they needed to be working on for the day.

'Jo's out on a joint op with Drugs and Fraud which affects us. As a result of what Sal told us was brewing. I couldn't say anything earlier because it was strictly under wraps but now I can tell you. They're raiding Louis Martin's house with warrants to search both his home and possessions, on suspicion of supplying drugs, and also those of Antoine Martin. He's suspected of money laundering. The drugs money.'

There was a murmur of anticipation from the team members. This was the best news they'd had on the case to date.

'Apparently Antoine's dad is a known, but as yet untouchable, supplier of high-quality coke, with a lot of friends in high places. As you know, Sal tipped us off via Virgil, knowing our interest in young Antoine. Fraud think that his supposedly successful online currency trading is simply a front to launder his dad's drugs money. Jo's gone in to see if he can find anything which would help us with our theories on Antoine's possible involvement in Derek Waldren's murder.'

'So you do think he had something to do with the Helen Reading killing, don't you, boss?' Jezza asked him, astute as ever.

'I didn't want to mention it sooner because it seems too far-fetched. But both Jo and I were struck by the fact that the crime scene up at Sykes reservoir was as clean and devoid of any traces of evidence as the woods up at Roman Lakes were when Derek Waldren was found.'

'What would be his motive for killing Helen Reading, if it was him?' Mike Hallam asked.

'Rubbing our bloody noses in it, because we couldn't get him last time, the little shit,' Maurice grumbled. Ted frowned at his choice of words but it was like water off a duck's back to Maurice. He thought Maurice was probably bang on the money with his theory, though.

'The on-tap coke supply would certainly confirm my thoughts when I saw him at the funeral, boss,' Graham Winters put in. 'If he's using, and his habit is maybe getting a bit out of control, let's hope it leads to a few slip-ups.'

'I have to say, as a father, that I'm surprised if Louis is letting his son sniff the nose candy,' Mike put in. 'He should know better than anyone the dangers.'

'Perhaps he doesn't know?' Virgil suggested. 'Perhaps Antoine is dipping into daddy's yayo without asking, making like da hard black man he pretends to be.'

'We clearly won't know any more information until we hear from Jo if he found anything of relevance to us. And I've no idea how long that will take. There's a chance of conflict over anything that's found, in respect of the different cases, of course. With luck, the items most likely to be of use to us – like any of Antoine's clothing, for example – won't be needed by either Drugs or Fraud.'

'Can I volunteer to interview Antoine, boss? Him being my

soul mate, an'all,' Virgil asked with a note of irony in his voice.

'Okay, before anyone gets too excited I need to make a point. I should have said this at the outset. Having Jo there today in no way indicates we can start going after Antoine. Not yet anyway, whatever today's search throws up. My orders from the Chief were quite clear on that. Until we know the outcome of the inquiry, we need to keep a low profile there, unless we uncover any rock-solid evidence of anything during the search. We've got Jo in on the raid to declare an interest. If he finds anything of significant help to us, then I'll have to follow the chain of command to get authorisation to take it any further.'

He sensed their disappointment at potential delay and hurried to reassure them.

'We'll regroup once Jo is back in, see if anything was uncovered which might be of help to us. And as soon as we can move, if there is anything, we will do. Remember, I'm as keen as any of you that Antoine should get sent down if he was involved in either the killing of Derek Waldren or that of Helen Reading.'

'I nearly did have to arm wrestle to get a look at anything which might be of interest to us,' Jo told them at the end of the day. 'With three units all claiming first dibs on anything we found it got a bit heated at times. Everything's being collated centrally and I've declared an interest in anything which looked useful, starting with the contents of Antoine's laundry basket. You were right, boss, when we were discussing it earlier. Piles of clothes dumped and not washed. It's all a very long shot. If it was him in the white van, if the clothes he was wearing on that day, more than a week ago now, are still there. Or if they've been washed, can the fibres still be matched to those found on Helen's clothing. You know the sort of thing.

'Next, we come to something really interesting to us.

Antoine's mobile phone. Steve, can you confirm Nigel's mobile number for me?'

Steve trotted it out from memory, not needing to consult his notes. Memorising numbers and data was a thing of his.

'That's what I thought. Fraud's techie type was very good. I persuaded him to check the call history for me at the house rather than waiting, in case it gave us a steer. Now, you remember there wasn't enough left of Nigel's phone after it had been under the train to get anything from it at all. But I got said techie to check specifically for the day that Nigel died. I couldn't remember all of the timings off the top of my head for that day. But at some point, and it seemed to me that it could well have been when he went back home after leaving here and before he went to the railway station, Nigel made a call to Antoine, and that call lasted well over fifteen minutes.'

'This was when me and Jezza were sat outside his house?' Rob queried. 'The time we assumed he was typing out the letter he sent to Steve, naming Antoine and the others?'

'They're going to send me a full printout of times as well as numbers for calls made and received. But yes, I would say around that time, from memory.'

'So something in that phone call was enough to tip Nigel over the edge? You think he phoned Antoine to warn him he was about to confess all and give him chance to turn himself in?' Rob suggested.

'Boss, Rob and I have both already told the Grim ...'

'DC Vine,' Ted interrupted her sternly. Gerry Fletcher's nickname was widely known and used, but Ted would not tolerate its use in a team meeting. It was his warning tone and even Jezza knew better than to ignore it.

'We both told Superintendent Fletcher that there was a brief moment – seconds at most – when we both had our eyes off Nigel, just before he went under the train. Suppose the phone call was enough to bring Antoine hotfooting in pursuit of Nigel, to make sure he didn't tell anyone what he knew about the night Derek Waldren died.'

'Did he have enough time to get there, between that call and the incident?' Mike queried.

'With those fast wheels of his? More than likely,' Jezza replied. 'Assuming he was at home at the time. He could have been anywhere.'

'Hang on, am I being a bit slow on the uptake ...' Maurice began.

'Wouldn't be the first time, bonny lad.'

Maurice ignored Jezza and carried on.

'I know Antoine's been in the frame for Derek Waldren's murder from early on, although we had no proof. But how has he gone from that to suddenly being suspected of killing Helen Reading, with no motive that any of our enquiries has dug up to date? And now to having killed Nigel, too?'

'All of this is just speculation at the moment, Maurice,' Ted told him. 'The only thing we have possibly linking him to Helen Reading is a witness statement that's tenuous at best.'

'Aye, and bloody wild speculation it seems to me, at that.'

'For now, it's all academic anyway,' Ted told him. 'We can't, for the moment, go after Antoine. If fibre tests from his clothes show up anything on forensic examination, anything at all to link him to Helen Reading, then we can see a way forward from there. And at the moment, we've no other suspects in the frame for that case. Jo, what's the situation with Antoine and his father?'

'Both arrested, boss, both taken for questioning to separate stations. The team doing the search of the property are very thorough and there are plenty of them, so I think it's unlikely they'll overlook much, if anything. They were still working when I came away. Adrian, from Drugs, says they're intending to hold father and son for as long as they can swing it. He doesn't think they have a hope in hell of getting a remand in custody or an extension of questioning time. Especially not since it's highly probable that Louis Martin's lawyer could be one of his best customers who will want him kept outside for as long as possible.'

'So for now, we ignore the Antoine aspect and we concentrate on Helen Reading. We need more information, more sightings. Anything we can get. Somebody must have seen something. I'm going to talk to the Super about a possible reconstruction of her last known movements. Jezza, would you be up for doing that? You've got the drama training and could be made up to look like her.'

'You'll need to speak to my agent, boss,' Jezza told him, grinning.

'DC Vine ...'

Chapter Twenty-six

It wasn't until early afternoon on Thursday that Ted received a summons to his Chief Superintendent's office. He imagined it was likely to be the result of Gerry Fletcher's inquiry, since the Grim Guardsman and his team had packed up and left the station the day before.

Ted hadn't yet received notification himself from Gerry but assumed he would follow the chain of command and inform the Chief Super first. Ted's hierarchy was complicated. When Jim Baker wasn't off sick, he was his boss for the cases he and his team handled. Superintendent Caldwell, the Ice Queen, was the person he reported to in Jim's absence. But Chief Superintendent Chris Higginbotham was the Divisional Commander. In charge of everything which happened not just in the division, but specifically within the station. Ted generally got on with him well enough, although Higginbotham did like to make sure everyone knew how important and busy he was at all times. Which was why being called to his office usually meant Ted being left standing in front of his desk.

The Ice Queen was already there, sitting in the only spare chair Ted could see. He never quite knew what to do with his hands whilst loitering there like a spare part so he hoped the Chief Super would be brief. Whatever Gerry Fletcher's findings were, good or bad, he'd sooner hear them without preamble.

'Ah, Ted,' Higginbotham said, looking up at him, his face neutral. 'I'm not sure if you've had your own copy yet, but I was just discussing with Debra what Gerry says in his report. Which is, of course, extremely thorough and detailed.'

Ted tried to curb his growing impatience whilst mentally taking the Chief Super out with a well-aimed karate kick.

'To cut to the chase, Ted, you and your team are to be congratulated. Gerry has nothing but praise for the way your investigations were handled. He gives special mention for the immaculate paperwork. The only caveat he has added is a recommendation that in future, in all similar cases where an expert witness is brought in, they are to be asked to state in writing whether or not, in their professional judgement, any worst case scenario could be possible.

'He stresses he's not apportioning any blame. It's just fire-fighting for the future. So well done, Ted. It's over, it's behind us all and now you can move forward. Please pass on my appreciation to the rest of your team for doing a good job, and keep it up.'

Ted managed to contain himself until he was alone in the corridor before he did an air punch of relief. Then he hurried back to the main office to see who was in. He called Jo in from his office before he told those assembled and asked someone to text the rest of the team members the good news, so they weren't kept waiting.

'Good news, for all of us. Gold stars and a clean bill of health all round. Superintendent Fletcher was complimentary about our paperwork, so well done everyone, and thank you. Now that's out of the way, and we've finally been able to drop any case against Tara MacNamee, that leaves our way clear to concentrate all our efforts on finding who killed Helen Reading. And once we get the forensic findings and more detailed info on the contents of Antoine's phone, we might finally be back on the trail to Derek Waldren's killer.'

Steve was in the office and he spoke up at that point.

'Sir, there's just a chance we might get a heads-up on the contents of Antoine's phone, and his laptop. Océane's part of the Central Park team who are working on data retrieval from the Martins' house. She knows it's of special interest to us so she'll make sure we're copied in on everything, as soon as possible.'

'Nice one, Steve, thank you. In the meantime, this definitely calls for a celebration. So tomorrow evening, after work, drinks are on me to finish the week.'

Ted and Jo had got together to discuss how things had gone when Jo had been to tell Tara that no action would be taken against her. There was always the worry, especially with a shark of a solicitor, like hers, that there would be an attempt at a claim against the police for the way things had been handled in arresting her as a suspect.

'I think it's highly unlikely she'll pursue it. She was so relieved when I told her it was all over that she just burst into tears. I was careful what I said. I didn't apologise, just repeated that it was standard procedure in such a case, being arrested but not charged, pending an investigation. I think she accepted that. I took someone from Uniform with me as back-up. Susan wasn't free so I went with Hilary.

'Tara's a strong woman. She's busily rebuilding her life, that's why she started back to work as soon as she could. I just wish we hadn't had to put her through it, but I don't think she'd want to go over it all again for any kind of a hearing.'

'I don't need to mention it, but I will anyway. Make sure your report is meticulous and prompt please, Jo. As we got house points for our paperwork from Gerry Fletcher, we've a lot to live up to. A couple of good results to celebrate tomorrow evening, then you and I can discuss what's happening between us for weekend cover.'

'Chief Constable for you, sir,' the telephone operator informed Ted as she connected the call. His first thought was that, despite Willow's advice and morale-boosting, he didn't yet feel ready for a rematch on the squash court.

'Ted? Jon Woodrow. A good outcome from Gerry Fletcher's inquiry, I hear. Well done. I never expected anything less of you. I can usually rely on you to do a proper job. So now feel free to carry on the case which was interrupted by the young man's unfortunate death. And if this Antoine lad needs putting away for more than coke and money laundering, I hope you'll see to it that it happens, and for as long as possible.'

'I'll do my best, boss.'

'That's good enough for me. Now, something really rather strange I need to talk to you about. I've been contacted by a senior officer from another force who is facing an external inquiry into one of his cases. A historic case. It needs to be done by someone from an independent force. One which is beyond reproach and suspicion. Said officer has requested you, by name, to conduct that inquiry.'

'Me, sir?' Ted asked in surprise. 'I've never conducted such an inquiry. I wouldn't know where to begin. Can I ask who it was who mentioned my name?'

'You remember me saying it was strange? It was Chief Superintendent Roy Marston. I know there's history between the two of you, and not in a good way. So I was probably almost as surprised as you are to get his call.'

Ted hesitated for a moment, trying to make sense of what he was hearing.

'Boss, this isn't some kind of a strange joke, is it? Only I can't imagine any reason at all why Mr Marston would want me anywhere near a case of his.'

'No joke, Ted, I assure you. It's to do with allegations of sexual abuse, made at a time when Marston was Duty Inspector at a station in the West Midlands. He interviewed two witnesses, both young girls. He claims to have passed the file to a Superintendent who's long since retired. It would appear that at some point the file went missing and no action was ever taken.

'I hear on the grapevine that you may know rather a lot about one of those witnesses, who's since come forward with damning evidence. And that you may know even more about how said witness came to be in a position where she can testify. Now, I'm not going to ask you about that because it would clearly compromise you. There are probably some things it's best I don't know about. But I wanted to ask you what you thought about Mr Marston's idea. Would you be prepared to run the inquiry? And don't give me any false modesty crap about not being up to the task. If even Gerry Fletcher can't find any fault with your paperwork, it's because there's no fault to find. So you're the perfect person to run such an investigation. It doesn't need to start immediately. I know you'll want to see your own cases through to put them to bed, finally. But after that, would you be up for it?'

There was another pause as Ted thought about it. The Chief put in, 'Believe it or believe it not, Ted, Marston does speak highly of your integrity.'

'Not, boss,' Ted chuckled. 'At least if he does, I bet that's all he speaks highly of.'

It was the Chief's turn to laugh. 'Well, he's clearly not your number one fan, that's for sure. But he does say that he believes you to be honest and incorruptible, which is what is needed in this line of work. It's all a bit irregular, I grant you, but I also think you'd be the ideal person for this. So can I take it you'll agree? And if so, will you call him yourself to tell him so, please?'

'Really? Should I be talking to him if I'm going to be running an inquiry into one of his cases? And that's still a big *if*. I might need to think about this a bit more.'

'Oh, I think you'd be a fool to refuse, Ted. It will look very good on your CV. And you're not going to be talking to him about the case. Not yet, anyway. You're just going to do him the courtesy of telling him whether or not you're willing to take it, since he asked for you in person. Which I think you probably are.'

Ted got the message loud and clear. The Chief wanted him

to take the case. He wasn't thrilled at the prospect but he knew when it was best to agree.

'I'll give him a call now, Chief.'

'Good man, Ted. I think you're making a wise choice. And before you start on the inquiry, you and I should meet again on the squash court.'

Ted decided he needed tea to fortify him for his forthcoming conversation with Marston. He couldn't begin to imagine how he'd found himself in the situation of agreeing to take the case. The Chief Constable could be persuasive at times and Ted had felt himself outmanoeuvred on this as surely as in any game of squash he'd ever played against him.

He took several swallows of his tea while he looked up Marston's number. Then he dialled it. The unmistakeable, slightly nasal and somewhat arrogant tones of Ted's nemesis responded.

'Chief Superintendent Marston.'

'DCI Darling, sir. My Chief asked me to call you.'

'Ah yes. Thank you for calling me, Darling. I expect you were surprised by your Chief's call?'

'I would say that was an understatement, sir. I'm still not sure why you asked for me.'

'I still haven't changed my opinion of you overall, Darling. I still think you're a cocky little sod, as I've told you before. I think you've been allowed to get away with murder for various reasons, mostly political. But even I have to admit, I do think you are a man of some integrity. I know you've stood up to me when you've believed yourself to be in the right and you've been unshakeable in your convictions.

'As I'm sure your Chief has told you, I'm facing an inquiry into a case that passed through my hands. I understand we can't discuss anything about that case. But I know I'm innocent on this, Darling, and I want that to be proved. I've made a lot of enemies in my time. I can think of a lot of officers who would jump at the chance to take me down, not because I did anything wrong, but because there's history between us.'

Ted tried to speak, but Marston cut him short. 'Yes, I know there's history between us, too. But despite whatever else I think about you, I think you are someone who is able to work in a detached manner. To keep personal feelings out of your professional life. I hope I'm right. I'm gambling on being right. If not, I'm going to look like a complete idiot when you decide to hang me out to dry.

'I don't need your answer today. You'll want to think about it. About the implications. I'm potentially putting my career in your hands, Darling, because I'm banking on being correct about you on this.'

This time Ted didn't hesitate. 'I'll do it, sir. So we probably shouldn't talk further until I need to interview you.'

The call ended with words Ted never thought he'd hear from Marston.

'Thank you, Darling.'

'Ted, are you sure you've not found Trev's stash? You're coming out with some very strange stuff of late,' Jim Baker asked him when Ted phoned him the following day to tell him about Marston's call. Trev had said something similar when he'd arrived back, late, after his karate session and a meal out with friends from the club.

'Honest truth, Jim. Marston, of all people, positively grovelling to me to help him out. I've never run this type of inquiry before so I hope I don't make a total cock-up of it and give him even more reason to think I got promoted as a PR exercise more than anything else.'

'Don't be so soft! You'll do a bloody good job, as usual. And the Chief's right. This will be a big tick for you. Who knows what it might lead on to? Anyway, you must be happy, with Gerry's inquiry wound up in your favour, plus no case to bring against your kidnap victim. Drinks in The Grapes tonight? I wish I could join you.'

'You're very welcome Jim, you know that.'

'Bella won't let me out to play at the moment. She doesn't trust me enough. But raise a glass for me, will you? And for god's sake come and see me when you get chance. I'm going stir crazy.'

All of the team members were in high spirits when they adjourned to The Grapes after Ted and Jo had called a halt to work for the day. They were no further forward yet on the Helen Reading case, pending forensic results, but at least their workload had been lightened with the news on Tara MacNamee. And the inquiry being over, with a favourable outcome, was a weight off everyone's mind. Now they were ready to let their hair down before starting again on the serious stuff.

Ted was halfway through his second Gunner when his mobile rang. Trev.

'Ted, I'm so sorry. I'm actually going to have to stand you up for once. A young woman came in with a big old beast of a Beamer that's broken. She's on her way to Hull for a ferry because her dad, in Germany, has had a heart attack and the family want her back as soon as possible. I can fix it for her, but it's going to take me a while. So I am sorry but I'll have to cry off to be a knight in shining armour. She's going to go out for a takeaway for us both. I hope you didn't book anywhere too expensive that might charge you for a late cancellation.'

Ted hesitated for a fraction of a second too long, realising, with a sickening feeling, that he had completely forgotten about his promise to take Trev out for a meal that evening.

'Erm, no, it'll be fine, don't worry ...' he began lamely.

'Ted! You bugger. You promised me, and you didn't even remember to book. And don't bother telling me yet again that you'll make it up to me because I clearly can't trust a word you say.'

Ted winced visibly as Trev ended the call. Jo noticed and asked, 'Oh dear, you in trouble, boss?'

'I was supposed to be taking Trev out for a meal tonight, somewhere special. Luckily, he's had to cancel because I'd actually forgotten to book anywhere and he guessed as much.'

'Take him out somewhere tomorrow night. Push the boat out, book somewhere really expensive.'

Jezza was sitting opposite them, not eavesdropping but unable to miss what was going on.

'Boss, you forgot to book? Seriously? That is bad. That is going to take much more than a meal out to fix. Take him away for the weekend. Somewhere romantic. What about Paris?'

'I don't like flying,' Ted started to protest. 'And we haven't worked out weekend cover yet.'

Jezza sighed theatrically. 'It's not about you, boss. And Jo, tell him.'

'You're off this weekend, boss. I'm covering.'

'Right, now give me your phone,' she ordered Ted, holding out an imperious hand.

'Why do you need my phone?'

'Because I'm going to book you the right sort of place, and sort out your flights. At some point you're going to need to enter your credit card details and I'm assuming you aren't stupid enough to do that on someone else's phone. Even if you have got yourself into this mess. Phone.'

Ted handed it over meekly. Within minutes, everything was sorted. Flights from Manchester were booked, with an overnight hotel and dinner in a Michelin-starred hotel. Trev would know instantly that he'd not come up with the idea himself. Ted just hoped it would be enough to get him out of the doghouse.

Chapter Twenty-seven

Ted put the fancy box carefully onto Jezza's desk as he made his way through the main office to his own before any of the team members were in. It was a box of hand-made chocolates from what Trev assured him was one of the best artisan *chocolatiers* in Paris. He'd laughed at Ted's shock when he'd seen the price tag; told him it had been worth every penny for Jezza's help.

'I know you do your best but this trip has been wonderful. I've adored every moment of it. Much better than a bag of chips and fish bits on top of Marple Ridge would have been.'

It had been the perfect gesture, Ted knew, and one he would never have thought of left to his own devices. Well worth the considerable dent in his credit card made by Jezza's choice of flights and venue. Trev had arrived home late on Friday, still furious with Ted for forgetting his promise to take him out to dinner. Ted's usual offers of red roses and wine, which he'd bought on the way home from work, had been rejected as inadequate. Not until Ted had produced the printed out boarding cards, hotel and restaurant reservations had Trev relented and hugged him. He'd finished off the booking Jezza had made for him when he got home and had found Trev's passport.

'I really am sorry I forgot,' Ted had apologised again, contritely. 'And I can't even take credit for the alternative plans. That was all Jezza's idea and she booked everything. But I really wanted to show you how bad I felt and to try to make it up.'

Trev had laughed delightedly.

'Well, much as I love you, I didn't really think you'd come up with an idea as romantic as this without a nudge from someone. Or as expensive. I bet your credit card is sobbing. I do try to make allowances for work taking over your life, you know. It would be nice if just occasionally I felt I was equally as important to you as dead bodies. People often complain there are more than two of them in a marriage. I have to compete with your whole team. But then I've only got myself to blame. Whatever possessed me to fall in love with one of the Lily Law?'

Ted liked to get in to work before the rest of the team every day, for a few quiet moments at his desk to wade through emails and other messages, including the Post-its which sprouted on his computer when he wasn't there.

Jo wasn't long behind him and came to find him for a catch-up.

'Good weekend, boss?'

'Really good, Jo, thanks. I'd never have come up with anything like that, on my own initiative. Jezza's a good'un, even if she can get a bit lippy. How were things here?'

'Blissfully quiet, for a change. A couple of drink-fuelled assaults but no bodies. It gave me time to think about how to proceed next, on the Helen Reading case.'

'I was giving that some thought, too ...'

'Ted, please tell me you didn't spend a weekend in one of the most romantic cities in Europe thinking about work?'

Ted looked guilty. 'Not all the time. I did have other things to occupy me.'

Jo held up a hand and laughed, 'I suspect we're about to venture into Too Much Information territory again.'

'Oh, don't worry. I'm a perfect gentleman. I always shut the bedroom door.'

The quip was the closest Ted ever came to discussing his

private life, about which he was obsessively protective.

'What I was thinking is that now the raid is over and Antoine's been arrested, there's no reason why we don't start talking to some of the other lads. Especially the ones Nigel mentioned in his letter – Jerome, Marvin and Donal.'

'I thought that too, Jo. Let's get those three spoken to before we tackle Antoine. Wasn't Marvin the one who tried to stop Antoine killing Waldren, according to the note? Perhaps if we lean on him now, he might start to crack. Especially if he knows Antoine is facing a possible prison sentence already. Then, based on what they tell us, if anything, someone needs to talk to Antoine, at length. If Drugs and Fraud have had him long enough and he's been cut off from his supplies, it might have loosened his tongue a little bit. I quite fancy that task myself.

'And let's not forget that Jerome's dad is a subcontractor for Louis Martin's property development business. You said Drugs and Fraud have seized all of Louis's vehicles, plus Antoine's wheels, for forensic testing. We need to get a look inside some of Jerome's father's vans as well, in case one of those was used to abduct and kill Helen Reading. If Antoine is going heavy on the coke lately, there's an outside chance he won't have been as careful with the clean-up as he was for Derek Waldren. Always assuming that was him and the others and that we're not going off on a complete wild goose chase.'

'I don't think you believe that any more than I do, boss. Do we need a warrant to search Jerome's father's vans?'

'It would be tricky to get one, at this stage. We've nothing concrete against any of them in the Waldren case, and never have had. Not to mention having nothing so far to make any connection to Helen Reading. Let's start with someone going round and politely asking at Jerome's father's firm about van movements on the day Helen disappeared. Try to pass it off as some sort of routine thing. Hopefully we can do it informally to start with. Find out if any of the vans were out then and who had access to them. Perhaps ask to check logs, see if any vans had unexplained mileage, anything like that. If they're in the clear on the Drugs front, they might be willing to cooperate with us to emphasise that.'

'Will do. When Drugs seized all of Louis Martin's vehicles I registered our interest in anything which might link any of them to either Antoine Martin or to Helen Reading's clothing. They were planning to have Forensics working on them flat out over the weekend and promised to let me know any developments as soon as they could.'

'Going back to what Nigel said in his letter, we also need to get a look at Marvin's car for any traces of Derek Waldren's presence in it, since Nigel said that was how he got him up to the woods. They might not have thought about cleaning that. They could probably come up with a plausible excuse if traces were found, but it's still worth a shot. There's an outside chance of finding traces to place it at Roman Lakes at some point.'

'Are we going to get them this time, boss, do you think? And do you seriously think Antoine was involved in some way in Nigel's death?'

'We're going to give it our best effort, Jo, that's for sure. I'm not sure about Antoine. It's possible that whatever he said to Nigel in that last conversation was enough to tip him over the edge. I doubt we could ever prove that. He's a nasty piece of work, for sure, so I'd like to get him for something. And speaking of getting the villains, try to free Rob up for as much time as you can. We'll hang on to Graham, to make up numbers. Rob really wants a crack at the bishop before anyone can claim he's unfit to plead, and I'd also like to see him brought to book, if we can do it.'

'Will do, boss.'

'Anything over the weekend from the reconstruction Jezza did?'

'We're wading through the usual timewasters. We did get

one person who said they were cut up at traffic lights by a white van and the time might just fit the one we're looking for. We're following that one up as the most likely.

'So shall I brief this morning, and are you coming to join us? Sounds like the rabble are arriving.'

'I'll leave it to you. I seem to have the world supply of meaningless emails to wade through since I went away.'

Jo grinned as he turned to go out of the office.

'Fine by me, boss, you stay and have a little nap after all your fun and games in Paris.'

He heard Ted throw something at his retreating back as he went out, chuckling, and closed the door behind him.

It was mid-morning when Jo got a phone call from his friend in Drugs, DI Adrian Jacobs.

'Jo? Adrian here. Tell me you love me.'

'I love you, Adrian. Goes without saying. What have you got for me?'

'You're playing with the big boys now on this joint op, Jo. Sexy crimes, sexy big budgets. So we've been slave-driving Forensics mercilessly all weekend to get us some results. And we have some which will no doubt interest you. Word of warning, though. These are only initial findings, not yet cross-matched.'

Adrian was clearly ratcheting up the tension, pausing for effect. Jo was trying to curb his impatience.

'Do you keep your women waiting this long, Ade? I hope you make it worth their while, if so.'

Jacobs laughed. 'Mucky bugger! One-track mind, you. No wonder you have six sprogs. Right, to cut to the chase, in one of Louis Martin's work vans they found clothing fibres. Like I said, no firm match yet to the clothes from the house, but some were dark fibres similar to jeans, others were white, and I'm quoting from the report here, "of a similar type to those found in protective coveralls". But that's it to date.

'Of course, we took DNA from both Louis and Antoine Martin, although both were reluctant to cooperate, so it might be possible to show that either or both of them had been in that van. Louis Martin might conceivably have had a legitimate reason to be there, as boss of the company. But it's hard to see what reason Antoine, a supposed online currency trader, would have to be in the back of a works van, which was where the fibres were found.'

'Now I do officially love you, Ade. Enough to stand you a beer and perhaps a curry when we can both find the time. Keep me posted on the final results, please. And can you do me another favour?'

'It will cost you more than one lousy beer. But go on, try me.'

'We really need to place Antoine in that van. Then we might be able to nail the slippery *bastardo*. But we also need to know who was driving it, if he was in the back. We took DNA samples of all three suspects in our earlier case, when they were cocky enough to think themselves untouchable. So could you ...'

'Get that cross-checked against any findings from the van? Consider it done, *amigo*. But it is definitely going to cost you more than one measly beer.'

Ted decided to phone Jim Baker later in the day to run a few ideas past him. As much as anything because he knew how bored Jim was feeling until he could get back to work. He would need to keep the Ice Queen involved in any developments but Jim could always help him keep things in perspective.

'Debs will tell you the same thing as me, and I know you don't need telling, but you need to wait until you've got some solid evidence before you make your move, Ted. Timing is critical. Get it wrong and his doubtless expensive lawyers will be screaming harassment.'

‘If Forensics can just give us something – anything – that puts Antoine in that van, then we can haul in the other three, say we have strong reason to believe that one of them was driving and see who will squeal the loudest to keep themselves out of the frame.’

Ted paused as Jo entered his office without knocking. The grin on his face told him it was going to be good news.

‘Got to go, Jim. Jo’s just come in, grinning like the Cheshire cat, so I assume it’s good news.’

‘Hispano-Irish cat, boss, but yes good news, though still requiring further work for a definite match. But with all the usual “subject to confirmation and on the balance of probabilities” stuff, Forensics say they’re pretty certain the dark fibres found on Helen Reading’s clothing are a match not just for those found in the van but also for the ones taken from a pair of unwashed black jeans found in Antoine’s bedroom. We’ve as good as got him, boss.’

‘Let’s not put the cart before the horse, Jo. There’s a long way to go yet. First off, we need Antoine in here, with his lawyer, for us to question. He’s on conditional bail, I imagine? Can you set that up, preferably for first thing tomorrow? I want the other three brought in at the same time. Exactly the same time, because I’d like Antoine to see for himself that the others are there. It might just rattle him, although no doubt they’ll all be in contact anyway.

‘I’ll take Antoine, if you can take Jerome. Marvin might be the one to crack first, with the right questioning. Mike to interview him, do you think?’

‘Mike’s good. Sympathetic, but not as much of a soft touch as Maurice. What about Donal Shaugnessy? I have a feeling he might be a bit of a hard man. Virgil?’

Ted nodded. ‘Virgil is ideal. I know he wanted a crack at Antoine but I’d like him myself. Set it all up, please, Jo. Tomorrow could be a billirant day.’

Jo looked at the boss quizzically. Ted laughed.

'Billirant. It's one of Trev's famous typos when he's texting a bit the worse for wear. He always insists on disabling the auto-correct on his phone and the results are often amusing. But I just have a feeling tomorrow will be a billirant one, for all of us.'

As Ted had expected, Antoine turned up with a high calibre solicitor, sharply dressed, on the ball. Ted doubted he'd let Antoine say anything at all, but he was prepared to try. It didn't help the lawyer's attitude that Ted was having to make a last-minute disclosure of the Forensics findings to date on the fibres found in the van. He was still waiting on final confirmation that the jeans found in Antoine's wing of the house definitely matched the evidence found on Helen Reading.

He explained the reasons for the interview, identified those present, and issued the standard caution. When he handed the forensic reports to the solicitor, a man called Tristram Penrose, he barely glanced at them, simply tossing them onto the table in front of himself with a look of barely-concealed disdain.

Ted had had the dark jeans which had been taken from Antoine's room returned from the lab. They sat in a clear evidence bag on the table next to him.

'Antoine, do you recognise these jeans? Do you own a pair like them?'

'Oh, please, Chief Inspector. Firstly, my client cannot possibly comment on an item of clothing he can only partially see through a bag. And secondly I would imagine that most young men of his age own something similar.'

Antoine looked amused rather than concerned. He'd been held in custody for twenty-four hours by Fraud but had had plenty of time since to top up with coke. From the looks of him, that's exactly what he had done. Ted wouldn't swear to it but he wouldn't have been surprised to learn that Penrose was also a user.

'Antoine?' Ted prompted in his usual quiet tone, totally

blanking the lawyer.

'I have lots of clothes. Including dark jeans. So?'

'Do you ever drive any of your father's work vans, Antoine?'

'Why would I? I have my own car.'

'Antoine, remember what I told you. You're not obliged to answer any of these questions.'

'And would you have ever had any occasion to be inside one of those vans, Antoine? Particularly in the back of it?'

Antoine merely shrugged in silence.

'So could you suggest for me why traces of fibres which match those from these jeans, which were recovered from your part of the house, should have been found in the back of one of the vans?'

Penrose sat up straighter at that and reached for the report, starting to flick through it.

'Antoine, as I told you, I'm investigating the death of a young woman called Helen Reading. Do you know anyone of that name?'

'Nope.'

'So if I tell you that I'm currently waiting on forensic confirmation that the fibres on these jeans, taken from your room, are a match for fibres taken from Helen Reading's clothing on the evening she was killed, that wouldn't concern you unduly?'

'I need an adjournment, Chief Inspector. Now. To consult with my client in private.'

Chapter Twenty-eight

'You want me to sanction a drugs search on a solicitor of the calibre of Tristram Penrose in this station on the basis of what, precisely?'

'I'm pretty certain Antoine is off his face. I imagine he's at the stage of carrying supplies with him wherever he goes now. Penrose had some time alone with him before I saw them, and I have a feeling he realised it would be obvious his client was using. There's just a chance he made Antoine hand over his supply for safe-keeping. Which means either one of them could be carrying.'

'Granted, but if we ask Penrose to turn out his pockets like a naughty schoolboy and he isn't in possession, there are going to be serious repercussions.'

'However, if Penrose and his client just happened to be walking along a corridor at the same time that a police drugs dog was walking the other way, that might be very interesting.'

The Ice Queen looked searchingly at Ted.

'Do you mean to say you have set this up before coming to get my approval, Chief Inspector?'

'It was time critical, ma'am,' Ted, as ever, opted for formality when he knew he was skating on thin ice. 'I spoke to DI Jacobs for advice on the drugs issue and he mentioned they still have a dog working at the house and at Louis Martin's business premises. Adrian Jacobs and the dog handler are on their way now. They should be here very shortly.'

'I'll need to at least let the Chief Super know, to cover both of our backs, should it be necessary.'

Ted could hear from the loud bellow of 'What?' in response to the Ice Queen's brief explanation that the Chief Super was not impressed. He heard snatches of the short conversation as she held the phone a short distance away from the side of her head to spare her ear drum. Penrose was well known, both professionally and socially. They were going to have to tread carefully.

'I managed to smooth his ruffled feathers. But I'm intrigued. How are you going to engineer this seemingly innocent encounter with the dog?'

'Unfortunately the recorder in the interview room we've been using has developed a technical fault, which will require us to adjourn to a different room.'

'For a fundamentally honest man, you can be surprisingly devious at times, Ted,' she told him drily. 'Please keep me informed constantly of all developments. This is very definitely an occasion where forewarned is forearmed.'

With four potential suspects currently being interviewed, space in the station was at a premium. Ted wanted to stage-manage the encounter with the dog so that it seemed as innocent as possible. Bill, on the front desk, phoned his mobile to let him know when DI Jacobs and the dog handler arrived. Ted had met Jacobs briefly on a couple of occasions. They greeted one another with a handshake.

'Good to see you again, Ted. This is Sergeant Lloyd, with Police Dog Axel.'

Axel was a grinning, tail-threshing Springer spaniel, which even Ted didn't find too intimidating. He briefly explained the plan and what he was hoping for, pointing out the layout of the ground floor. It needed to look natural as the two officers and the dog walked past Penrose and Antoine. Ted went back to the interview room where he'd left Penrose in conference with his client.

'I'm sorry to interrupt you, Mr Penrose, Antoine. Our technical team tell me there's a slight problem with the recording equipment in this room. Clearly we want to make sure our interview is recorded properly once we resume so I've got someone coming to take a look at it in a moment. If I could possibly ask you to adjourn to our conference room in the meantime, I've arranged some coffee and biscuits for you there and we should be able to get started again very quickly, if you're ready to proceed.'

Penrose huffed as he picked up his papers, making his feelings known. Still apologising, Ted showed them out into the corridor then led the way towards the conference room. Jacobs and the sergeant, with his dog, were walking towards them and did no more than nod politely in acknowledgement. All except PD Axel. As soon as he drew level with Penrose, he plonked himself down on his hindquarters, tail wagging faster than ever, staring up at the man and whining in excitement.

It was clear that the solicitor knew instantly what was going on. His face drained of colour, his lips pinched in anger.

'What's the meaning of this? What is that dog doing here? Get it away from me. I don't like dogs.'

'Mr Penrose, is it? DI Jacobs, sir, Drugs. Young Mr Martin and I have already met,' Jacobs told him, holding up his ID. 'This police dog is trained in drug detection. He is indicating to us that you possibly have drugs in your possession.'

'Both of them, guv,' the dog handler told them, watching his dog gazing from Penrose to Antoine and back again. 'He's giving a strong indication on both these gentlemen.'

'I therefore have reasonable grounds to suspect that either or both of you may be in possession of a controlled substance, which gives me the right to search you. Is there an interview room we can use, please, DCI Darling? I'll need to record the full procedure. And can you spare me another officer as a witness? I'll need to let the sergeant and Axel get back to work.'

'We can go back into the room we've just come out of. That's empty at the moment.'

'I thought you said the recording equipment was faulty?' Penrose demanded, glaring at Ted.

'I'll give it a thump. I've just remembered that usually makes it work again.'

With his suspect being spoken to by Drugs, Ted was free to find out how the rest of his team members were getting on with their suspects. Jezza was tasked with observing the various interviews via monitors so she could alert the boss of anything which needed his immediate attention. Ted slid into a chair beside her.

'How's it going?'

'Jerome thinks he's in a bad gansta movie because he's pleading the fifth amendment. Refusing to say a word. It's a Mexican stand-off. Or perhaps a Spanish one, as it's Jo. I'm glad it's Virgil in there with Donal and not me. He looks ready to lamp someone at any moment. He's not even bothered with a solicitor. He's just bluffing it out with a "prove it" attitude to everything. And DS Hallam is definitely winning by a pin-fall against Marvin. I wouldn't like to be one of his kids caught out doing something wrong. He's very persistent. Marvin may have been the goalie on the old team but he's having difficulty defending against a verbal striker like our Sarge.'

Ted smiled at her word play then turned to watch Mike in action via the monitor. Marvin Gray had requested a duty solicitor and it looked as if he'd been allocated the office junior. She was leaning forward in her seat, vigilant as a tennis umpire, but Mike was totally ignoring her, continuing with his unrelenting questioning of Marvin which had the young man visibly sweating and constantly licking his lips.

'So you have no alibi at all for the evening Helen Reading went missing? And you maintain you've never met her, nor even heard of her?'

'I never said that. I seen on the telly about her being missing, like, but that was all. I didn't know her, and I never went near where she disappeared from.'

'How do you know where she disappeared from, Marvin?'

'You don't have to say anything, Marvin. You're not obliged to answer these questions. Inspector, my client has already told you, several times, that he didn't know this lady. So if you have some evidence to the contrary, it's high time you produced it.'

Mike simply inclined his head in acknowledgement of her presence before repeating the question to Marvin.

'They said. On the telly. I saw that reconstruction thing. They said what road it was in.'

Ted leaned forward and used the intercom to speak to Mike through his earpiece.

Mike listened then asked Marvin, 'Have you ever driven or been a passenger in one of Antoine's father's work vans?'

His words seemed to surprise Marvin, whose eyes widened for a moment before he said, 'No, never, why would I?'

'We have evidence which shows that Antoine was a passenger in the rear of one of his father's vans the evening Helen Reading disappeared, with a possible sighting of it in the vicinity where she disappeared from. Which means that someone was driving the van, if Antoine was in the back. Now, we have your DNA on record and it will be checked against any found in the van. Is there anything you'd like to tell me?'

'Marvin, you're not obliged to say anything. Inspector, if you have some evidence pointing to my client, you must disclose it to us. You know that as well as I do.'

'Marvin, it's true, you don't have to answer my questions. But if you have nothing to hide, there's really no reason not to. Is there? Were you driving that van? Or were you with Antoine at all that evening?'

'Not that evening, no. That weren't me.'

'Nice one, Mike,' Ted said quietly. 'Now let slip the dogs of war.'

'Shakespeare, boss?' Jezza asked in surprise. 'I somehow

didn't think that would be your thing.'

'Oh, my dad was well read, even if I'm not. Besides, Trev's watched the film about a hundred times. He has a thing for John Gielgud.'

'But you were in a vehicle with Antoine at some point when he was committing a criminal offence. Is that what you're saying, Marvin?' Mike pounced on the wording.

'Marvin, don't say anything. You don't have to. Inspector, I want an adjournment to take further instruction.'

'Very shortly, Ms Allen. I'd just like to hear Marvin's reply to my question.'

Marvin was looking increasingly desperate. From the way he was shifting about in his seat, Ted imagined he needed the lav, and soon.

'You see, Marvin, in a letter Nigel wrote shortly before he died, he says you were present in the woods near Roman Lakes on the night Derek Waldren – probably known to you as Badger – was murdered. Nigel says that in fact you lent him your car to get Derek up there. And that you came shortly after. You, Antoine, Jerome and Donal. What do you have to say about that?'

'Yeah, I know he said that, but it was a lie.'

'How do you know he said that, Marvin? That letter was sent to us here, directly. The contents have never been made public. We believe it was written very shortly before Nigel died. So how do you know what was in that letter? We know Nigel spoke to Antoine on the phone shortly before his death. Did he also phone you? Did you phone him? Or did Antoine tell you about the call.'

The solicitor kept making a valiant effort to interrupt Mike's flow. He totally ignored her and ploughed on with his questioning.

'How do you know what Nigel said, Marvin?'

'It wasn't me! I didn't do anything.' Marvin's voice had gone up now, shrill, almost breaking in his evident fear. 'I tried to stop Antoine. With Badger, I mean. It wasn't what any of us had agreed to. We were just meant to frighten him. Hurt him a bit, to let him know we were serious about him giving himself up to the police. But Antoine's a mad bastard. He was high as a kite, getting off on the risks we were taking. I couldn't stop him. He was out of control. But it wasn't me with that woman. I swear to god. I've been keeping out of his way. He's completely crazy.'

'And who else was with you, up at Roman Lakes that night, Marvin?'

'Me, Antoine, Jerome and Donal. Don't tell them I told you. They'll kill me. I want police protection. Twenty-four hour. Lock me up, if you have to. Just keep that mad bastard from getting anywhere near me. I'll tell you. I don't want to go down for this, so I'll tell you. But only if you can protect me from Antoine.

'When Nigel phoned Antoine and told him about the letter he was sending to the police, Antoine said it would be the last thing he ever did. Nigel told him he was getting on a train and heading to Liverpool for a ferry across to Ireland and he'd never be found. He had some distant family there, I think. Antoine told him he'd find him, wherever he went, if it took him the rest of his life. He said he might as well jump under the train as get on it because he was dead either way.'

'Thank you, Marvin. You've been very helpful. Ms Allen, we'll take a break now and I'll arrange some refreshments. Please take as long as you need to talk to your client. There'll be a PC outside the door at all times. Just inform them when you're ready for me to come back. If your client needs a break to use the facilities, again just ask the PC outside to arrange an escort for him. For your own protection, Marvin, as much as anything. Antoine is still in the building.'

Mike left the interview room and came to find Jezza. Ted was letting both Virgil and Jo know the latest and asking them to join him.

'Bloody masterful that, Sarge,' Jezza told Mike appreciatively.

'I'd second that, Mike. Let's scoop up the other two and adjourn upstairs for now. I think we've all of us deserved a brew. I have a bit of interesting news to report, as well.'

They opted for Jo and Mike's office, which was bigger than Ted's. Ted went to find his own teabags while Jezza put the kettle on. For once she wasn't accusing anyone of sexism for letting her be the one to brew up.

Mike recapped on his interview with Marvin and finished up with, 'I think it's probably all over bar the shouting with him. Whatever his solicitor says to him now, I don't think he's going to stop singing. He's clearly hoping to get off being charged and to get witness protection. I imagine we'll have to charge him with something though, boss?'

'Conspiracy to commit GBH, for starters, I would imagine,' Ted replied. 'I'll have to talk to CPS at length for their advice on a holding charge. I doubt we'd ever get a conspiracy to murder to stick. But we can't ignore the fact he lent his car to get Badger out to the woods and he's admitted they intended to hurt him and frighten him. There's got to be a charge there we can stick him with.'

'But is it enough to take Antoine down, though, boss?' Jo asked him. 'Jerome is denying everything, when he can be bothered to say anything at all. He would clearly back Antoine's alibi for the night Badger died, and I imagine he'll alibi him for the night Helen Reading disappeared, too. So if all that's stacked against Antoine at the moment is the money laundering charge … Well, white collar crime. It's hardly in the same league as two potential charges of murder.'

'Ah, well, there might just be a bit more stacking up against Antoine in the shape of a tasty charge of possession of a Class A substance, namely cocaine. That could get him seven years for possession, possibly much longer if we could show he was also supplying.'

He told them of his set-up with the police dog, which had them all laughing in appreciation.

'Boss, you little tinker, that was inspired. I think you need to take a weekend in Paris more often,' Jezza told him.

'My credit card is still recovering, Jezza. Don't forget, everyone, that we're still waiting on confirmed forensic results on the van. If we have clear evidence putting Antoine in direct physical contact with Helen Reading, inside that van, and evidence of who was driving it, I'd say we were close to wrapping up a solid case.'

'My money's on Jerome for the driver. He's Antoine's right-hand man in everything. I wouldn't be surprised if he's a user, too. My strong feeling is that when Antoine says jump, Jerome's only question is how high.'

'And what about Donal's involvement in it all? Virgil, what are you getting from him?'

'Apart from dark, murderous looks and sullen silence, boss? It's only a gut feeling but I don't think Donal's involved in, or interested in, anything else. Certainly not the Helen Reading killing. He just wanted Derek Waldren to pay, as the man he saw as being responsible for the suicide of his kid brother. Plus he has a seemingly watertight alibi. He plays guitar in a group and they had a booking for the night Helen disappeared. Not just his word on that either. He did tell me about that, in a smug sort of way. The group's relatively popular in Manchester, especially with the Irish community. A biggish venue and lots of people filming them perform. Whoever was driving the van for Antoine that evening, I'd bet money it wasn't Donal.'

Chapter Twenty-nine

'The main supply was in Penrose's pockets, but we did find sizeable traces in Antoine's. Enough to charge him with possession,' Adrian Jacobs told Ted after he'd finished searching both men. 'If this is all right with you, Ted, and your gaffer, I've summoned up my sergeant and I'd like to interview them both here, to save time. I know your murder case trumps my Drugs one, but I'd like to question them as soon as possible, while we've caught them *in flagrante delicto.*

'Penrose is denying everything. He's not a user, never touches the stuff, he was just trying to help out the son of an important client by confiscating his stash before he was spoken to. A momentary lapse of judgement in the heat of the moment, wrong thing for the right reasons, blah-blah-blah. Funnily enough, he's refused our offers to get him a solicitor of his own. I suspect he doesn't want anyone knowing about this, especially not the firm he works for. He's in for a shock, because I intend charging him with possession at the very least.

'I've confiscated their clothes, given them coveralls. Forensics will be able to tell from their threads whether or not our Mr Penrose really is a nose candy virgin, but I'd bet my meagre pay cheque that he isn't. And yes, before you say anything, we'll make sure anything untoward on young Antoine's clothing is reported to you. How does that fit in with your interview plans?'

'I'm sure we can share Antoine between us, as long as he's allowed his breaks, by the book. If I get the test results I'm hoping for this afternoon, I think we might be able to charge him with Helen Reading's murder. It largely depends on whether his loyal sidekick can be persuaded to talk, based on those test results. I'm sure my Super will give us an extension to question him, if necessary, based on all we've got going on.'

'Ah, yes, you got the Ice Queen in the station lottery, didn't you? Is she as frosty as her reputation?'

'She constantly makes me feel incompetent, probably without intending to. She does brew a good cup of coffee, though. I'll need to update her shortly, and probably the Chief Super too.'

Jacobs laughed as he said, 'I imagine he'll be cacking himself about Penrose. They're probably in the same Lodge or something. Look, I doubt we'll get finished with our bit before late afternoon, so perhaps we could have a swift half together before we head back to the big city? You, me, Jo, my sergeant, maybe yours too. Mike Hallam, isn't it? I know him.'

Ted left Drugs to carry on with Antoine for now and went to finish his discussion with Jo and the others. Their suspects, apart from Antoine, were all currently on a refreshment break.

'What's the plan now, boss?'

'We need to get a full written statement from Marvin, as long as he's not bottled it during the break and wants to retract what he's said so far. Or been told by his brief to say no more. Then we'll need to put the contents of that statement to Jerome and Donal and see what they have to say to that. I'd also better arrange a couple of officers to babysit Marvin when we've finished with him. I'll check with CPS about a holding charge. They might be happy with a slightly lower offence for him, but I'll push for a murder charge for Jerome and eventually for Antoine. I don't think we have a hope in hell of bringing charges against Donal. We'd never break his alibis and it's all just hearsay that puts him at the scene. Everything hangs for now on the forensic results and when we get them. I'll keep you all posted on that.

'The other thing which will need doing as soon as possible

is to question again all the other team members about their alibi for Antoine and the others on the night Derek Waldren was killed. Mike, I know that means a lot of legwork but call up Leona and Charlie from South Manchester, if they've nothing more pressing on. I think you can safely leave Marvin to stew for a bit while you sort that.

'Let's try to get round as many of those as we possibly can whilst we've still got the ringleaders tucked away in here. That way, they can't tell them what to say.

'Tell them all that we now have an eye witness who says it was the four of them, Antoine, Jerome, Donal and Marvin, who killed Waldren. And that Nigel was with them at the time. Make sure that they mention all five. If Marvin isn't mentioned, they'll all know immediately who the informer is and that could put him in serious danger. We need that to start happening as soon as possible.

'Jo and Virgil, you need to pile the pressure on Jerome and Donal. Stress the eye witness in the Waldren case and hopefully, before too much longer, we'll also have something to place Jerome in that van for the Helen Reading one. And make it abundantly clear to them that the very least they're facing is conspiracy to murder so they're likely to be going down.'

'Is it worth getting your witness to the van incident to see if he can ID either Jerome or Antoine, boss?' Jo suggested.

'Mr Baines? He did say he didn't see the driver, but he might have glimpsed him without realising it. All he said was that he saw a black youth, and that could possibly have been Antoine. But it was as vague as that. Anything's worth a try, though. Mike, can you have a word with Kevin Turner and see if he can spare anyone to set up a photo ID? There'll be a mugshot of Antoine once Drugs charge him, which they will. As soon as those results come through, we can arrest Jerome on suspicion and get his photo, too. See if either face means anything to our Mr Baines. It would be a bonus if he could pick out one or the other.'

'Jezza, can you be monitors monitor again, please. In charge of watching the screens. Let me know immediately of any developments.

'Adrian's suggested we should have a drink with him and his sergeant after work, anyone who's interested. We might have something to celebrate, if Forensics comes through with the goods.'

The Ice Queen suggested that she and Ted should go and brief the Chief Super together on the latest developments.

'You'd better be damn sure Drugs are right about this, Ted,' he said warningly. 'The repercussions if you've got it wrong don't bear thinking about. I know Penrose through the Lodge, not to mention Louis Martin through the Rotary Club. I'm shocked to hear this about him. And what was a sniffer dog doing in the building anyway?'

'Just routine, sir, checking out a suspect thought to be carrying,' Ted replied evasively.

'Could Drugs not at least take them back to their own territory to charge them? That minimises the potential damage to us if you have got it wrong.'

Higginbotham was playing politics, as he often did. If they were right and got a good solid case out of it, he would want to claim the lion's share of the glory. If they were wrong, he would have no hesitation in throwing Ted to the wolves.

'And what about the rest of it? How close are you, realistically speaking, to a conclusion on the two murder cases?'

'Waiting on final forensic confirmation, sir, but one of the suspects has started to talk. And I think it would waste a considerable amount of time moving Antoine from one station to the other. Especially when DI Jacobs is already in this neck of the woods.'

'All right, fair enough. Make sure everyone knows that any

suggestion of immunity from prosecution is out of the question on a murder case. Is there a lesser charge which could apply to this lad Marvin, if he does testify? Discuss that with CPS, see what we can offer him. But let's try to get some closure. If this station manages to wrap up two murder cases and a Class A drugs one, it's going to look very good on our statistics. Very good indeed.'

Ted was in with Jezza, watching Jo and Virgil at work, when his phone pinged for an incoming email. The screen told him it was the anticipated report from Forensics.

He told Jezza so as he got up to go. 'I'll pick the report up from my desk then I can print it straight out. Let Jo and Virgil know there may be an important development.'

Ted sprinted up the stairs, full of anticipation. These findings were pivotal to the development of the case. If they could place Jerome in the driving seat of the white van, he was going to have a lot of explaining to do, having already said on tape that he'd never had occasion to drive any of the vans. Antoine probably wouldn't have been in white coveralls if he was planning to get out of the van to abduct Helen Reading – or anyone else, if she was just a random choice – hence finding his traces. He risked drawing too much attention to himself if he was wearing a white CSI-type suit in the street if anyone had seen him. But sitting in the driver's seat, Jerome could well have been suited up and wearing gloves.

Ted scan-read the report on his screen whilst it was printing out. It was detailed, as ever. Initially there was nothing there to get excited about. No fingerprints, sweat traces, stray hairs, skin cells. As he'd feared, it looked as if whoever was driving had been wearing protective clothing and gloves.

Then Ted's eyes fell on a passage which filled him with elated excitement. There were traces of saliva and nasal mucus secretions on the van's steering wheel. Someone had sneezed. The traces were smeared and smudged as if a rough attempt had been made to wipe them away with a sleeve or similar. But the minute traces had been analysed and compared to traces already provided.

The person who had sneezed in the driver's seat of the van was Jerome Brooks. The results were conclusive. There was more good news in the shape of confirmation that the fibres from Antoine's jeans were a positive match not only for ones found in the van but also for those found on Helen Reading's clothing.

'Gotcha, ya little bastard!' Ted did a double fist-pump, then leapt up from his desk, snatching the print-out and hurrying back downstairs.

He put his head round the door to tell Jezza briefly what the findings were, then went into the interview room where Jo was with Jerome. Jo introduced him for the tape. Jerome had also decided to dispense with a solicitor. Given his stubborn refusal to say anything, he'd probably thought he didn't need one.

Ted sat down next to Jo, facing the young man. As usual, his voice was quiet so Jerome subconsciously moved slightly forward in his chair to hear him.

'Jerome, do you have any legal training?' Ted asked him by way of an opener.

His question seemed to have caught Jerome by surprise because, despite his intention to say nothing, he said, 'No, I don't. I'm a painter and decorator. But I don't need any 'cos I'm not saying nothin'.'

'I see. That is your right, of course. I'm here because I've now had the confirmed results of forensic testing on a van belonging to Antoine's father, Louis Martin. A vehicle which we have reason to believe was involved in the abduction and murder of a woman called Helen Reading. It would appear that someone sneezed on the steering wheel. Traces found have been matched to samples which were taken from you when you were interviewed before. Can you give me any explanation how that could have happened, when you've previously told us you've never been in any of those vans?'

Jerome looked smug, grinning all over his face. 'Easy, that. Someone's trying to frame me so they got something of mine and smeared it on there.'

'I see,' Ted repeated. 'Well, that might indeed be the case – in a crime fiction book or a television drama. However, we're in the real world here. That kind of thing is very rare. And why do you think the sample was smeared, Jerome? If someone was driving and sneezed, would they necessarily then smear the steering wheel, to use your own word?'

Jerome's eyes narrowed. As so many suspects before him, he'd clearly been dismissive of the short, slight, quietly spoken officer opposite him. Now he was revising his initial judgement.

'Depends,' he said. 'If you gozzed all over it while you were driving, you'd probably wipe it with your sleeve. It would be a bit gross to hold it with snot on it.'

Ted wondered if Jerome realised he'd revealed exactly what had probably happened. He didn't press home the advantage. He had other, more important things, he wanted to talk to him about.

'Setting that aside for now, Jerome. We've now had an eye witness come forward who places you at the scene near to Roman Lakes on the night Derek Waldren, also known as Badger, was murdered there. To be precise, you, Antoine, Marvin, Donal and Nigel.'

'No comment.'

'This is an eye witness who is prepared to testify against you in court. Based on their statement to us, I have officers, right now, interviewing the rest of the members of the former football team on which you all played who provided you with alibis for that night.'

'You can't have a witness who would testify ...' he blurted, before stopping himself short.

'Why is that, Jerome? Is it because Nigel was the one who

was threatening to talk and he's now dead? How do you know Nigel was going to talk, Jerome? And what do you think he wanted to talk to the police about?'

'Well, I didn't, but if anyone did, it would be him ...'

'So you are saying there was something for him to talk about?'

'No! No, you're putting words in my mouth.'

'Would you like to take a break to organise a solicitor for yourself, Jerome?' Ted asked him pleasantly. 'You're entitled to legal representation. Just as you are at liberty, as the caution told you, not to say anything.'

'No. No, I don't need one. I haven't done anything. I just meant that Nigel liked to cause trouble. He was well jealous of the rest of us because he never made the team. We let him tag along with us but he was never really one of us. I wouldn't put it past him, before he topped himself, to do something that would stir up shit for us.'

'You're surely not suggesting that it was somehow Nigel who smeared your DNA in Louis Martin's van, to make trouble for you? After all, those vans are presumably cleaned periodically and it is some time since Nigel's death. The thing is this, Jerome. We can place you in that van. Unless you can offer a really plausible explanation for the forensic findings. And it's only right that I am open and honest with you about this eyewitness. So I must tell you that this is someone who is still very much alive. And prepared to testify against you.'

There was a definite flicker of fear in Jerome's eyes at that news. His brain was clearly racing as he tried to work out who would have been the first to break ranks and go against the pact of silence.

'What Inspector Rodriguez and I are going to do now is take a short break. I'll arrange some refreshment for you, if you'd like something. But you are not, at this stage, free to leave. I'm going to take legal advice as to what you're to be charged with, so I would very strongly suggest to you that you use this time to arrange a solicitor. I'll send someone in who can sort that out for you. In the meantime, as I told you, you are not yet free to leave, or to contact anyone except your solicitor.'

Chapter Thirty

Ted and Jo went back to the monitors to see if Virgil was making any progress with Donal. Jezza was still observing what was going on, making notes and ready to alert Ted immediately to anything he needed to know. In response to Ted's question, she told him, 'At least he's changed the record a bit, boss. We're now alternating between "no comment" and "load of bollocks". But in a nutshell, news of an eyewitness doesn't seem to worry him in the slightest.'

'He knows we have absolutely nothing on him except the eyewitness. No forensics, nothing. I bet his alibi for Badger's death, at the cage fight, will be impossible to break. Even if Marvin swears in court that Donal was there, Donal only has to deny it and produce a few dozen witnesses to say he wasn't and he walks free. No wonder he looks so confident.'

'If we could get Marvin or possibly even Jerome to say Donal had been present when they were discussing what to do about Badger, we could check his alibis for those dates and times,' Jo suggested. 'Then we could possibly get him on conspiracy to murder, or to commit GBH, at least.'

'I think that's all we can do with him,' Ted told him. 'Much as it goes against the grain, I think we might have to accept that he's the one who got away on this one. Get Virgil to take him to the custody officer and have him put on pre-charge bail with conditions. I want him banned from going anywhere near any of the other football team members, for any reason, for a start.'

'Watching him on screen, boss, I honestly don't think he

would bother. As I read him, he did what he thought needed to be done for his kid brother. I suspect he wasn't bothered that it went further than the original plan and Badger ended up dead. But now, as far as he's concerned, it's over and he wants nothing more to do with it, or with any of the others.'

'I agree, Jezza, and it will be interesting to see if Virgil still feels the same about him. I think we bail him and forget about him for now. We've certainly nothing to charge him with as things stand. Let Virgil know, please. Meanwhile, Jo, I think you and I should go and discuss with the Super, probably in conference call with CPS, who else we charge and with what. I'd dearly love to get Antoine remanded in custody if we can. With him out of the way, the others are far more likely to start to break apart.

'And as soon as Drugs have finished with him, if he's sorted himself a replacement solicitor, I think I need to put the forensic findings to him and hear what he has to say. While you go and see what more you can get out of Jerome.'

As Ted and Jo headed for the Super's office to see if she was free to discuss the situation, they were hailed by Bill on the front desk.

'A heads-up, if you haven't heard yet, Ted. Your lad Jerome now wants a solicitor. It's being arranged for him as we speak so there might be a slight delay before you can interview him again.'

'Thanks, Bill. You know Adrian Jacobs, from Drugs, don't you? A few of us are having a drink with him when we knock off this evening, if you fancy joining us?'

'Aye, why not? I'll let young Steve know I'll be home a bit later and to keep my tea hot for me.'

'You've got him cooking for you now, have you?'

'He's not a bad cook,' Bill told him. 'He's even got me eating a bit of that Chinese stuff.'

Ted laughed as he went on his way. Bill had always been so set in his ways, refusing to try anything from the nearby

Chinese takeaway, except their spare ribs of which he was less suspicious than most of their other dishes. Steve's new lodgings seemed to be working well all round.

'I think there's enough to charge Antoine with Helen Reading's murder. Forensic results put him in direct contact with her, and in the back of that van, shortly before she died,' Ted summed up for the conference call. 'I'd like to put him up for a remand in custody on the grounds that I believe he's very likely to attempt to interfere with witnesses.

'Apart from the eye witness statement from Marvin Gray, I've nothing yet to charge him with Derek Waldren's murder. But I think there's a strong possibility that his alibi for that one will start coming apart at the seams. There's also a slim chance Jerome might start to talk in an attempt to do a deal for himself in the Waldren case. As far as Helen Reading goes, I can place Jerome in the van, but showing he had any involvement in the actual killing is harder. He'll probably argue that he was just there to drive the van and he believed it was simply going to be an innocent prank. Although that won't hold up if we can show Antoine has killed before. He could still argue he couldn't have exerted much of an influence either way over Antoine if he was driving and Antoine was in the back. Certainly not physically trying to stop him, if he admitted being naive enough to think Antoine hadn't intended to kill her.'

'Have you got any link between Helen Reading and either Antoine or Jerome?' the Crown Prosecutor they were speaking to asked Ted.

'Nothing that's shown up so far. As far as we can tell at the moment, she was probably a random victim. Someone who just happened to be in the wrong place at the wrong time.'

'I'm never sure whether it's better or worse for the victim's families and loved ones if it's pre-meditated or random. Can you connect Antoine to the tights she was strangled with? But presumably not Jerome?' she asked.

'Not yet. There were no traces of Antoine's DNA on the

tights, so he probably had gloves on when he strangled her. And nothing at all linking Jerome to either the victim by direct contact, or to the back of the van. I suspect that if Jerome touched her at all, to dispose of the body, for instance, he was wearing protective clothing, so there'll be nothing to find. We got lucky with that sneeze, which is about all we have on him.

'Drugs and Fraud seized a lot of paperwork from the house which is still being gone through. There's an outside chance that if Antoine bought the tights himself there could be a receipt somewhere amongst it all which shows the purchase. One more thing in our favour.'

'I agree, from what you say, that you can safely charge Antoine for Helen Reading's murder. We can prepare a pretty robust objection to any bail application. Despite his having no previous convictions, other than the odd speeding ticket, he's facing Class A drugs charges as well as murder charges. We can't rely on the money-laundering charges to help us much. But his likelihood of attempting to interfere with witnesses should hopefully work strongly in our favour.'

'I was hoping we could make Marvin a protected witness and redact his name from the statement before disclosure.'

'Well, I think that would be reasonable. But it's clearly not going to take a genius to work out who the informant is if only five of them were allegedly involved and one is now deceased. I know you hold out no hope of getting anywhere with Donal Shaugnessy. But how likely is it that Jerome might also agree to testify? He must be under no illusion, though. He's facing serious charges, whatever he offers up by way of a bargaining chip.

'I'm sure I don't need to spell out for you, Ted, the complexities of the principles of secondary liability, *Actus reus*, that sort of thing. Was Defendant Two actively encouraging or assisting Defendant One in the commission of the crime? And, more importantly, can we prove that?

'But on balance I'm inclined to think you could charge

Jerome as a principle for now, exactly the same charge as Antoine, then we can take a more informed view when we have any additional information. Also dependant on what he may have to say for himself if and when he starts to talk. Who's his solicitor?'

'He didn't have one originally, Val, but he's since asked for one. I don't yet know who it is.'

'Is it critical to your inquiry if he's bailed?'

'Probably not. If he talks, he's very likely to go to ground to avoid Antoine, in case he's also bailed. We'll need to keep him under obs, just in case.'

Once the conference call ended, the Ice Queen looked at Ted and Jo with a hint of a smile.

'Well, gentlemen, I don't want to start counting our chickens before they hatch. But it does look as if we might have something of a result before the day is over. Well done, both of you, and to all the team.'

While Ted was waiting to be able to start questioning Antoine again, he was following the progress of his officers who were chasing up all the former football players about their alibis. For the time Derek Waldren was murdered, all of them had provided alibis for each other, claiming they were all together at Antoine's house the whole evening and the night. Nigel's letter had indicated that he and four of the others were not. They were instead up in the woods when Derek Waldren was killed. Once the others learned of that, there was a chance some might change their original statements, seeking to cover themselves.

In the days leading up to Nigel's death, they'd all been gradually changing their stories concerning him to indicate they couldn't swear if Nigel had been with them all that evening. But they'd stayed solid in their mutual support for the rest of them – Antoine, Jerome, Jordan, Marvin, Wayne, Will, Sammy, Terry, Alan, Gary.

Now Ted's officers were telling them there was an eyewitness who gave the lie to what they had all previously said and the wheels were starting to come off. Maurice was alone in the office, collating all the information as it came in. Ted went to see him for an update.

'Young Terry, the one with the Scouting background, was the first to crack, boss. Graham went to talk to him in the shop where he works. I don't know if it was Terry's Baden-Powell conscience or being worried about a police visit at work, but he wants to retract his earlier statement. Graham's told him he needs to come in and do it formally so he's fixed up a time first thing tomorrow.

'Leona's had similar success with Will. Looks like we're all in for a busy day of statement taking tomorrow, and with a bit of luck, with their alibis in tatters, perhaps Jerome and even Antoine might realise they're on a hiding to nothing now.'

'We're working on a remand in custody for Antoine,' Ted told him, outlining his discussion with the CPS. 'As soon as Drugs have finished with him, I'll be going back for another crack. They're arresting his solicitor, too, for possession, but I doubt we'll be lucky enough to get him banged up on remand.'

Maurice's desk phone rang. He answered it, looking at Ted as he said, 'Yes, he's here. I'll send him down now.' As he hung up, he said, 'Antoine's all ready for you, boss. Go get 'im.'

Ted found Antoine, looking sullen and subdued by all that had been happening to him, sitting none too patiently in an interview room with his new solicitor, whom Ted knew socially as well as professionally. Ted's former partner Philip had been a Crown Prosecutor. The two of them had been out for a meal once with Joel Taylor, who now sat opposite Ted.

'Mr Taylor,' Ted acknowledged him as he sat down.

'Chief Inspector,' he responded. There was still a bit of an edge to his attitude. He'd sided with Philip after he and Ted broke up, inevitably. 'I understand you were behind a bit of a pantomime involving my client and a police dog.'

'No pantomime, Mr Taylor. But the Drugs case is of no interest to me, nor any relevance to what I wish to question your client about. I appreciate you've come in rather on the last minute in this and some of the disclosures I need to make are slightly delayed, so we'll come to those when they're available. My apologies, but they come from an eyewitness whose identity is protected so they are being prepared with anything which could identify them being redacted.

'But turning first of all to the forensic report, with which the defence has already been served. Antoine, I want to come back to fibres from jeans found in your bedroom being an exact match for those found on the body of Helen Reading. What can you tell me about that?'

'No comment.'

'Antoine, I think Mr Taylor will agree with me that at some point you are going to have to explain your connection to Helen Reading. There really is no doubt about the forensic results placing you in close physical contact with her.'

'Who's Helen Reading?'

Antoine was starting to sniff now, wiping at his nose with the cuff of the sweatshirt he was wearing. Taylor was sitting quietly for the moment but Ted knew he would leap into action at the least sign of his client needing his protection.

'Helen Reading is the woman whose body was found in Sykes Reservoir just over a week ago. She was murdered. The body was found after an anonymous tip-off by a member of the public using an unregistered pay-as-you-go phone. For the tape, I'm showing Antoine Martin and his solicitor an inventory of property seized during a raid under search warrant of premises you occupy, Antoine, in a wing of the house belonging to your father, Louis Martin. You'll see that the list includes, together with your own registered phone, another unregistered phone. The contents of both are currently being examined by a police expert, particularly the unregistered one.

'So I'll ask you again. Did you know Helen Reading? Did you ever come into contact with her for any reason? Can you explain how the results in this report show that your jeans came into contact with her clothing at some time?'

Taylor leaned closer to his client and had a muttered one-sided conversation with him. Ted deliberately moved his chair back from the table so as not to be seen to be eavesdropping.

'My client has no statement to make at this time. I request time to take instruction.'

'That's fine, Mr Taylor. But I have to tell you both that I am not satisfied that Antoine has provided a suitable explanation for the findings. I am therefore going to take you now, Antoine, to the custody officer, where you will be charged with the murder of Helen Reading. There is the strong possibility that a further serious charge connected to the murder of Derek Waldren will be forthcoming. And I should warn you both that I intend to raise vigorous objections to any application you may make for bail.'

It was a lively group who got together in The Grapes at the end of the day. Ted tried to buy the first round but Adrian Jacobs insisted he was in the chair.

'You played a blinder there with the dog idea, Ted. Getting Penrose was a double bonus. We suspected all along he was into the stuff. We so nearly had Louis Martin once before but Penrose shot us down in flames with a load of highly questionable character references and alibis. It will be worth the price of a round of drinks to see that smug bastard taken down and, with any luck, struck off by the Law Society. So cheers, Ted, here's to you. Though what fun you get out of that glass of piss-water, I can't imagine.'

'Well, someone has to play the grown-up,' Ted told him.

He always hated to come the heavy-handed boss but he was a bit concerned that Jo had attacked his first double whiskey like a drowning man thrown a lifebelt. If he was planning on making an evening of it, Ted hoped he wouldn't be stupid enough to drive.

Mike Hallam saw Ted's look and lifted his half a shandy in his direction.

'Don't worry, boss, I'm in the driving seat tonight. We sorted it out between us before we started. Even without a grown-up telling us to.'

It was good to see Bill socialising, for once. He knew Adrian Jacobs' sergeant from way back and they were having a good old gossip over their pints. Bill could be a solitary man. Too many years on his own since his wife died young.

In no time Jo was heading for the bar for the next round, taking orders.

'This one's on me. Boss, another Gunner?'

Ted drained his glass but stood up to go.

'You're fine, Jo, thanks. I think I'll get off home.'

Adrian Jacobs and his sergeant both started making clucking noises as Jacobs laughed, 'Hen-pecked by that bloke of yours, Ted? Won't he let you stay out to play?'

'Some of us have an early start. I want to question Antoine first thing tomorrow, before we put him up for remand. So I'll say goodnight all, and try not to get yourselves arrested for anything.'

Trev clearly wasn't expecting him home so early. He was in the kitchen, his phone in one hand, the other clutching a doorstep of a bacon, lettuce and tomato sandwich. He had his earphones in and occasionally broke off chewing to say something out loud. Ted recognised the language as Welsh but had no idea what it meant. Trev jumped guiltily when Ted came in, taking the earpieces out.

'You're back earlier than I expected, so you caught me slacking and snacking. I was polishing up my Welsh grammar before I speak to Annie. Who, incidentally, says it's so long since she spoke to you she's forgotten what your voice sounds like.'

'Did she really say that or is that you embellishing?' Ted asked him as he moved forward to kiss him, almost treading on Adam in the process.

'Your clothes smell beery. Have you been in the pub?'

'I had a swift one but left them to it. I live with an insanely jealous man who thinks he plays second fiddle to my team. Even though that's not true.'

'Did you have a good day? Were you celebrating?'

Ted briefly told him about their successes. When he mentioned his trick with the drugs dog, Trev laughed delightedly.

'Ted Darling! You devious little detective.'

'The Ice Queen said something very similar,' Ted told him, picking Adam up for a quick cuddle.

'Did she indeed? I hope she knows only I am allowed to call my man that. I shall sort her out. Handbags at dawn!' Trev loved to camp it up when he was in a good mood, as he clearly was to see Ted home earlier than anticipated, for a change.

'Let's go out for a spin on the bike,' Ted suggested. He eyed the glass of red wine on the work surface. It looked hardly touched. 'Are you all right to drive or do you want me to?'

'Absolutely fine, officer. Where are we going? I haven't started supper yet so that will have to wait until we get back.'

'We did Paris for you so let's make it chips and fish bits on a hilltop somewhere which is more my style. I'll go and get changed.'

'A fish supper with my favourite policeman. I can't think of anything better.'

Chapter Thirty-one

Ted had arranged to interview Antoine further first thing, before his remand hearing. Joel Taylor didn't look thrilled at the early start but Ted knew it would be reflected in his hefty bill. He wondered how long it would be before the Martin family money started to run dry. With Louis's vans all impounded, he wouldn't be able to do much with either his property development business, or bringing in new drug supplies to replace those which had been impounded.

Adrian Jacobs had told Ted he was hoping to get Louis Martin put away for a long stretch. He was confident, even with Martin's connections, that this time he had enough on the man to do so. He also reported that during the search, Louis Martin's wife had turned up, seemingly unaware of what had been going on in the family home, and furious with her husband and son in equal measure. She hadn't stayed long. Just enough time to screech at her husband that she was going straight to her solicitor's office to file for divorce.

Ted wondered, as he often did, whether she really had been completely unaware of where her husband's, and her son's, money was coming from. Had she been aware, she would almost certainly have wanted everything put in her name to try to protect it. No doubt her solicitor would advise her she potentially risked losing everything if it was deemed to be the proceeds of crime.

'I have some more disclosures to make, Antoine, Mr Taylor, and again I apologise for the short notice. These are things I've only just received.'

Océane had clearly been working late the day before. Her report on the unregistered phone was waiting for Ted when he got in to work that morning.

'This document, as you can see, shows the calls made and received by the unlisted phone found in your bedroom, Antoine. I'd like to draw your attention to two in particular, made the weekend before last, to this station. The first was a tip-off about a body in a lake at Reddish Vale. The second, from the same phone, mentioned a body in Sykes Reservoir, which is where Helen Reading's body was subsequently found. These are transcripts of those calls. I can arrange for you to hear them if you wish. Did you make those calls, Antoine?'

'You don't have to answer at this point, Antoine,' Taylor told him.

'That's true, Antoine, you don't. But at some point I am going to require some answers. You see, the fact that both these calls mention water makes it improbable that they were just a prank of some sort. Someone guessing that there was a body to be found, not to mention guessing that it would be found in water. If it was just a guess, it's something of a coincidence that on only the second call, the police teams were led straight to where the body was. That rather suggests that the caller knew that information. Which could suggest that the caller was, in fact, the killer. Or had at least been present when the body was dumped.'

'You're surmising rather too much, Chief Inspector,' Taylor told him. 'You've not yet established whether or not it was my client who made those calls. You certainly can't deduce whether or not the caller was connected to the death of the unfortunate woman.'

'Not at the moment I can't, no,' Ted replied pleasantly. 'But I do have an eye witness who saw Helen Reading being snatched from the street and bundled into a white van. Antoine, traces of your clothing fibres have been found both in a white van belonging to your father's firm and on Helen Reading's clothing. Do you have anything to say about that?'

'I don't know Helen Reading.'

'Yet your clothes came into contact with her clothes at some point shortly before she died.'

Antoine shrugged, seemingly unconcerned. 'Maybe I bumped into her somewhere. In a shop, or something.'

Ted produced another item in a sealed evidence bag.

'Again, I'm sorry this is late, it's only just come into my possession. This is a supermarket till receipt for earlier that same day, Antoine. So you did indeed go shopping. And this item on the receipt is the purchase of a pair of tights, amongst other items. Who were they for, Antoine?'

'Is this relevant, Chief Inspector?'

'I wouldn't be asking if it wasn't, Mr Taylor. A similar pair of tights was used to strangle Helen Reading.'

'They were for a friend,' Antoine put in.

'I see. And did you give them to this friend, since the search of your premises didn't reveal a pair of tights anywhere. If so, could I please have the name of the friend, so one of my officers can verify your statement?'

Antoine maintained a sullen silence.

'Fair enough. Now, back to this eye witness. They are, as we speak, being asked to do an ID from photographs of the make and model of white van they saw, together with the person they saw get out of the van and bundle Helen Reading into it.'

For the first time, Ted saw a flicker of something in Antoine's eyes. Not fear, exactly. More a realisation that he might not be as untouchable as he'd thought he was.

'Another point. Your own phone, not the unlisted one, shows that you received a call from Nigel Denby, shortly before he met his death under a train. You spoke for some time. What did you say to one another?'

Taylor made a noise of impatience. 'None of this is relevant or admissible in any court of law.'

'Did Nigel tell you he intended to make a full confession about what happened the night Derek Waldren was murdered? Did he, perhaps, tell you that he intended sending a statement to us here at the station, naming those who had been involved in the killing, and that he would be naming you?'

Ted slid a copy of Nigel's last letter across the table. Taylor picked it up and scanned it contemptuously.

'Hearsay. You know this is of no use to you without corroboration.'

Right on schedule, as agreed, there was a brief tap on the door and Jezza's head appeared in the gap. 'Boss, have you got a minute?'

Ted excused himself, paused the recording and went out to join her in the corridor.

'What news, Jezza?'

'The best, boss. Jerome's solicitor is advising him to cooperate in any way he can to try to save his own skin if we agree to go for a lesser charge. Jo's with him now and he's spilling his guts about everything. He's admitted driving the van when Antoine grabbed Helen Reading. He maintains he thought the idea was just to waste police time, by giving them another missing person to worry about. But he realised, from the sounds in the back as he was driving, that Antoine was actually throttling the life out of her. He admits panicking and carrying on driving. He also admits helping Antoine to dispose of the body later on, but he denies having anything to do with the killing itself.

'He's also admitted being present when Badger was killed. He confirms that Marvin tried to stop Antoine from going all the way and says he also tried to stop him, although I doubt that. And the rest of his former team are slowly turning against him. The alibi now is barely holding up. Have we got him, boss? Can we finally nail the little bastard?'

'Don't jinx it, Jezza. We're nearly there but there's still a bit of legwork to go. Keep me posted of any further developments, please.'

'Sorry about the interruption,' Ted said as he returned to the interview room and restarted the recording. 'You and your client will be getting copies as soon as possible, Mr Taylor, but once again this is a statement from a protected witness which will need to be redacted. I can tell you, though, Antoine, that we now have another eyewitness statement to your involvement in the murder of Derek Waldren. I'll take a short break now to consult with CPS but I believe that, by the time you appear in court shortly to answer the charge of murdering Helen Reading, we will be seeking to add a second charge of murdering Derek Waldren.'

Seeing Antoine's eyes widen, Ted went on, 'And before you mention your previous alibi, Antoine, I have to tell you that your friends who provided it are rapidly changing their statements. You no longer have a credible alibi for your whereabouts on the date in question. Which is one of the reasons for opposing any application for bail which you may make. We have reasonable grounds to be concerned about interference with material witnesses. Plus, as your home is still a crime scene, we would not be happy about you being released with no fixed abode to return to.'

Chief Constable Jon Woodrow missed nothing which happened in the force he headed. Ted had no idea how he kept his finger on so many pulses at once. Woodrow had phoned him later that morning to congratulate him on the news that, as they'd hoped, Antoine's bail application had been refused and he was now remanded in custody on two charges of murder.

'I know it's short notice, Ted, but I have a window early evening and you and I need to talk some more about the inquiry into Roy Marston. What about a game of squash and a discussion afterwards?'

Once again, Ted had realised it was more than an invitation. He'd intended working late, having already told

Trev there was no way he could make either the junior self-defence club, or their judo night. He'd just have to push the paperwork back to the next day. If his biggest boss of all summoned him, he had no choice but to go.

Ted had had a good day. Not just Antoine safely in custody, but he'd also had confirmation from CPS that they could charge the bishop with the historical sexual abuse of minors offences. He'd left that privilege to Rob to see to. He'd earned it, with all the diligent work he'd put in on the case.

Buoyed up by the successes of the day, Ted was feeling positive enough to win one game against the Chief, for the first time ever, before being reminded of his player ranking and soundly thrashed in the best of three.

They were both in high spirits when, after their showers, they went to order food. Ted had no idea what time he'd be home or what Trev's plans were for food so he opted for a healthy-looking quiche and salad option with his fruit juice.

'Mr Darling is paying today, Larry, for having the temerity to win a game,' the Chief laughed. 'I had to up my act to put him firmly back in his place.'

When Larry brought their food over to the table they'd selected, he set Ted's plate down almost reverentially in front of him.

'Congratulations, Mr Darling. You're one of the very few players who's ever won even one game against the Chief.'

'A good day today all round, Ted. You and your team have brought in some good results. Well done. And you've clearly been sharpening up your act on the squash court. Now, back to this inquiry. Once you've got things wrapped up on your own cases, I suggest you hand over to your DI and you head down to the West Midlands for a first look at the paperwork there.

'Up to you entirely how you run things, of course, but I'd suggest taking one or perhaps two of your own team with you until you see what's needed. Did you have anyone in mind?'

'Maurice Brown,' Ted said immediately. 'He can be a bit of a skiver but he's the best at plodding through things picking up any inconsistencies. I have to confess I'm really not all that sure how to proceed on something like this.'

'Nonsense. It's a case, like any other. Run it as you would anything else that came your way, and above all, forget that it's Marston, and forget any history between you. I know I can trust you to be professional and impartial. After all, even Marston acknowledges that. If you need any help in how to run it, talk to Gerry Fletcher. I'm sure he'd be happy to give you any pointers.

'I'd like to see you start at the beginning of next week. We need to boost public confidence in our ability to police ourselves. If there's any suggestion at all that files were deliberately lost or misplaced in a case of serious sexual abuse of children, I want to send out a clear message that it's being dealt with rigorously and it won't be tolerated in the future. Not by anyone.

'This is going to turn into a high-profile inquiry. From what I've heard of this mysterious witness who's going to testify, there will be some very well-known heads to roll. And if there's any question of a police officer having deliberately blocked a case, they need to know that, retired or not, we will find them, we will extradite them if necessary, and they will go to trial.

'I know you can do this, Ted. Marston's right. You may have your faults – god knows, you can be a stubborn sod at times – but I don't think you can be bought at any price.'

Ted and the team were all in high spirits for their get-together in The Grapes at the end of the week. They'd finally had some good results and things were looking promising for seeing some justice being done on cases they'd almost given up on.

Rob had arrested the bishop and had him charged, although it was no surprise that he'd been granted bail. His legal team were busily trying to make a case for him being unfit to plead. Luckily, Rob had been chatting to some of the staff and former staff in the home where the bishop lived and discovered he was not at all popular. He could be difficult and seemed to delight in getting people into trouble. He'd even succeeded in getting two of the care workers dismissed and they had been more than happy to testify that his supposed lapses in memory could be summoned at will, and that a lot of the time his mind was as sharp as ever.

With Antoine safely on remand in custody, all of his former team-mates had retracted their earlier statements, which had previously provided him with a watertight alibi. Not one of them would now support his claim that he had been at his home with all of them on the evening when Derek Waldren was killed.

Jerome was increasingly talkative as he tried everything he could to get himself a lesser charge than murder. He'd admitted that it was Antoine's idea to kidnap someone. Antoine had seen on the television news that Ted had been tied up in the Tara MacNamee case and thought it would be amusing to create a smokescreen in the shape of another disappearance. Jerome confirmed that she was just a random stranger they'd seen walking alone. They'd been out cruising, looking for someone. Antoine was clever enough to be on the look-out for cameras which might catch them.

When Jerome had spotted a lone woman walking hurriedly and purposefully, head down against intermittent rain, Antoine had told him to stop the van while he got out and dragged the unknown woman inside. Jerome insisted he hadn't known Antoine intended to kill her. Antoine was determined to show how superior he was to the police, convincing himself he had got away scot free with killing Derek Waldren.

There'd been a breakthrough when Baines, the witness who

claimed to have seen someone bundle a woman into a white van, had not only correctly identified the make of van from photos as being the same as the one seized from Louis Martin, but he'd also picked out Antoine from a set of photographs, albeit tentatively. The team would now need to arrange a VIPER video identification to see if he could pick him out again from more images.

All the team were in the pub after work on Friday, even those with homes and families to go to. The week's results called for a celebration for all of them. Ted had warned Trev he would be late home and had offered to chauffeur anyone who needed a lift. Clearly not all of them would be fit to drive home afterwards, especially as Jezza had challenged Jo to a dual with the tequila slammers.

Ted's phone rang with a withheld number. Sighing, hoping it wasn't going to be something to spoil the fun if he couldn't, after all, do the promised taxi run, he picked up the call.

'Ted? Harry. Are you near a TV? Put the news on. And thank you.'

Ted glanced across to the television set high up above the bar. It was already on a news channel, but the sound was muted. Ted leapt to his feet to move closer, catching Dave, the landlord's attention, and gesturing for him to turn up the volume. A news reporter he recognised was doing a piece to camera in front of a familiar background.

'Whitehall is in turmoil with the news of the arrest of at least three senior members of the Cabinet. There's been no official statement yet, but the Metropolitan police are promising to issue one at any moment. Rumours are rife but normally reliable sources are saying that the three men concerned have been arrested on charges relating to historical cases of child abuse. One of the accused is said to be a member of the House of Lords. The others are thought to be senior Secretaries of State, although no identities have been revealed at this stage.

'As the news breaks, there is wide speculation that the leader of the Opposition is trying to bring an emergency motion for a vote of no confidence in the Government. Further updates are expected shortly.'

The End

Lightning Source UK Ltd.
Milton Keynes UK
UKHW011812230719
346692UK00001B/64/P